THE CHESTMAKER

THE CHESTMAKER

JL SMYSER

To all the language arts teachers I've ever had...

If this is bad, it's your fault.

PROLOGUE

The cellar salivated a briny slime, and above our heads was anarchy.

A silhouette transferred match fire to a lantern. My father—his loose wool shirt damp with sweat and seawater—was armed with a pistol. I fiddled with the button on my shirt cuff. My pants were filthy, and no amount of spit-shining would rub the dried Scarlet Muck off my boots. I tried kicking off what I could with my heels, but my father stopped me.

"Pay 'tention to the sounds, Archie," he commanded in a whisper—ear smashed against the cellar door.

Sounds? No sounds down in this damp place. Just the stench: mold, ale, soggy potatoes.

He pulled his peppered beard away from the door. "I think they've passed, but we can't be sure. Keep ready."

"Are they going to hurt us?" I asked.

He came down the stairs to embrace me. "I don't know. We may not make it through the night." He was not very adept at encouragement. Craftsmanship, debate, and machinery he could fixate on for hours, but consoling others was not his strength.

After a crash of glass resounded through our shop above, my father pointed his pistol at the door. By the increasing gusts of his breath, I knew it was only a matter of moments.

The treasury was looted first.

Then the shop's stock.

The workroom.

Bedrooms.

Then...

The door creaked open. My father squeezed the trigger. A wet hiss followed the click.

A voice trailed down to our ears. "Wet gunpowder. Isn't that the worst?" Soon after, footsteps clunked down the warped stairs. A brittle plank cracked under their weight halfway down. "Bloody ol' wood," the voice cursed. "Sage advice… Wood needs to be properly prepared for a damp place like this." The imposing pirate, half in shadow, halted at the bottom.

My father was soon by my side. He handed me the lantern and wrapped a free arm around me. I held up the light but couldn't quite see the intruder's face. Unarmed, but one couldn't be sure there was no pistol under that bucklecoat.

My father raised his pistol above his head—which I didn't know at the time was meant to bludgeon me as the only way out of a fate worse than death. But it was the pirate who stopped him.

Holding up hands, "Don't do that, mate," they said earnestly. Their gaze flicked to every corner of the cellar, searching for something. "I'm only here to peruse your lovely home. Nice collection of ale you have." One hand motioned toward the ale barrels on the rack against the wall.

My father's grip hurt my shoulder.

"Chestmaker, are ya?" the pirate asked.

My father nodded while lowering the pistol.

"Thought so. Saw your product upstairs. Crew's gunna take some. I apologize for that. Admirable craftsmanship, though. The boy, too?"

My father was barely audible: "Steadier hands than I. Smarter, too. He'll design better chests than me soon."

From upstairs, a voice yelled down, "Captain Gildeye? Anything you need help bringing up?"

This pirate answered, "Nothin' down here! Finish up and move on to the next!" Attention aimed back to us, the pirate asked, "Have any more treasures down here?" My father shook his head. "Don't lie to me. I've been nothin' but kind so far."

"Don't need treasure. Got my boy."

A grunt of acknowledgment from them. Then, "I used to know that feeling." Their attention focused on me. I drowned in those eyes, wanting nothing more than to be free of them. "Having someone worth fighting for. That's more valuable than gold."

I nodded, but didn't understand.

The intruder pointed to a single barrel of ale. "I'll take that and be on my way." They unlatched the ale from the rack and hoisted it over a shoulder. The venture back up the stairs was a tricky one, but eventually the pirate captain successfully hobbled up and out of the shop.

It's hard to remember everything from that night. I know some people died and buildings were burned down. But what they don't tell you about pirate raids is that what happens after is dreadfully worse. People have nothing left to lose. Desperate and angry, average citizens riot for what little resources are left behind. Ten years ago, that's what it did to us. Land was worth murdering for and food was as good as gold. Made people distrust their own neighbors. Put a functioning economy into shambles and erased a culture of festivity and community. The pirates had spread anarchy to Tyro Archipelago like a disease.

It was, as the charter barons would later call it, an imbalance.

THE ARTISAN

Salvatorre's Cases, Coffers, and Chests (No Coffins). The sign is askew. After sweeping the Scarlet Muck off my porch, I use the broom handle to straighten it. If only straightening out my debts could be as easy as that.

Returning inside, I dust or rearrange the unique treasure chests lining the shelves and floor space of my cramped shop. One side of the room has the ornamental designs—encrusted with quartz and stones in intricate patterns, or inlaid with mother of pearl, or delicately painted. A customer in search for their perfect chest could find the epic sea battle depicted on one, while another could settle for a bejeweled sunset. Some are cedar, some mahogany, some spruce. A few have an aged visage to them as if they were fished from the ocean after an era or two of being lost. I had rusted them myself, actually, and frayed the leather handles. The wear and tear tells stories—always lies, but the customers don't have to know that.

But the ornamental designs are nothing compared to my famous gear-lock chests presented on the opposite wall. They are much more useful while riding the waves. I serve all kinds of sailors: pirates, privateers, soldiers, explorers, traders—all of whom want to protect their treasures from one another. Nothing beats the infectious excitement a customer has when they learn the secret to a chest.

A mechanism inside one releases a paralytic dart at someone who might dare open a chest not their own. Many have secret compartments or false openings. There are a few with magnetic locks. Or a key made to look like something other than a key. I've even got a few puzzle boxes to hold small trinkets or scrolls.

The chest of any home or ship is the centerpiece, tying the whole living space or treasury together. It is functional art. Even passed down as family heirlooms. As an artisan, I have to know what will suit the customer the most. Class and dignity or cunning tricks? Something to hide wealth or show it off? That is the challenge at which I excel.

I spit-shine one with an armored casing and a seal to prevent water seepage. It is this design which gained me some acclaim when a famous explorer went above the pole into uncharted waters and disappeared. Her valuable work was recovered only because they found the chest I made for her completely undamaged. The subsequent interest in my work was overshadowed by her miraculous reappearance and thus never really brought in more customers. But for a brief few days, my design was printed in papers across this polar quadrant.

Upon the top shelf, where the smaller ones are displayed, I reach for a coffer with a quincunx keyhole—a unique five-hole design which cannot be picked open by traditional means. It can only be unlocked with the key, or with a hatchet and determination. Unfortunately, I lost that key I worked so hard on. Nearly tore the floorboards up searching for it. Can't easily sell a chest with no key. I sigh at the loss, take the chest down, and place it out of sight until I decide what to do with it.

Behind the counter in the back of the shop are stairs leading up to my living quarters one way and down to the cellar the opposite. Between that ascension is my workshop. The round door creaks open to a windowless room—dark and dusty. I flip an iron switch with a rubber handle. The exposed wires bring electricity to the crackling bulbs. A quick proliferation of light whips the darkness away like a blanket to reveal my unfinished pieces. There are some half painted or not yet lathered with varnish. Metal scraps are scattered around the perimeter. A rack on the wall holds my tools: hatchets, saws, clamps, molds, hammers.

There's a single chest almost finished in the center of the room. The deadline for this piece is today—a turnaround of only three days. The buyer will return later, but I've been having an exceptionally difficult time with it. In the center of the front where a keyhole would normally go is a small clock instead. Had bought it from Kalloway the gearsmith, dismantled it with precision, and reassembled it with a connection to the locking mechanism in the chest. The inside lining is a plush fabric over two sets of spruce planks. Between those sets are the components and springs I tightened and set just right—or perhaps not right considering I couldn't get the rusted thing to work. My work with levers and gears has always been exceptional, but spring-work is where I always needed my father's advice. I squeeze my hands between the chest walls and fiddle with the cogs, but am unable to see exactly what I'm doing. There's a snap between my fingers and I pull out a broken tin rod the length of my thumb.

Groaning, I throw the pieces and pace the room. Berating myself, I rub the smooth surface of the button on my cuffs. The frustration clears after a moment.

I love a good challenge, but perhaps I was foolish to believe this could be done in such a short amount of time. I nearly asked Kalloway for advice with the clock yesterday, but the inner workings of a chest must be a secret between the maker and the buyer. No, I have to figure it out on my own. This is a gear-lock chest—my specialty. I cannot sour the Salvatorre name.

My father also occasionally got in over his head like this, and I was always there to solve his problems. I surpassed him at some point with my fixation on all things mechanical. People around the island take advantage of my skills to fix their generators. Though underappreciated and underpaid, I take these jobs to gain experience and perception. To embolden my visions of the craft. This issue is simply a matter of thinking around the problem, not through it.

The tin rod is too rigid. A wood rod is too weak. Perhaps twine around the rig in a certain way might achieve a similar result, but such delicate material should rarely be used in a chest. They easily fray over time. It needs to be something between both. The solution creeps into my mind with trepidation. A copper wire might achieve what I seek. I discard the idea. No copper wire at any of my workstations. Buying some would require hopping on an air balloon to get to the other side of the archipelago. There is hardly any time for that. Every reasonable solution leads to a tapered end. I am not going to make a flimsy product. No twine. No wood. My designs are meant to last.

A memory enters my mind like a flare of light. There should be copper wire down in the cellar.

Ran out of lantern oil, so I rush down the rickety stairs with a lit candle to the empty ale barrels. A few years back, my father broke one of the barrels and fixed it with a couple strands of copper wire. I don't use the barrels, so the wire is free to take. I unwind the strands and wrap them around my fist.

With my mind cluttered, I forget about the warped and cracked stair I always avoid. My boot crunches through the plank, and my chin bashes against a step. I tumble backward to the cellar floor. White shirt—now bronzed with powdery dust and dirt—has a few drops of blood. I press a palm to my chin to stop the bleeding. My free hand reaches for the candle which landed on the staircase.

A silvery item under the broken plank catches the flickering light. A minor glint promising fortune. I stick my hand down past the splintered wood to retrieve the shiny. A key. A five-pronged key to be exact—the one I made for the quincunx keyhole. A lucky find, but how did it even get down here?

After pocketing the key, my gaze through the staircase falls upon another curiosity. Another glimmer off a strip of metal with an oxidized patina. I gently stick the candle a little bit farther in past the wooden shards. The stairs swallow the light and reveal an enclosed chamber of stored bricks, planks, and the centerpiece of it all that has me so curious. A chest. The flame flickers close to it. It's an old chest with designs I can't decipher from here.

Getting just a bit closer, the flame touches the center design. It looks like some kind of rune.

Click.

The stairs need replacing anyway, so removing them shouldn't be a problem. As I begin tearing one off, a jingle rings through my shop. The front bell. Someone entered. I scramble up the stairs to the shop. Some woman in a flamboyant blouse and bodice peruses my stock.

After setting the candle and wire down, I teeter over to her and ask, "Was that door unlocked?"

Nodding, she asks, "I apologize, were you not open yet?" She stops looking around as if to avoid offense.

I stutter, "No, but I can make an exception."

"I don't wish to be a hassle." She pauses, looks at my clothes. "Are you all right? You've got blood on you."

"I'm fine. No hassle."

Truthfully, she couldn't be more of a hassle. Bad timing with that chest under the shop. My mind keeps snapping back to it. Is it my father's? How long has it been there? I want nothing more than to rush back down. Maybe treasure? Surely not here. He wouldn't have kept hidden treasure around here without using it during the lean months—and there were plenty of those.

She breaks through my obsessed thoughts: "You're fairly young to be drawing such notoriety."

The notoriety is not because of me. For generations, Salvatorres have been chestmakers in this quadrant of the southern pole. In fact, I've been hard pressed in carrying on our good name with Ozma trying to run me out of business ever since my father died. He's been cracking down on anything that might bring imbalance to the delicate equilibrium of the archipelago. That includes me. A chestmaker is worth less than a flake of fool's gold to the charter barons.

"You made all of these yourself?"

I reply, "Most. A couple are leftovers from my father, and some I've bought from traders that I cleaned up. I was taught to treat every job as an art, and then try to be the best at it."

She stares at—no, *through* me, like she can detect every flaw in me and my work. It's not an abnormal feeling. It comes from everyone. It helps to look away from her gaze. I spot a speck of mud I missed on the floor and imagine its destruction.

"What is the gimmick for this one?"

"Gimmick?" The chest she gently touches is a fairly nice piece. Upon its spruce and iron frame is a painting of an aquatic tentacled beast in a clear blue sea. Its tentacles flow up to the top of the chest and emerge from the paint as porcelain which cradles a statuette ship. The interior is plush velvet.

"Aye. Don't all of your pieces have gadgetry within to make some kind of gimmick?"

I stumble over my response. "N-no, not all of them. That section is purely decorative. Treasury centerpieces. This section over here are the ones with the… gimmicks." I fiddle with the button on my cuff. "This piece is lined with a cozy interior to make all of your valuables feel… comfortable, I suppose." What am I saying? Objects can't feel comfortable. They can't feel anything. And furthermore, what could possibly be hidden in the cellar? My curiosity is a rampaging warship anchored at the docks.

"I'm sorry if I've offended you. How much for it?"

"Twenty."

"That's a fair price." She reaches for a pouch. Her fingers descend into it and open like a floating jellyfish. She pockets a few coins and hands me the whole pouch. I notice a ring on her finger with a certain signet I've never seen before. "I promise that is twenty."

I don't count it. I want to get back downstairs.

It's not a heavy piece, so she doesn't need help carrying it. She cradles it, and I open the door for her. She glides down the thin, cobblestone lane toward the docks.

Across the lane, Kalloway the gearsmith is taking down the signs on his shop. The ones for discounted timepieces and children's gadgets.

"Are you closing down?"

He grunts affirmatively, then says, "Couldn't pay my taxes anymore. Ozma made me sign a rusted villein contract. Had no other choice."

Traditional arts and trade work has all but disappeared along Tyro Archipelago. This marks me as the very last of the artisans in the Port Ov Krakau. The charter barons have systematically pushed the others into villein serfdom for the sake of balance. To them, what is balance if not lucrative business? Our valuable crops are traded to nearby islands. Coffee, sugar, cocoa, rubber, various fruits, and medicinal herbs. Each island in Tyro has its specialty. The target on my back is now the biggest it has ever been.

"Couldn't you leave? Move to another island, I mean?"

He scoffs, "You're foolin' yourself. I'd need enough money to fund safe passage across the sea. Not cheap. Pirates are everywhere nowadays."

"And sometimes the real pirates are right here at home."

He throws his signs down, looks around to see if anyone heard, and faces me with a reddened face. "You watch what you say, lest you want to end up like your father."

I step back. "What do you mean?"

"Forget it. Just clamp your tongue and go back to your work. Don't draw unnecessary attention to yourself."

Kalloway has always been the grouchy neighbor, but something lingers beneath his words now that feels paternal. Protective. A remainder of something that once thrived here.

If I could just scrape together enough coppercuts, I wouldn't have to keep my head down. I could go anywhere else. My craft would be valued. Respected. Treasured. Anything other than what it is here now where the people have all but forgotten what Tyro and Krakau used to be.

Marching up the cobblestone lane is a huddle of villeins going to the Obitzu Bayou to work. On their shoulders is a bundle of stilts and basket-scythes used to traverse the bayou and collect the coffee cherries within. Kalloway folds into the huddle and disappears up the road with them.

I close my door, lock it, and sprint to the cellar.

The last of the plank shards are ripped away in my feverish curiosity. The rusted thing is too heavy to pull out in one heave. It takes several to get it out from under the staircase. The size of it is surprising. Standard-size chests are about half this. Getting it up to my workroom is a tricky task, but my determination gets the job done before I have to open up shop. By the end, I am sweat-drenched with aching arms, but now even more eager to open it.

Under the electric illumination of the workroom, I can admire it. However, there isn't much to admire. There's no sign of paint or extra decoration. What really draws my eye is the lock. Or is it multiple locks? It's a sequence of five, I deduce, along a complicated yet beautifully crafted escutcheon, but none have a slit for a key. They are ivory depressions with runes. Overall, it's an impressive piece. Something to be proud of. Unfortunately, I have to destroy it.

I retrieve my sledgehammer and prepare my stance for a formidable strike. These locks, while great in an earlier time, are probably weak from age. However, I want to preserve them to study later. A well-placed strike against the wood should unseal this mechanical monstrosity. I hoist the hammer and bring it down on the wood. It neither splits nor cracks. Instead, the sledgehammer flies from my hands and bounces across the floor.

Strange. Perhaps there are multiple layers of dense wood. That could explain the size and weight.

I try again, but aim for the metal braces on the second strike. Again, nothing breaks. Preserving the runes aren't going to work, after all. I try once more with a side swing straight into them. A crack rumbles through my arms. My immediate assumption is that I broke the lock. A distinct confusion invades me when I witness something wholly unbelievable. The shards scattered across the room are not from the chest, but from the sledgehammer. What's left in my grip is a handle split down the middle. I can barely wrap my mind around the force needed to splinter a chunk of metal like it's brittle stone.

Deciphering the lock is the only clear way in, but that'll have to wait. The timepiece chest has to be finished before the client comes to pick it up. I find the copper wire and fix it into place. After a few more adjustments, it works perfectly. It's a unique chest which can only be opened at a set time.

There is no rush of customers when I unlock the shop door. There never is. The Port Ov Krakau doesn't have much to attract visitors, so the usual browser is gathering supplies before hopping pebbles to another more important island.

The sailor I made the chest for enters with a pudgy hand resting atop an extended gut. His coughs unload spittle into a stringy beard. He purposefully scrapes muddy boots on my floor to remove the muck, then locates me by a rack of smaller chests.

"Where is it, boy?" he says, breath smelling of fish. I heave it out of my workshop and drag it to him. He stops me with a foot against the chest. "Don't scuff the bottom, kid."

"Not a kid."

He laughs. "Could've fooled me. Never be a sailor. Your body couldn't handle it." He pulls out a coin pouch and dumps some coppercuts and tinstrips into my palm. After hoisting the chest up to his shoulder, he goes for the door.

I mumble after scanning the currency.

"Wha's that?" he grunts, barely cocking his head toward me.

"This isn't enough. This is twenty coppercuts and ten tinstrips. The chest is fifty coppercuts, or forty coppercuts and fifty nickelcuts, or five hundred—"

"Enough of that salted shite." He swivels fully and lumbers back to me. "You said it's twenty-one coppercuts for one of these specially designed chests."

Now I'm under this sweaty, pudgy giant looking up with fear clearly plastered all over my face. It's not the right time for me to reply, but I do. "That's just for the chest. Labor and supplies for a custom design requires me to ask for…" My voice tapers at the end, leaving me silent and desperately trying to find anything around the room to look at besides those bloodshot eyes. My throat is dry and swollen.

"That is no way to do business, boy. Be upfront with the price from the beginning."

"I—"

"Clamp your tongue. I'm leaving now. Hope you've learned something. And clean yourself up. You've got blood all over yourself. Disgusting." He stomps out and slams the door.

Perhaps he was right. Was I not clear about the price?

I pocket the money. I planned on buying food with that income, but now my cabinets will be empty for another night. This is hardly enough to cover the cost of the materials bought to make the chest.

The chest!

I am propelled to the workshop to study my strange discovery. With that interaction out of the way, I give it every shred of attention. The bell will alert me if anyone else finds their way in here.

How can a chest shatter a sledgehammer like it did? How can it have five locks with no keyhole? I feel trapped within it, anxious to get out. It's a bit comforting to think of myself in a box where I must use my every wit and whim to find the door. But this box, this mysterious chest, just won't reveal its secrets to me. Hating to admit it, I can't decipher this without help.

I don't usually talk to people on the island. I fix generators here and there, and fail to haggle prices at the store. Generally speaking, I am ignored. The exception to this is Grifton. He's never shown a sliver of greed, and I know he'll love to help. Sneaking it to him is the ordeal.

It's clear the day is dead, so I close early. I wheel to the front a barrow and drag the chest to the porch, this time utilizing logs of firewood underneath to roll it. With this method, the chest is loaded into the wheelbarrow within minutes. A tarp from storage covers it well.

Each island in the archipelago has a charter baron who makes the bylaws to optimize land usage for the preservation of balance. In our case, we have the smallest island of the bunch and half of it is covered by the Obitzu Bayou, which is hardly habitable. The healthiest pastures are utilized as farmland, leaving the port town on the Scarlet Muck to be a cramped nightmare. The distance between homes is hardly a bricklength, and the lanes are thin. Trying to weave between the Krakau residents and the wandering animals is already difficult without the added bonus of trying not to tip over a sagging wheelbarrow. Chickens cry from their coops while kids play on porches. Some older folk stare me down while picking their teeth with wheat stems. Hot air balloons dot the sky, each floating passengers across the archipelago. A butcher screams his deals and a woman tells him to clamp his tongue.

We are a lively but not lovely people. Not since the pirate raid a decade ago.

My destination is the Brewed Bay coffeehouse by the docks. Grifton's own popular eatery and the only source of brewed coffee on the archipelago. The rest of our coffee beans are exported to other islands. Ozma enjoys it enough to not target Grifton with inane fines and bloated taxes like the rest of us.

I'm not dependent on him, but he's the one I need to approach if absolutely necessary. He settled here a few years after the pirate raid, and my father loved coffee. They became close friends, and he is almost like an elder brother to me.

I store my wheelbarrow in his shed with the bags of cherry husks and barrels of beans. I lock the shed behind me, depositing the extra key in its hiding spot in coffeehouse generator.

"Little Salvatorre!" A man bounces off the porch of the Brewed Bay. I'm not little anymore, but I'm stuck with him calling me that. "Welcome back," Grifton says, half laughing. His single thick rope of entangled hair whips around his back. He grabs my shoulders and looks me up and down. "Get in a fight with a pirate? You got blood on you."

"I'm aware."

He guides me inside and gives me a wet rag to clean myself. The coffeehouse is furnished with beautiful stained-glass tables. Imprisoned in the large fish tanks along the wall are the meals for the week, swimming from one dead-end to another. Electric sconces along the wall provide some light, but the bulk of it is from the sun through the windows with a perfect view of the island's bay. A few customers are here, but it's an unusually slow day for the place.

Grifton serves me a conch-cup of filtered water along with a salmon meal on a dried lily pad plate. He also gives me two pitaya fruits, which I hold on to for later. I fix things for him every once in a while and in return he gives me free food. I thank him and scarf it down without saying much. During which, he brings out a basket of mud with worms in it. He slides a few in each tank. We watch the fish nibble on the wriggling prey.

Finally, he asks, "Is there any particular reason you're here, Li'l Salvatorre? You look to be in a hurry."

"Did my father ever mention anything about some kind of runic sequence lock?"

His attention gathers completely on me. "No, I don't believe so. But that seems interesting. Why do you ask?"

The folks eating nearby don't care enough to eavesdrop, but I motion for Grifton to come closer just in case. He takes a seat near me. Coffee fumes cling to his breath.

"I found a chest in my cellar. It had these runes but no keyhole."

"A chest? Did you bring it?"

"In your shed."

"Let's take a gander." He tells customers he'll be out for a moment. They wave him off. "How big?" he asks me on our way to the shed.

"Two bricks."

"Two bricks? Rust, that's as large as you are! How did you haul it all the way over here?" Opening the shed answers that. He unwraps and folds the tarp, sets it aside, and examines what I brought. "This is fantastic. And you say it was your father's chest?"

I shrug. "It must've been."

"There are initials on the side here. Faded, but do you see? I don't think 'GS' would stand for anything but Galvan Salvatorre."

I hadn't seen the initials before. No chestmaker carves their initials in a chest they might sell, so it must've been his. Why wouldn't he have told me about it? What could he have kept from me?

"Do you recognize the runes?" I ask.

"A little. I remember a book I read about the prohibition runes."

"The what?"

Grifton scrunches his face. "The prohibition? When islands all across the pole made alcohol illegal."

I shake my head. "I know what prohibition is. What about the runes?" My father educated me well enough, perhaps even better than most people on the island, but these runes are new to me.

"Well, the grog-mobs, who kept supplying the alcohol, needed a form of communication to not get caught. I think these are the same runes they came up with. But that was my grandparents' generation. Why your father used them on this is odd."

"Do you recognize which ones these are?"

"I believe this triangle within a triangle is the rune for fire. This spade with a loop is water, maybe. The skull and crossbones is obviously poison. I don't know what this rake-shape is. And this last one looks like a volcano, but I don't know if that's what it symbolizes."

"I don't know if any of that will help, but I appreciate it." I wheel the barrow out. He stops it with his foot. It reminds me of the client from earlier. Had I said something to offend him? Sometimes I get too blunt and people react negatively.

He asks, "Do you need help with it?"

"I like the challenge."

"I'll still stop by after I close up. I'm curious."

Grifton removes his boot and reminds me to put the tarp over it. As I wobble back through the cobblestone lane, he returns to the coffeehouse. The return home is on a slight incline and takes me nearly twice as long to get back.

14

Along the way, a little neighbor girl tugs on my shirt and asks if I've got food under my tarp. Her ribcage can be seen through her rags. Her parents use her to beg for food from people who visit the port, but I wonder how much of it she actually gets. To stop her from looking under the tarp, I sacrifice one of the pitaya. I make her promise to eat it before running home to her parents.

For hours I study the strange chest in my workshop. I touch every inch of it with a magnet. I search the cellar and the rest of my home for clues or keys. No success. As the answers continue to elude me, I grow frustrated. I wield a fire stoker and whack it, stab it. No damage. This wood is hardy. Must be something special. Carving it with a knife doesn't work, either. How did he get his initials on it?

Maybe I shouldn't open it. My father left it out of his notes for a reason. Left it hidden. But why not give it a regular lock and dump it in the sea or bayou? It must be something worth keeping.

I inspect the fire rune: a white triangle within a white triangle carved into an ivory depression. White? The other runes look like slivers of metal underneath the ivory. Why is the fire rune different?

Because this rune's already unlocked!

I fetch a conch from the kitchen and fill it with water from the cleaning bucket. I heave the chest over so the runes face up. My hand trembles pouring it into the water rune. It slowly fades away as if being drained through pores in the ivory. The water seeped in completely and—

Click.

The spade with a loop is now white—unlocked. The depictions are the keys. Never would have figured it out had I not already accidentally unlocked the fire rune when I first illuminated it with the candle under the stairs.

What a magnificent contraption. No doubt it needs a lot of inside space for a mechanism to every rune. Makes me wonder if there's anything in the chest besides machinery. It wouldn't surprise me in the slightest if my father made a huge puzzle box. Though I do find it strange how even I bested him in chest mechanics and yet he could piece together something like this. There are still so many tricks of the trade I need to learn.

Despite deciphering how to unlock it, the last three runes still bewilder me. Where am I supposed to get poison, and what did the other runes mean? How would it even know the difference between poison and water if both are in liquid form? I spill more water on the other runes just to be sure my father was thorough in his design. None percolate through like before.

Poison? What kind of poison? It was prohibition, so the skull and crossbones might have been first utilized as a symbol for the alcohol itself.

I run back to my kitchen. Elevated on a stool, I reach toward the highest cabinet over dishes I've been ignoring for several days. My fingers crawl around the cabinet like a spider until I find the last bottle of rum my father ever purchased—unopened. As I scamper back to the den I wonder how it could distinguish alcohol from water. Perhaps there's a density or buoyancy discrepancy. The rubbery odor hits me when I pull the cork. I haven't smelled anything like it in a while. The rum has a black tinge to it that stains the ivory. My mouth drops open when the rune accepts it and unlocks.

The rake-shaped rune looks a little like a primitive depiction of a lightning strike across the sky. It won't hurt to try electricity, and I can vaguely picture how a lock may work around such an idea. I flip off the lights and don rubber gloves. Using only the dim glow of a single lantern, my fingers fumble at one of the light bulbs to retrieve the wiring. I disassemble the light, leaving the wires attached to the switch. Plier teeth biting down on the wires keep me from touching them directly. After lifting the chest upright and shuffling it closer to the switch, I touch the wires to the rune and slam the lever into position.

Another faint *click*. It worked perfectly.

I rewire the bulbs, flip on the light, and study the runes. All are white except for the volcano-shaped conundrum. Perhaps it means lava, but heat should work just the same if that were the case. It could mean land or dirt or igneous rock. How could any of those unlock something? Or it's something else entirely.

There's a knife on the workbench that gives me one idea. I clean it off, sanitize it, then plunge the tip of it into my finger. If there's a theme, perhaps blood is the last key. Blood, water, electricity, fire, and a lot of alcohol—Grifton might say those are ingredients for a hardy person. Drops of blood stain the ivory. The minor sacrifice is not accepted. Silly idea, anyways. Grifton might say that, but my father was not the type. And he always paled at the sight of blood.

I return to the kitchen with the rum, and leave it there on the small dining table. The salt water I use to rinse my finger stings. I clean the wound, bandage it, all while pondering that final rune.

Volcanoes. Islands. Soil. How could a mechanism detect dirt? Wasn't any stranger than wood that can't be carved or a shattered hammer. It's settled. I take a handful of the dried red soil from the front road and rub it into the red-stained rune.

Click.

Vapor seeps from the crack. My heart changes its tune. I reach over to fiddle with the button on my cuff. A musty stench permeates the room, like when the bayou winds drift into town. I reach down to open it, but the top swings open on its own.

This is… more than a puzzle box. It's an enigma. No, an impossibility. Muscles weak. Shaking.

Why did I need to open this? Why did I persist? I need out—

Lungs constrict.

I can't—

I don't—

"I don't understand," I whimper aloud.

"I said the same when I was locked inside this damn thing," replies a raspy voice from a man now freed from the chest.

THE STRANGER

A thin and scruffy man stretches out before me like an unfolding scroll. He groans. Shakes every muscle. His balance is that of a young child learning to walk.

"Help me, please," he groans. I remain still. Seeing this, he proceeds alone, leg stretching over the side of the chest.

What a stumbling mess with that unkempt hair, and I can see every vein across his skin. I sidle around him to investigate the chest. His wandering hands search the room for something substantial to hold himself up. The workbench is his choice, but I don't like how close he gets to the tools.

"Who are you?" I finally speak while peering inside the chest. It's not lined with cushions or textiles of any kind. It's plain wood—a most uncomfortable thing to be locked in.

"Shadir. Do you have rum?" He palms his forehead and retracts his question. "Water. Do you have water?"

"Yes."

Another staggering observation about the chest is the lack of mechanical innards. The box is completely empty.

After a moment of nothing, he asks, "Can I have some?" As I leave the workroom, he adds, "And food, if you can spare it."

I return with a conch cup of fresh water, and the last pitaya Grifton gave me. I am reluctant to give it up, but this man is as starved as that child from earlier.

After handing those over, I step back and fiddle with the button on my cuff. This must be some kind of scam or convoluted attempt at thievery. Picked me because he knew he might get away with it like that man I sold the chest to.

"I'm Archie Salvatorre. Explain yourself."

"So you're Salvatorre's son," he says through a groan of pain while massaging his neck. "I've been locked away a long time. That bastard put me in there."

"My father died a year ago. Don't play tricks on me."

"He died?" He stares off into his own memories—reliving something, or many things, or maybe faking it. "Shame." His yellow teeth rip into the pitaya. Eyes widen as if it's the most delicious thing he's ever eaten. He devours it in a few quick bites. Spittle and juice run rivers through his hairy chin. "So you're all alone here then? Or is your mother—"

"It's just me."

He clears his throat, releasing a gust of rancid breath through the room. "Archie, right? How old are you?"

All he has is questions for me, but I'm the one who should be interrogating. I reply, "Nineteen."

"Bloody Baldeva," he says, shoving his face into his hands. It looks like crying before he looks back up with dry eyes. "Your father put me in that chest at least twenty years ago. Probably a lot more."

"Why are you doing this to me?" I ask. Before he can answer, I say, "Somebody put you in my cellar to play a jest on me, or to steal from me, didn't they? Why are you lying?"

"I swear I'm—"

"Was it Ozma? Is this his trick?" I leave the workroom again, saying, "Stay here. I will return with my pistol."

"Wait!" His knees buckle and he falls. His bony arms struggle with the load of his body. When he raises his head, a gun barrel nearly touches his face. Shadir puts a hand up to block it, but a bullet will still tear through him at this range. "I swear there is no trick here. There is magic in this chest."

"No, there isn't. Get out of my workroom. I'm not going to be made a fool."

In disjointed, awkward movements, he eventually raises himself and stumbles through the shop. The barrel of my gun jabs his back the whole way.

He croaks, "Gilligan would be upset with you." I pause, anchored with confusion. Shadir notices and continues, "He'd be upset with his son kicking out a friend."

"When were you supposedly locked in that chest?" I ask.

"The seventeenth year of the Ape Queen calendar. I swear—"

"Does the name Galvan have any meaning to you?"

"No…"

"Galvan Salvatorre is my father. Gilligan Salvatorre is my grandfather. The year today is the twenty-third of the Star Koi calendar."

After a long calculation, his breathing becomes shallow gasps. "Fifty-six years? I'm almost… *eighty* years old."

A jest? A theft? Neither make sense with something this elaborate. I barely remembered my own grandfather's name. For another person to go out of their way to find out that information to use against me is strange. And no one led me to look under the stairs. I found the chest by chance, and got lucky opening it. Manufacturing all of that would be impossible.

"Go to the kitchen," I demand, and gesture the way with the pistol.

He does, and chooses to rest at the small dining table with the newly opened bottle of rum.

"You have rum just laying out? Bold. I've known folk who were hanged for less. Or is prohibition over and done with by now?"

"Too many people got sick and died before they realized alcohol is sometimes safer than water."

He chuckles a bit. "Brilliant irony. May I have some?"

"You can take it when you leave. I don't want you to sodden your brain until you've explained yourself."

"It'll take a lot more than this to get me drunk, but very well. Me and your father—grandfather, I suppose—we were great friends growing up. Just a couple scrappy scammers down by the docks. Then dipped our toes into smuggling for the grog-mobs. Helped fund our trips to other islands."

If he's lying, prying deeper could trip him up.

"If you were friends, why did he lock you in the chest?"

Sucking in a lungful, he prepares for an answer. Eyes drift around the room. Thin, veiny fingers scratch at his beard. Finally, he lets out, "On our trip, we found something. An Arwellian ruin undiscovered by anyone since the flood."

This morsel of information attracts me. I've always been interested in those who lived before the flooding of the world. Most of their ruins were sunk, but some were built on higher elevations and avoided complete destruction. Had I been born a few generations earlier, I would've wanted to sail around the ocean to find them. Alas, that is not my fate in such a day and age. An Arwellian ruin in the southern pole that hasn't already been picked clean by explorers and plunderers probably no longer exists, but there's no way for me to disprove his tale.

Shadir continues, "It was an island infested with predators. An amazing discovery on its own, but in the ruin itself was something strange. I can't begin to explain it. This thing was unnatural. Hard to remember details, like a fuzzy dream. But I remember the power emanating from it. And the magic used to curse us."

"So you're sticking to this *magic* story?"

"Clearly, you've never seen the gold priests along the Port Ov Aslo." Then, with a bite of disdain, "But I'm not here to convince you. What we saw wasn't mind tricks or sleight-of-hand. It was real, and we couldn't let anyone find it. As the navigator and cartographer, I made the map to the island, and had it memorized. So after I burned all the maps, Gilligan wanted to hide me from those who would come looking for them. I told him I would not cower under a rock forever. So he took it upon himself to create a chest with the ability he gained and sealed me inside." The mention of the chest aggravates him. He's shaking, and his fists tighten. "My closest friend did that to me. Can you imagine that?"

"No."

"Well, try to." He buries his face into his hands.

It's clear he needs time to clean himself, rest, and gather his thoughts. I let him be for a span so I can finish my end-of-day chores. Because he's so feeble, I choose to believe he can't run off with anything of value if left alone. Even so, the pistol is kept with me at all times.

As I rub grime off my shop door with a wet rag, he kneels before one of the load-bearing columns in the middle of the shop. Carved in that wood are initials and lines marking different heights of children. One of them was from my grandfather when he was growing up here. No one else could possibly know that. Not even Grifton.

He then inspects my chests, and smirks as if wading through good memories. He chooses one and finds the secret compartment in a manner of seconds. No average person should know about a chest's secret as casually as that. Though it is a reliable design passed down through the family.

There is some truth to his story. I can't deny that. But to what extent? And what do I do about it?

Later, he says, "I want to go to the cemetower. I assume Gilligan is there?"

"Yes, my father showed it to me once. I'll take you."

The bustle of the island died down substantially. The sun wades in the ocean, slowly sinking. We step over the mud-bathing frogs and crimson snails of the Scarlet Muck. Stale wind from the Obitzu Bayou commingles with the salty sea air. And when the sun finally dips below the horizon, it is the bright blue and green lights of the Aurora Tide which keep us from stumbling around in the dark.

Shadir takes it all in. "Never thought I'd enjoy the sight of Krakau so much."

Our brisk walk takes us a little outside of the port town and up the ocean-side cliff which overlooks the harbor. We come upon the torch-lit tower ascending hundreds of bricks high and descending several bricks below the ground.

Every bit of land is important to the structure of our society. It's vital to not waste space burying our dead, but burning bodies is a dishonor.

The idea of keeping the dead is strange altogether, but I think I'm the only one who believes that. Although, it does bring some business to my shop. It's not uncommon for families to lock up valuables with their dead. They employ me to make small ornamental chests to put with the bodies.

The crypt is peaceful at night, I have to admit. Statues strike beckoning poses. Lilacs and roses give calming aromas. Volunteer crypt-keepers keep it maintained, and light it well for those needing a late visit.

The entrance has load-bearing supports to hold the weight of the swirling staircase. There are some stacks of books, gardening tools, and broken statues, but nothing of value. Religious cantos and prayers are chiseled into the wall. The meanings of them are long forgotten. We go up the stairs.

The bodies are placed inside the walls in stacked crypts. Names and dates are carved on the stone slabs that seal those crypts. I haven't yet come to see my father since he was put in here. Don't see the point in it. I grieve, of course, but the dead can't hold a conversation. Even if I did go to his crypt, I wouldn't be able to stop thinking about how he isn't in there in one piece.

Shadir finds his mother first, then his father. Wasn't sure if they died before or after he was locked away, and it felt too sensitive to ask. Just how much the world changed without him is probably overwhelming. Assuming he told the truth, no one from his previous life is alive. People don't live as long as the ancient Arwellians used to. He scrambles around the crypts, finding others, and reading out the names of those he knew. He's trying to hide the sea in his eyes, but I can see the tear drops dotting the floor.

Eventually, we stop at my grandfather's crypt. Shadir's face contorts with all the anger and heartbreak and betrayal trapped inside, but words fail to reach his quivering lips.

"Let's go," he says to me. "I wanted to say something to him, but it seems useless now. He can't hear me."

When we head back to the shop, the nightly glow of the Aurora Tide is enough to make it back without a lantern. This high up, we can appreciate the sight of the entire port. Shadir's glistening eyes take in the natural beauty. It sits between the glassy bay and the dark mass of the bayou—as ominous as it is dangerous. On the opposite side from us is the farmland, and quite a ways beyond that is the bug-swarmed aura of lamp lights powered by a generator. A wrought-iron fence surrounds a gaudy house there.

Shadir notices this, and asks, "What is that down there? Seems like a waste to be using so much of their generator during this bright of a night."

"The charter baron manor." They claim to need the extra space others don't in order to efficiently bring balance to the island. A small price to pay in order to keep anarchy and barbarism out of our lives. "Built a few years ago."

I refrain from saying more. I was told to clamp my tongue by Kalloway. Maybe he's right. I have no idea what this man will say, or what he believes. Maybe this whole thing is one of Ozma's tricks.

Wait and see.

"Seems wasteful," he says, remaining pensive, but that is not enough for me.

Awaiting us on the porch of my shop is Grifton, fiddling with a book's spine before seeing us. A look of excitement transforms into confusion.

He uses the book to point, "Never seen you before."

"I'm a distant relative."—"This is Shadir."

We said those at the same time. Luckily, there's no contradiction. Reluctantly, I follow along with the lie.

"Shadir?" Grifton says, looking the stranger up and down. "Nice to meet you. I'm Grifton. Owner of the Brewed Bay by the docks. Freshest brew on the island."

"Only brew on the island," I add.

"Didn't know the Salvatorre family had distant relatives."

"On my mother's side," I say. Grifton knew my father well, but not my mother. "I actually didn't know he was coming to visit."

That in itself was strange to say. People don't really visit Krakau anymore.

Shadir waves a grimy hand through his mangy beard. "Sorry for the appearance. Long journey."

Grifton holds up the book. "I found in my collection this historalogue with a grog-mob rune translation in it. Figured I would bring it by—"

I stop him. "No need. Already opened the chest."

He chuckles and shakes may shoulder. "You were always a clever one, Archie." To Shadir, "Couldn't ever beat him in card games. What was inside?"

"Nothing," I say. "Just a puzzle box."

"May I take a look?"

I nod and usher him in. Shadir makes interrogative nonverbal cues behind Grifton's back which I shrug off.

After a quick investigation, Grifton says, "Strange design. Perhaps it was just a project your father started working on and couldn't finish."

"It's probably that," I say, gently guiding him back out. "Might sell it if I figure out how to make it work."

"Well, let me know if you do." He gives one last skeptic's look at Shadir. "Nice to meet you. Come by sometime. I'm as famous for my coffee as the Salvatorres are for their chests."

After Grifton departs, Shadir says, "I can't let anyone know who I really am. People won't understand."

That I know. Barely understand any of it myself.

Every rational voice in the world would tell me I shouldn't let him stay, but something compels me. My father wouldn't have. I don't want my hospitality to die out like his did. He kept us safe during a questionable time, I acknowledge that. But I don't want to keep fearing the world like he did. Maybe it'll be my last mistake, but I make the offer.

First, he bathes and trims his mane. Natural color has almost completely returned to his skin. I give up my bed for him. If what he says is true, he hasn't had a good night's rest in fifty-six years. My father's old room is full of storage, so I roll out some extra blankets in my humble treasury to sleep there.

I have a main chest by the hearth. Designed it myself. Looks quite fancy, but holds no treasures. It's a decoy in case of another pirate raid. A hidden chest is in my workroom. Looks rather dusty and unassuming—certainly not something to steal. The mechanism within the chest makes it special. The main storage is empty, but the secret compartment at the bottom keeps my money safe. It locks every coin in place to avoid a jingle when moved.

Earnings for the day are spread across my floor to count. Four customers today, though one didn't pay enough. Might break even, but I still haven't counted the pouch from that woman who came in early. I retrieve it. Feels heavier than normal coppercuts. I dump the pouch. Gold coins bounce and spin across the floorboards.

Lightheaded, I check to make sure they're real. They feel real. In the soft light of the candle, they have a polished glint. This is absolutely real gold. She misunderstood what I meant when I said that chest costs twenty. She thought twenty gold.

I rub the face of one and turn it over in my palm. This isn't just a doubloon, but a crown with some queen's head on it. A servant to royalty perhaps. A tide of excitement comes while imagining my chest adorning some grand treasure room in a castle. But that ebbs as quickly as it flowed. Doubt surges in its place. She may have purchased it out of pity.

They're shinier than coppercuts. I rub my thumb over the face of the monarch I don't recognize. What can I do with them? I can't exactly spend it in the archipelago. That could draw suspicion.

I should've corrected the mistake when I had the chance. I was naive. Foolish to get so caught up in the runic chest that I didn't count it.

But it's not my fault. She made the mistake. Based on dress and jewelry, she comes from a much more affluent society where a craft like mine would garner more attention and value. What a place that would be.

Tides wash me away from this place.

And what about this stranger in my bed? He could kill me for these. I check to see if he snuck down, fully aware of this feeling as paranoia. It's hard to shake out of my head. My luck could swing heavily in the other direction to make up for this mistake. But I never believed in luck before, so why is it coming up now?

I fit the coins into my secret compartment. After hiding the chest again, I return to my makeshift bedroll and blow out my candle. Sleep evades me for quite some time as the world of my mind consumes me like sporerot. I wriggle in place, turning over one way and the other like a fish out of water.

The next day I wake to brushing sounds. Peeking around the corner, I find Shadir scratching at the Scarlet Muck and sweeping it outside. That is generous of him, but I can't know for sure if he's doing this to get on my good side.

Approaching him, I ask, "What is this for?"

He pauses. "Just to thank you for letting me stay here last night. It was the first good night I've had in… well, you know."

I'm particular about my chores. I scan his work. Adequate, not perfect. "So you'll be leaving after this?"

"I guess so," he says before brushing a pile out the door.

My scrutiny moves across the inventory to the column with the initials. Whoever he once had, family or friends, they're long perished. There is nowhere for him to go.

I wonder aloud, "You and my grandfather were close? Was this shop like a second home to you?"

He chuckles. "Yeah. We were rascals running around this place. Then we grew up into louts, and the locals hated us. We wished for ages to get off this pebble. When we finally did, all we could dream about was getting back and running this shop together." Shadir stealthily slays a tear building in the corner of his eye. "More valuable to me than all the gold in the world… at one point."

What Shadir said is familiar. The voice of the pirate from the raid comes back to me after all this time.

"Having someone worth fighting for. That's more valuable than gold."

Before being sucked deeper into that memory, the door swats open, cracking a hinge and knocking the bell off. An elegantly dressed man eyes the two of us before closing the door behind him. He corrects his disorderly lapel before addressing us. "Which one o' you sold a chest to Lady Pero at such an exorbitant price?"

My stomach drops like an anchor. On his belt is the same symbol as the woman's ring from yesterday morning. The one who gave me twenty gold coins. A meek gesture professes my involvement.

The man practically snarls like a bayou gator when he stamps closer. "What kind o' grift you runnin' in this swampy trash heap?"

"I don't—"

"I'd rather not be on this island longer than I have to be so fetch me what you stole."

My throat feels like I swallowed a cannonball.

Because I don't respond in time, the man targets Shadir. "Is the shop owner an idiot? If I am not given a full refund, I'll have to discuss this with your island's charter baron. I'm sure they'll want to avoid a conflict with their biggest trading partner, the *Aronian Kingdom*."

This can't be happening. I can't lose everything because of a mistake that was barely my fault. Ozma is already looking for any excuse to put me under contract. I can't go in there. The bayou. Not after…

I have to give the money back, even if it means losing the chest they already took.

Shadir leans the broom against the wall and says, "Excuse me, good sir. Archie did not tell me we were graced with such a fine lady. How much did she pay for the chest?"

"Aye, twenty-two gold, it was. I expect it in full."

"Twenty-two?" I finally manage to sputter. "No, she spent a flat twenty."

Shadir says, "I believe this conversation needs a mediator. Let's go to the charter baron and see if they'll help us."

"Shadir, stop," I whimper.

The man scoffs, "I will not bother them with the likes of this unless it is to exile you both off the island."

If only that were the worst thing they could do to me.

"Please, I insist," Shadir says. He places one hand on the man's shoulder and ushers him out the door. "We'll bring the money and have this all sorted out."

"Unhand me! I will be given what I'm—"

Shadir places a deft foot in front of the man who then tumbles off the porch and into the dirt. This is followed by a tantrum that arouses interest from nearby Krakau folk and the villeins marching up the lane.

"You fools! Swamp-heathens, the lot of you!" Dusting himself off, he says, "The gallows for you when I tell the charter baron."

As he hauls tail down the lane, I turn to go get my chest. I don't have twenty-two gold, but I can give what I have and see if that will satisfy him. Before I take another step, Shadir grabs my arm.

"He's not going to do anything. That man's a scammer. He's not Aronian. The woman was in on it."

"How do you know?"

He lets go of my arm. "His accent. Diction. Attire. None of it was

Aronian, unless things seriously changed in the time I was away. He saw you as a scared, naive target. Preyed on your natural fears. Expected you to pay back more than what you got because you don't know fake from real. Then they sell the chest still in their possession at an inflated price on some other island. Your grandfather and I practically invented that one, although these two may have perfected it."

"But they gave me crowns. Real gold. And the woman was so nice."

"A convincing touch, but it's all to confuse you. They let your anxiety boil inside all night so you'll be more susceptible in the morning."

My face flushes. Gullibility nearly destroyed me. It could've been the end of my shop had I fallen for it. "Will they come back for the crowns?"

"I don't know. It's a lot of money to lose."

Though flustered, I know my next decision is the reasonable choice. "Stay here," I say. "You stay with me as my employee. Help me run this shop. Protect me from people like them."

Shadir is genuinely surprised by the offer. "Archie. Thank you, but are you sure?"

I rub stress out of my face. "No, not really. But you better take the deal now before my other instincts kick in."

"I'll start right away. Now."

We shake hands. Smiling, he picks up the bell that was knocked off the door and sets it back in place.

My actions are foreign to me now. Population control is under the domain of the charter barons. I've just created an imbalance.

THE CHARTER BARONS

Shadir has the idea to bring down a few chests to the docks. Many sailors don't have a reason to leave their ships, so they never make it far enough up the lane to view my stock. While I manage the shop, he displays them out there. I was hesitant at first, so I had him take one at a time. But after several days, he takes two or three and occasionally sells out.

I'm in my workshop fixing a piece of a puzzle box a customer broke when the front bell jingles. Now every time I hear it, my insides are squeezed of all courage. I worry those scammers will return, or perhaps Ozma. That's the worst-case scenario. But this time it's Grifton paying a visit.

"In the workshop!" I call out.

"You look happy to see me," he says.

More like relieved, but I won't say that. "Looking to buy a chest?"

Although I jest, he responds, "In a way, yes."

Grifton already has a Salvatorre chest. I remember when my father sold it to him. "Oh, well I suppose the one you have is a bit dated. If I remember correctly, it's a standard tumbler lock with inlaid obsidian. Tricky, that obsidian. Brittle. Don't think my father used it much after that."

"Good memory. Actually, I was hoping to purchase the runic chest you found."

My eyes dart to the corner where I keep it. Studied it earlier, but there wasn't anything I could learn. The inner mechanism is small and simple. Deadbolt locks unconnected to anything except the runes. The rest of it also lost its invulnerability, as if unlocking it dissolved any imbued magic. Bloody waters, I can't believe I'm considering magic now, but there is no other explanation I could make of it.

"I still need time to study it. It's a strange lock."

He meanders over to the corner, studies the chest in and out. Our conversation is diluted with prolonged silence. He kneels by it and touches the inside. He's not a chest enthusiast, but even an average person would know there is something off about it.

"I saw that man out by the docks. The one you claim to be a relative. He's selling your chests. Why?"

The accusatory tone is what catches me off-guard the most. He's upset more than confused. No, not upset. Cautious. Skeptical. I should've considered he'd pry into Shadir's presence.

"He's helping me."

"We both know this shop isn't profitable enough for you to hire an employee. Who is he, really?"

"It's as I told you."

"You would tell me if you found something in this chest, wouldn't you? Valuable or dangerous?"

I stop working on the puzzle box, but don't take my eyes off it. It's my refuge. An oasis away from this moment. "There was nothing in it. Shadir has nowhere else to go. I'm offering a place to stay for his help. That's all."

"You understand how suspicious this all looks? You find a chest and now have an employee. You are not a great liar. I see straight through you."

A pang of rage emboldens me. "Not your well, not your water." I walk over and slam the chest shut. "And this is not for sale."

"Very well." On his way out, he adds, "Truth or not, you need to be careful. You don't have official approval from the charter barons. They will notice him eventually. You and I both know they'll get you on anything they can."

He means well, I know he does. But I have to start solving my own problems.

Before closing time, Shadir returns from the docks with one chest leftover and a bag of various legal tender. I count and sort them while he does closing chores.

Shadir pauses his work to reminisce by the post. He does that every once in a while. The broom hairs tap uselessly against the floorboards as he fixates on the initials carved there. "Whatever happened to this place?"

I avoid answering that and pretend to be too focused on hiding the money away in my unassuming chest.

But Shadir continues, "People here are strange. People used to talk to each other. Jest and quip. Haggle. Offer drinks. I haven't seen that yet."

"People aren't like that here."

"Disappointing. But I suppose I shouldn't be surprised. It's been a long time." He returns to sweeping the Scarlet Muck outside, but is more vigorous with it. "And what does everyone do to pass the time? Krakau used to be vibrant at night. Little gatherings. Lively parties. Building muck castles around bonfires. Grifton's coffee place used to host dancing nights. Nothing like that ever happens now?"

Putting the chest in a safe place, I say, "I have bits of memory like that when I was young. But nothing was ever the same after the pirate raid."

"Oh." He slumps with the clarity. "Rusted pirates ruin everything."

After closing, Shadir prepares crimson escargot for dinner. It's a popular meal around here, although the texture of snail is appalling to me. But his long-lost family recipe makes it surprisingly edible.

Last night, he got drunk off that rum I gave him. Turns out, decades of not having a drink made him much more of a lightweight than his pre-chest era of debauchery. In a moment of vulnerability, he admitted to reciting many various things while trapped in the chest. Recipes, songs, stories—over and over again so he wouldn't forget. He rarely speaks about what it was like in there, but every time he does I can hear a nugget of torment in his voice.

After washing the dishes, we play card games until the sun sets, and the Aurora Tide drapes across the sky.

During a particularly bad hand, he slaps his cards down and states, "I'm tired of losing to you at cards every night. Get a rusted lantern. We're doing something else."

"Something else?" I repeat, blankly.

I lock the shop behind me and follow Shadir down the lane. Lantern in hand, he silently guides me to a pier on the bay.

"Keep an eye out," he says.

"For what?"

"*Merfolk.* Who do you think? Other people. We're takin' a skiff."

"Are you feigning anchor or just crazy?"

Shadir swings a leg over the edge of the skiff. "Never did dumb things with friends before?"

"No. Never really had friends."

Wobbling, I follow him in. He grabs me, pretends to throw me off balance, and then laughs. I don't. Smart people have a healthy fear of the ocean, especially at night. We sit and prepare the oars, then match rowing strokes.

"No friends at all? No one to steal a skiff with? No one to chase around or dare to get close to the bayou?"

I shake my head. "But don't pity me for that. I didn't want to grow up a hooligan."

"*Oof.* Cuts deep, that does. Though I deserve it. The most dangerous thing Gilligan and I did was lure one of the gators into town with a chicken we stole. We were… idiots."

"Sounds like it."

"Well you don't have to agree with me that easily."

"Don't mess with the bayou," I say, repeating a lesson my father taught me.

I'm exhausted by the time we get to the middle of the bay. However, the effort is worth the sight. The Aurora Tide above is mirrored perfectly by the still obsidian water below. For a moment, we're hovering between dimensions. Ribbons of light embellish the world. Tyro awaits on one side, and the deep, dark world on the other. I'm stable here in the center of this breathtaking realm.

Shadir scratches something into the side of the boat with a knife he brought.

"You vandalize the boats you steal, too?" I ask. Except, it doesn't look like he is doing it for fun.

"Nothing noticeable. Just something else we used to do. Put our initials everywhere. 'G' for Gilligan. 'S' for Shadir. Like leaving behind a trail."

I relax into the nook of the skiff. All worries vanish in this overwhelming peace. I never knew such an escape could be so close to home.

<hr>

A couple weeks pass without Ozma coming to investigate. The two scammers haven't shown up either. Shadir tells me not to worry, but that's difficult. Who wouldn't be desperate to get twenty crowns back before it's all spent? Although none of it has been spent yet. I haven't had the need. For the first time ever, I'm making a profit. However small that may be. There is actual, real hope that I might earn enough to fund a safe voyage to another island and set up shop in a place that will appreciate my work. A place where I can be of value without being an imbalance.

Shadir is adamant about bringing in customers and pulling his weight. After the few days of trial, his assistance became essential. He cleans faster than I do, greets the customers with an amiable smile, and sells a few chests down at the docks every morning. Stock almost ran out a few times, but I have ample time to make more while he minds the shop. With that extra time, I've developed several new techniques in my craft.

Shadir understands me. The chests are shelved in the right positions. He doesn't muddle with my routine. Never tries to take advantage of my hospitality. I let my guard down around him now, which is not something that comes so easily nowadays.

Though I haven't spoken to Grifton much after he inquired about the chest, he was right. Someone will get suspicious soon. A visitor is fine, but keeping someone hidden in my home without disclosing it to them is illegal and detrimental to the community. I'm not certain if a neighbor will snitch on me. It's hard to tell what people will do around here. Many of them wholeheartedly believe the charter barons are the only ones who know how to keep the balance of the island. They've sacrificed community and trust for blind safety. That's why I have to leave. No one will ever change things here.

After bringing up the population issue with Shadir one afternoon, he hovers in the door frame of my workroom making suggestions. "I can make a plea. Next time someone passes away, I'll be on the list."

He'd be near the top. Birth permits are of lesser value to the charter barons compared to a full-grown adult who can work. But not very many people find themselves willing to live here save for the occasional refugee from other islands.

I'm fiddling with a chest inspired by the electricity rune. Though my focus is mostly on that, I respond, "Anyone who hopes to live here must start in villeinage. Unless you have the funds to buy yourself out of it. Grifton did that, but he's the only one who has. Probably expensive."

His eyes widen with an incoming idea. "What about the money from the scammers? That must be more than enough. And since I already have a place to stay, I won't be paying for island space. I'll take the crowns to them and pretend I'm moving here from Aronia."

Pausing my work: "I suppose that could..."

To use those crowns for that would not leave any for—

"I'm sorry, Archie," he says after seeing the distress grow on my face. "I shouldn't have suggested spending such a fortune on me. After all, what am I to you but a stranger you found in a box?"

"I'll consider it," I say and divert partial attention back on the chest. "But as you've noticed, this place isn't like the home you remember. Surely, you don't want to stay here for long."

His hand rubs the back of his head. "The politics of this island is much more muddled than it used to be. We didn't have to worry about the charter barons or being serfs. Our biggest threat was pissing off the grog-mobs. I mean... not everything was sunshine and rainbows, but as long as they were kept happy the people lived as they liked."

"After prohibition failed, there was a takeover of the charter council by the grog-mobs."

A jingle at the storefront alerts us. I get up but Shadir puts up a hand to indicate he'll handle it. I follow him out anyways, paranoid and curious. In the store is a young girl in a bucklecoat. Perhaps a trader's kid. The look on a child's face when they see a secret compartment or unique mechanism is one of the many joys I get from this craft.

"Good evening, young lady," Shadir says. "Shopping for a parent? We've got some nice puzzle boxes. Or perhaps a coffer for—"

"I'm okay," she says, then peruses at her leisure.

"Okay..." Shadir mumbles. He pretends to wipe clean the counter with a wet rag and gets my attention to continue the conversation. While not completely hushed to a whisper, he is quieter than before. "I suppose that would have been the next logical step for them. But we used to elect charter barons. I take it things have changed?"

"They changed the charter so now they elect their own, claiming they know what is best for the balance of the island."

This girl keeps sneaking looks at us. Finally, she interjects at Shadir, "You the Salvatorre on the sign?"

Shadir flicks a thumb at me. "That'll be this one."

"Archie," I say. "Are you looking for a specialized chest design? I'm good at—"

"Nope." Her curt responses are like the lid of a chest snapping down on fingers still rooting around inside. This rudeness doesn't disturb me, as I'm used to it by now. However, the pistol holster peeking out from under her bucklecoat does raise a concern.

When she's perusing the chests again, Shadir says, "What is all this talk of balance and imbalance I keep hearing about?" But before I could answer, Shadir hollers at this girl. He claps to get her attention. "I see those shifty eyes of yours. Used to have 'em myself. Don't think I don't know what you're doing. You won't get away with stealing anything." He shoos her out the door, but she leaves with an interesting grin. Almost menacing.

"You think she's with those scammers?" I ask, returning to my chest in the workroom.

"I don't know. Could be children being children." He joins me in the workroom again and grabs a measuring tool to flip around in his hand. Then he balances it on a finger. "You had once said they've been trying to run you out of this place since your father passed."

I snatch the measuring tool from him before he breaks it.

Trying to immerse myself into the work, I explain it as bluntly as I can. "About eleven years ago, people in the archipelago were spreading anarchist ideologies. There was talk of Baldeva's revolution. The barons called it an imbalance that could destroy the island."

"People have been using that ol' scare tactic for generations. Got a good dose of it myself growing up."

A splinter sticks in my thumb. I bite it out. "The infighting destabilized us. Weakened us. Not too long after that was the pirate raid I told you about. People died. They burned down stores. It changed everything. The culture of the island you remember died then. And the charter barons cracked down on these imbalances. Told people to watch out for them."

The weeks since getting out of the chest have been kind to him. But he hasn't been able to ignore everything around him. He's seen the starving girl. The villein serfs. The questionable sailors who come through and cause trouble.

He says, "They send people into the most dangerous part of the island to collect coffee cherries. People starve while they live in a manor away from everyone else. They squeeze the life out of shops like this. How is that not imbalance?"

"A lone chestmaker in this place doesn't generate much income. My craft is of no value to them, and neither am I. Income generates through trading our goods to other powerful nations. That keeps our heads above water. As much as I hate it, disrupting that ensures we drown." One of the springs is bent, so I replace it while trying to change the subject. "The lever needs some grease. Can you hand me that—"

"Archie, please look at me." I finally do. "Things can change here. I will make sure of that. You deserve to be a chestmaker. I don't know what I can do right this moment, but I will do something. I just need you to make a decision about that citizenship plea. We don't have much time." He waits for a response that never comes. Craning his neck to check the storefront, he says, "The day is dead. I'll lock up. I can't express how much I appreciate what you've done for me. Feels like the old days with Gilligan."

I have a similar notion of gratitude, but can only express it as a head nod. But he's been here long enough now that he can decipher what that means.

The following day, our routine is broken. Shadir is touching up the arrangement of chests on the shelves when he sees a commotion outside through the windows. He calls me over. A crowd is moving out of the way of a group of four. Two mercenary guards with double-barrel shotguns and two unarmed individuals dressed in fine clothes.

"Charter barons?" asks Shadir.

"Yes. The scrawny one is Ozma. He's the current baron for the Port Ov Krakau."

"And the well-fed woman who screams at everyone?"

"Ozma's mother, Stellagard. She was the previous baron here. Although, through Ozma she still pretty much runs everything."

They already collected our taxes, so this is an unusual time to come down from their manor. And with guards? They're not here for money. They're looking for someone.

I grab Shadir's sleeve and pull him back. "I think they're coming here. They know about you."

We can't go out the front door. They'll see us. Maybe the cellar. No, they'll look everywhere. I pull Shadir back to the workshop.

"There is no way out of this room," Shadir says.

Frantically pacing the workshop, I say, "I know, but... the chest!" I still have the runic chest in the corner of the room. "Get in there. Maybe they won't look inside. I'll put some things on top of it. Make it look inconspicuous."

"This isn't—"

"Shadir, now!" I yell, and then go back to the front window.

They have made their way close to our porch. But we are given a bit of time when that begging child I gave the pitaya to approaches them. She maneuvers around the legs of the guards and tugs on a loose part of the woman's pants. I can't hear what the girl says, but I know she's asking for food or money. Stellagard is startled by her, and a guard pushes her away with a boot so hard that she falls to the ground.

Shadir hovers over the chest, looking deep into it like it has the depth of an ocean trench.

I yell, "Shadir, we have no other option!"

Stellagard is loud enough to hear even from inside. She's demanding the parents show themselves. When no one steps forward to claim the child, Ozma states she might be old enough to climb the trees in the Obitzu Bayou. They're about to force her into villeinage. She's just a kid.

"Shadir!"

He snaps, "I can't! I just can't do it! I can't go back in there."

The girl's scream grabs my attention. She is kicking at the shins of both barons from the ground. I grit my teeth, reach for the door handle, and storm outside. Stellagard raises a hand to beat the girl. I squeeze between the two guards in my way, knocking them off balance, and grab her arm before it strikes and yank her back. I position between them and the girl.

Ozma says, "Archie Salvatorre. Exactly the person we were looking for." He snaps at one of the guards. "Hit him for assaulting my mother."

A firm, gloved hand is about to strike my jaw when Shadir yells from the shop's porch, "Don't you dare touch him, you coral-brained cur!" Shadir gets between us.

"What are you doing?" I ask.

"I have not made a mistake," he responds, still keeping focus on the guards.

Stellagard says, "See here, son. A watchful eye on your people is important. These greedy, filthy toads will do anything to break the law. Handle it." She gives him a hearty slap on the back. He steps forward and straightens his clothes.

"Who are you?" Ozma asks Shadir. "You are not on our list of citizens."

"Archie's relative. I'm visiting."

"Visiting, you say?" Ozma smirks. He's been wanting to get rid of my shop for a long time. And now, he finally has the chance. "According to statute thirty-two of this island's bylaws, a visitation must be brought to the attention of your charter baron and must not consist of more than five days. According to rumors, you've been here for quite some time now. A few weeks I'd wager."

I step forward. A guard crosses his shotgun over my chest to keep me from doing anything rash. But all I want to say is, "He's leaving today. You don't have to do anything. We can forget about this."

Shadir says, "No. We'll negotiate. Pay the fine. Whatever it takes to stay here. This is my home too."

"Negotiate?" Stellagard says, amused. "We are not here to negotiate. It's a pity you couldn't learn the lesson from your father's death. Galvan Salvatorre was a dissenting voice. We should've suspected his son would also break the law."

Also break the law?

Ozma adds, "Negotiations are for citizens who don't put the island and citizens at risk of total imbalance. We should've fed them both to the gators when we had the chance."

Stellagard mutters, "Quiet, Ozma."

The words burrow deep into me like the snails in the Scarlet Muck. The image of his mangled body stains my vision again. I always knew something was strange. They found him in the bayou. He constantly warned me never to go in it. Never. It's the most dangerous place in the archipelago. He was terrified of it. Casually getting killed by an alligator didn't make sense.

Shadir pushes the nearest guard away and advances on the charter barons. "Bastards!" he yells as he flails a fist at them. It lands on Ozma, and they tumble to the ground together. The guard Shadir pushed gathers himself and presses the shotgun into Shadir's back. He doesn't attempt to get up. But he does say, "I will not have my home ruined by swindlers and crooks."

I am frozen. As frozen as the day Grifton brought me what was left of the body. I twist the button on my cuff. It hangs by a thread now.

Stellagard says, "We are a ballast in an otherwise unstable place. People like the filthy beggar child who just ran off—they need us. Without us, it is chaos. You two are an imbalance that needs to be culled for the greater good."

A crowd gathers, refusing to interfere or interact. They'll do nothing. They'll watch, and then return to their mundane lives as soon as it's over. That is always how it is.

"Attention, citizens of the Port Ov Krakau!" announces Ozma. "Your neighbor, Archie Salvatorre the chestmaker, has broken one of the most sacred laws of our archipelago. He has harbored another person for weeks. If we had not caught on to this egregious act, the balance of our island would have been pulled asunder into chaos. For this, I charge him with breaking the balance laws of the Tyro charter." Ozma looks into my eyes. "Plead guilty to betraying your neighbors, and I might give you mercy."

Mercy is villein serfdom. Mercy is slaving away in the bayou where the snakes and gators and greenticks are. Mercy is execution by nature.

Shadir says, "Archie, don't you dare. You're guilty of nothing!" He looks out at the crowd. "Your charter barons pay for mercenaries like this to protect them, but who do they pay to protect you? Don't you have anything to say?"

They don't. They won't. That is not who they are.

"What do you say?" Ozma prods.

I stutter, "I am… an imbalance. I am of no value to this island. But please, allow me to exile myself. I cannot go into the bayou."

Ozma states in a lawful voice, "With the power given to me by statute three of the charter, I hereby sentence—"

A bell tolls in the distance. It's a sound we haven't heard in a long time. The warning bell was installed decades ago, and the last time it rang was during the raid ten years ago. Pirates are at our shore.

The screams of people running up the lane from the docks confirms it. Someone announces what they've seen. "A black flag raised in the harbor! They're coming!"

Stellagard and Ozma share an entire conversation with a single look. The mother says to the guards, "Forget about them. Get us back to the manor. We'll be safe there."

The mercenaries move around Shadir and I to accompany the charter barons. They run away, leaving their citizens alone to deal with the pirates.

THE PIRATE CAPTAIN

I have flashes from the raid so long ago. The sinking dread is intensely familiar—a nightmare ripped straight from my memories and hafted to reality. The crowd dispersed like rodents when the barons took off. I don't know where that girl went, but I hope she's making her way back to a safe place.

Freshly dosed with adrenaline, I tell Shadir, "Let's go back inside for now."

Shadir nods and bounds up the porch steps with me close behind. I lock the door behind me and go to retrieve the pistol in the chest under my bed. Peering out the windows, there's not much to see yet. The piers are not visible from here, but there is hollering fading in and out between the rings of the bell.

"The cellar," I mumble.

Shadir declines. "The cellar will not stop them. We need to get all of our valuables and lie low outside of town until they leave."

His plan makes more than enough sense, but I can't seem to control the desire to flee downstairs. The cellar isn't safe and yet I insist on crawling to it like a roach. Anchored, I fiddle with the button on my cuff. It comes off, falls to the floor, and rolls away.

Shadir breaks through my anxiety, saying, "Grab your money and some canned food. Hide your best chests. Then we leave. Do you understand?"

I do what he says. After preparing everything and leaving the shop, we creep up the lane, looking over our shoulders every few steps. A group of six or seven of them come up the lane behind us. As far as I can tell, no one has been severely harmed yet. I don't hear the usual sounds of looting. No splintering doors. No crashing of glass. None incite violence, though they do wield weapons. They march with purpose without pillaging. They're not doing much raiding, it seems.

One of them points at my shop and they halt. I had left the door unlocked so it wouldn't be broken down. They invade without delay.

"Shadir, wait," I call out. He halves his long strides and looks back at me. "They stopped at the shop."

Shadir whispers, "Perhaps the scammers are responsible? No, that can't be possible. Did the woman ever see you with the chest?"

"No, never. The only other person who knows about it is—"

They trickle into my shop until only one person remains outside—Grifton.

Shadir pulls me out of sight before we're spotted. We squeeze between two houses. He whispers, "Change of plan. These pirates are after me. They know who I am. I won't blame you if you decide on leaving me behind, or ratting out where I've gone. But please help me get to the docks first."

The docks. *Toward* the pirates. The farmland has nowhere to hide and the Obitzu Bayou is hardly survivable. Stealing another boat is Shadir's only option.

"Wherever you're going, I'm going too."

He nods, and then pulls me out the other side to the space behind the buildings.

Our circuitous route will take us past the pirates to the heart of town and back to the bay. We duck behind every house, hedge, and heap of firewood—scurrying along and popping our heads up like rodents smelling the air for predators. The pirates spread their herd to check every lane and alley, but they don't have the numbers to check everywhere at once. Other Krakau folk close shutters and lock doors.

Shadir waves me over to a grey picket fence. I kneel beside him. My heart, beating like it is, feels like it has every intention of giving us away. Most of the pirates have bypassed us and the lane is clear. We bound over the fence and hit our top speeds. The cobblestone soon transitions into the Scarlet Muck, slowing us down like the snails that traverse it. I whisper a trail of apologies when I hear the crunching of shells. I usually avoid them as best I can.

When we make it to the docks, Shadir scans for a suitable vessel. He doesn't want a skiff this time, but also doesn't want a large one with no crew to support it. He nods to a sufficient sloop several bricks away. It's something we can manage together.

We pace ourselves into a jog. With hardly any coverage, the distance feels like leagues. The salty tide gently laps the sloop tied to the dock. Shadir tugs and strangles the boat's dock-knot like it's a snake trying to bite him.

"Where do you think you're goin'?" asks a light voice behind us. I swivel and point my pistol. The pirate tenses but does not waver. "Put it down."

It's the bucklecoat girl from yesterday, but this time she's got her pistol aimed at me from her hip. Every joint in my body locks. Of course she was with the pirates. They used her to stake out me and my shop before coming in full force. How can a pirate ship employ someone so young? Even with my gun aimed at her, she keeps a calm and snarling demeanor. There is a demand in her eyes, one I cannot shake free from.

Shadir steps in front of me and grabs my pistol. He says, "I'm not asking you to kill or be killed for me, Archie." He turns to the girl. "You just want me. He is not part of this."

"The captain wants him. Archie Salvatorre, grandson of Gilligan Salvatorre. In what rusted town are *you* important?"

Why do they want me? Who am I to pirates other than a chestmaker?

Shadir tries to introduce himself, but she snaps back, "Clamp your tongue. And throw the pistol into the water."

When I take too long to do as she asks, Shadir pulls it from my grasp and tosses it in for me. He uses this moment to position himself where he can push the girl in too, but she takes precautionary steps backward. She's not so easily taken advantage of.

She takes us to one pirate in particular with the sharpness and bearing of a chiseled statue, dressed in a dark blue bucklecoat with epaulets on the shoulders and furry cuffs. This man searches through my chest, and furrows his brow at the cans of food. He tells the girl, "Good work, Edia. Here… extra food rations," and tosses her a can.

Sardonically, the pirate girl says, "Thank you, Ald—" A staggering glare from the leader stops her. Edia corrects herself: "*Captain.*" She practically spits her spite at him.

We're promptly tied up and taken to their docked ship.

It's a two-mast, whiptail-class quarvette equipped with a single line of gungills on one side. It is roughly forty bricks long and ten bricks of beam—the width at the widest point. The grey color is possibly from the wood on Alcutta Island. I once bought some of their lumber a while back for a project. It's a beautiful color when fresh, but over time the color wares and dulls, especially when constantly wet. On the mast is a black flag with two fish depicted, an ugly blackscabbard eating the end of a silvery daggertail—like a sheath and knife. I begin to narrate all this information to Shadir, but he shushes me to avoid a pirate's scolding.

After boarding, the captain orders us to kneel. I do so, but Shadir has to be forced. The loading ramp is pulled up. Some of the crew return to duties around the ship, but many stay with us at the center, encircling us. The anchor is raised and the ship drifts towards the middle of the bay.

The captain says, "I don't want to spend any time on your nonsense. I want no sly remarks, jests, misdirection, or incorrect answers. I want the truth, and nothing but." The man circles us like a hunting shark.

"What truth?" I ask, not expecting the swat at my head afterward.

"What did I just say? Where's the map?" He snaps fingers and points somewhere. Two crewmates bring forward the runic chest. "When we searched your shop, we found this. It's the chest you found, innit?"

"It was empty," Shadir lies. "Saw it myself when he opened it."

"And who are you?"

I answer for him, "Shadir. My employee." We swap glances. He wants to lie, but I make it clear he shouldn't. The girl already knows.

A smug grin grows on the captain's face. "Perhaps named after your grandfather? You a local?"

Shadir nods and squirms in place.

The captain bellows, "What are the chances of that? I've got the grandchildren of both Gilligan and Shadir on my deck. I absolutely must go fishin' today because I'm bursting at the seams with luck." The crew doesn't laugh alongside him. They seem unsure of what they're supposed to do. "If there was no map in that chest, then where could it possibly be?"

Shadir smirks. "A map to what? Buried treasure? How quaint. You're chasin' folk tales."

The captain's tone sinks into deeper aggravation. "I said not to make any jests." He unbuckles part of his coat and rifles through his inner flaps to pull out a pistol. He loads it and presses it against the back of Shadir's head. "You know what it's for. I can tell. It's all over your faces. I only need one of you. So perhaps Archie will tell me to save you, or you tell me to save yourself. Either way works."

A few moments pass in silence. I say nothing, mostly because I've no idea what's happening and what they're looking for. Is he talking about the Arwellian ruin Shadir mentioned? If that's it, why does he refuse to tell them? Either one of us can lie, but following up on that lie would be impossible. He has to tell them something.

Shadir says, "Neither of us have an answer for you. Whatever they did has nothing to do with us."

"Fine. Say hello to Baldeva for me."

A spray of red follows the crack of the pistol. The ring in my ear is like a scream. My hand instinctively cups it. I look over to see Shadir go limp on the deck. My mouth is agape, trying to net a breath. My lungs are too startled to get more than a sip of air. He did it. He shot Shadir. I can't bare looking at the body for more than a second.

"Your turn, Archie." He puts away his weapon, opting to deal with me using two hunks of metal that look like rings welded together. They're nickel-knuckles. One punch with those on can crack my face like an egg. He kneels before me, making sure I get a good look at his hands.

Gasping for breath, I say, "I don't know anything about it."

"Even if it has nothin' to do with the chest, you have something of value."

"I've never had anything of value in my life!"

"Check every facet of your memory. It's something important. Something that your family would have kept stowed away in a safe, secretive place. Was there anything you weren't allowed to look at? Any place you weren't—"

A voice cuts him off, "Are those my nick-knucks?" All of the crewmembers crank their heads to a position behind me. The feminine voice continues, "Those are my nick-knucks *and* my bucklecoat, Aldrezier."

The captain, now known to me as Aldrezier, is stunned. "How did you get out?"

He rises and stumbles closer to the back end of the ship. I'm free to turn and look at the confrontation. My eyes gloss over the body of Shadir to find any signs of life, but there's no surviving what happened. I rotate as best I can and see three noteworthy figures. Across from Aldrezier, a woman stands in front of a hatch leading to the brig. The girl who caught us earlier is with her. This woman holds an air of authority, and walks with determined steps. Her wool garbs are underneath a vest of shark leather and breeches, a neckerchief, a gold belt buckle, and gator-leather boots. She casually holds a pistol, no doubt loaded, and walks toward us. The crew parts to let her through.

"You lost," Aldrezier says. "The fleet is mine now. The crew is on my side!"

She makes eye contact with just about every member of the crew. They shift in place and refuse to compete against her stunning gaze. "I have to hand it to you. You chose a perfect time to start this mutiny. You've utilized the gaps in the crew's knowledge to confuse them. I'm assuming you've told them I knew the map was on Tyro Archipelago all this time, and that I've been putting off ransacking the place." She now directs her speech to the crew. "He did tell you this, yes?" A few nod. "Did he tell you raiding this place would've caused more harm than good? Did he fail to mention I planted Grifton on this island in the first place?" The crew hesitates to reply, but it's clear they were fooled.

"Stop talking," commands Aldrezier, lifting his pistol with intent.

She ignores him. "This archipelago has been raided before. There was no guarantee anything of value was still here. Grifton was once my helmsman, but he wanted to retire from piracy, and so I asked him to stay on this island to look for anything strange that may come up so we could sail elsewhere. And he befriended the Salvatorres. That's efficiency, right there. That is being a captain."

"This isn't true." Aldrezier tries to weave more lies but can't spin them fast enough. "You've been lying to us this entire time!"

"Then why are the rest of the crew hesitating to help you. One ship is a nice get, but I am curious how you were going to convince the rest of the captains in the fleet that *you* are now the grand captain. They would've hunted you down."

A crewmate flanks Aldrezier and swipes the pistol from him.

"She's gotten people killed," he pleads to the crew.

"I do what I have to do. You think you'll be better? I have significant doubt about that. You see, if you had not been so mutinous, I could have warned you about what we were looking for. The Salvatorre lad probably hasn't a rusty idea where the map is. Had you not been so treacherous, I could have told you the person we were looking for is the very man you just shot in the head. Shadir himself. He had the map in his head, not on paper. Now you've dismantled decades of work with a single bad decision. It would be shocking if any of these fine people wanted you as their captain after this."

"I didn't know!" Aldrezier pleads to the displeased crew now closing in on him. "We can still come back from this." A strike to his gut silences him. They strip the traitor of his accoutrements and take him to the brig to be dealt with later.

The woman addresses the crew, "You're fish off the hook for this. Be thankful I like you all so much. But don't let the words of fools trick you again."

"Cursed seas," someone says.

Whatever that crewmate is reacting to sends a wave of gasps and awe through the rest of them. A few start pointing in my direction until all of them know what I don't. Then I sense it. Motion and sounds next to me. Shadir's body rises from his pool of blood. The bullet hole is barely a scar—healed as if it's just a flesh wound from ages ago. I back away as much as I can with tied hands. After a moment of struggle, he's back on his knees looking straight at me. I receive a message through his eyes—an apology for not telling me about something.

The magic within the chest wasn't what kept him alive all these years. My grandfather wasn't the only one cursed with magic.

Other than Shadir, the only person unfazed by this miraculous recovery is this captain.

"Cut them free," she orders. "They're both welcome on this ship as friends." The two who approach us to cut our bonds do so with the urgency of a hesitant kitten. She bellows at the others, "Get back to work! And someone get to swabbing this deck before it stains." After we're freed, she meets us. "I am Isadora Rubias, captain of the *Prey Empress*, grand captain of the Blackscabbard Fleet, the Voice on the Wind, the Pirate of Providence, and whatever other random titles they've given me over the years." She gave a dismissive wave to the extra accolades.

"I'm Archie," I croak, transfixed by her in every facet. Eyes the color of honey or brass. Scars which tell stories beyond my years. She presents herself to the world as if welcoming any attempt at her life to be tried and failed.

"I know who you are. I know who both of you are. Actually, I apologize for bringing you into this, Archie. We got word from Grifton that you found a chest hexed with magic, and immediately after, you were seen with a suspicious man named Shadir. I hauled our asses over here as fast as I could to get the chest and its contents. But last night, Aldrezier locked me in the brig at gunpoint, and then fabricated everything to form a mutiny against me, as you've clearly seen. Edia, my young ward over there, came to free me while the crew was distracted."

Shadir, still getting a hold on his senses, says, "Great, we're up to speed. Now are we free to leave?"

"You are not, sir. I've been looking for you for a long time. You traveled with my grandfather. He told me about your immunity to time and injuries, but I was unsure you could survive something like that. I feared everything was lost when I saw you dead. Good to know you can still lead us to the ruin."

"What ruin?"

"You know very well what ruin. The Arwellian ruin you tried to pilfer around fifty-five years ago."

Shadir tries wiping blood out of his hair while saying, "You'll never get that information out of me. If I could die, Gilligan would've put a bullet in me long ago to avoid telling anyone where it is."

"I'm sorry to hear that." Captain Rubias orders two passing crewmates to take hold of Shadir. "Put him with Aldrezier for a bit until he can make rational decisions."

Positioning myself between them and Shadir, I plead, "That man is my… employee. I demand to know why he deserves such treatment."

"He's the only one who knows the way to where I need to be. None of this concerns you if you do not wish it to. Therefore, we'll drift back over to the docks so you may disembark before we leave." Although her voice is stern, it isn't like how most people address me. Most talk to me like I'm unintelligent, a child, a survivor in need of pity, or a combination of the three. This is different. Respectable yet still commanding.

The crewmates move past me and hoist Shadir away.

"I hate pirates!" he yells.

"Who doesn't?" says Rubias.

A shout of warning cuts through my impulsive reply, which is probably for the best. Someone up on the mast points to the etherward horizon. In the vast slab of blue, are two dots of orange and red—two ships entering the bay.

Rubias shouts to her crew above, "Are those the flags for Aronia's Kingsguild?"

"Aye, captain," yells one of the men on the mast with a spyglass. "They're huntin' us down, but the mornin' sun's in their eyes so we may have an advantage."

They must've been nearby and heard the bells. Now they're coming to offer aid to protect their commodities. I can't really go back to port to face the charter barons, nor can I hang around on a pirate ship about to be skewered by cannons.

What a fortune I netted this day.

Rubias turns to me, saying, "I'm sorry for this, Archie. We have to leave. I'll have to throw you overboard. We're close enough to shore. Can you swim?"

She doesn't stop to let me answer that. When she closes in to grab me, I reach for the pistol holstered at her side. I back away and aim. Deep, yellow eyes stare down the barrel, more exasperated than worried. Feeling surrounded by other pirates, I move to the bow of the ship, hop onto the banister, and angle my feet for the best balance.

"Give me back my friend, let us off, and leave this island forever."

Rubias has a small snort that punctuates her laugh. "I don't have time for this. Leave him be." Any nearby crew backs off and gets to work. "It won't be my fault if you get blown to pieces by the Aronians."

The crew scrambles, latching ropes and steering the rudder wheel. Rubias pounces up the stairs and commands the hind crew to start all the propellers for full speed. Her voice booms across the ship to direct the deck chief to unfold the masts. Crewmates tug on lines until the great black canvas releases and slips down to catch air—a giant lung taking a deep breath.

From my vantage point, I am treated with an amazing sight: the ship slices through water, the crew jumps from rope to rope along the mast, others scurry underfoot in the hull, and the captain stands tall against the enemy. It's all a machine—well-oiled, flawless cogs spinning to produce tremendous speed for this aquatic steed. It's a quarvette, a slim, quick, and agile beast. With the whiptail propellers swirling at the rear, this ship is as fast as one could get for its size. The classification of ships are named after types of ray fish, and whiptails could outpace any prey by skipping across the ocean's surface like a thrown stone. This beauty was built from the bottom up for speed, which the captain takes full advantage of.

Coming at us are two manta-class galleons—sluggish, bulky things with a third mast but much more burthen to pull. Even without the orange flags, I can identify them by the color. They are famously crafted using trees with a reddish hue. Although they aren't warships, two of them together could easily take on this ship. The First Lord Admiralty Captain, a mouthful of a title, stands atop the raised stern on one galleon, spyglass in hand, and it feels like I'm his target. Of course, he probably doesn't even notice me. He's looking for the ship's weak spots, but I feel like one of those spots.

There's a shot in the distance. Surely cannon fire can't reach us. The gungills on their flanks aren't even aimed at us yet.

"Mortar incoming!" yells someone at the front of the ship. It's a different weapon mounted on the deck and fully operational at this distance.

I instinctively look for a place to hide, but I'm defenseless without knowing where it'll hit. A moment later, a burst of wood cracks near the banister. Another mortar shot strikes the water, but a third hits near the crew who are turning the horizontal push-wheel that moves the rudder and changes the ship's direction. Some of them are knocked from their position, now incapacitated. The others struggle to keep the ship maneuvering toward the incoming ships. There isn't anywhere to run because they're positioned as a blockade to the exit of this bay.

I run to the crew's aid and help a few up who can still move. I find a place on the wheel and join the push. It turns, but I doubt my puny weight is helpful alongside the muscular men and woman pushing with me. Nevertheless, Rubias sees me helping and gives an appreciative nod, granting me an impassioned fuel.

"Should we return mortar fire?" asks the deck chief.

Rubias says, "No, weave-maneuver straight between them."

Seems crazy. The cannon fire of both together will pulverize this ship in one go. But the crew follows orders without questioning it, and that gives me hope we'll get out of here alive.

I follow the commands of the deck chief. We push the wheel one way for a few rotations, then turn around and push the other way. If one mapped our trajectory on the ocean it would be a winding line. As they near, the two galleons converge to intercept us. When they do so, we keep the ship straight and speed right through the middle of them. Their plan is to ram us on both sides, but we swim just a little too quick for them. Their prows hit each other, and they can't commit to a cannon release without firing upon themselves too, causing havoc in their ranks. Their captains no doubt simmer in their anger as we dally away from the dual wreckage.

When we've distanced ourselves enough from the galleons, my time on the wheel is over. The crew celebrates at this time, clasping hands and patting backs. No one perished, but a few injured by the mortar shots are taken to the infirmary below deck.

"I'm sorry, Archie," the captain says coming up from behind me as I gaze at my home island getting farther and farther away. "We can't return you home today. There will be more coming. Also, I believe this is yours." She hands over my chest. I had forgotten about it. The secret compartment is intact and my money is safely tucked inside. "Is there anything they took that I can return to you?"

"Not really. And this is yours." I give back the pistol. "Am I your prisoner like Shadir?"

"Of course not. Shadir is not a prisoner. And you helped my crew. It would be dishonorable to keep such a person with your luster as a prisoner." She strolls over to the captain's cabin at the rear of the ship, waving me over.

Dishonorable? I want to question her about what honor a pirate has, but decide against it. "It is mighty bold of you to say Shadir is not a prisoner when he is being held in the brig."

She stops and motions at a man with a red and inflamed face. Skin flakes off his bare torso. He was the one commanding us at the wheel earlier. "Captain," the man pleads, "I was suspicious of Aldrezier from the moment he told me you were locked in the brig. But that is no excuse. I should've acted sooner."

Waving the apology away, Rubias says, "Archie, this is Salmon Mako, the deck chief. Salmon, please release Shadir from the brig. Then get yourself to the infirmary. You may have a bit of sun poisoning." He looks at his shoulders and shrugs. "Also, meet me in a bit and we can talk about your promotion." A smile cracks across his red cheeks. It looks painful but that doesn't stop him. Rubias enters her cabin and awaits my entrance to close the door. "Salmon is a hard worker. Sometimes he works too hard. Deck chiefs are second-in-command. Now that Aldrezier is no longer the captain of the *Prey Mantas*, he'll take over."

"Are you not the captain?" I wonder.

A flippant child's voice in the corner of the room startled me. It's the girl, Edia, saying, "The beautiful and fierce Isadora Rubias is grand captain of the entire Blackscabbard Fleet, forty ships strong." She is a well-versed child with an attitude of salt that rivals the sea. I guess around eleven years of age. "She can't watch over all of them."

Rubias smiles at the girl. "Keep studying. Don't mind us."

"I won't. Not 'nless you start spouting secret plans and such."

"I'm teaching Edia how to be a captain. It's not all pillaging, plundering, and anarchy. You've got to know politics, trade routes, and the like." I nod like someone interested. "How do you factor in to all of this, Archie?"

I say, "Apparently my grandfather knew Shadir. Put him in that chest your crew took. I found it under my basement stairs and unlocked it. Told Grifton about it. Apparently he told you. Here we are."

"You had your own shop, didn't you?"

"Still do, I think. I make artisan chests."

"I'm familiar with your work. I hear you're one of the best chestmakers in the polar circle."

"You've heard of me?" I say, stunned. I'm more surprised to hear of the polar circle bit. I knew I had always been a solid competitor in this small slice of the world, but not as far as she says.

She places her various items on the table—her pistol, nick-knucks, and a leather-bound journal. "I've seen Salvatorre chests decorating all kinds of homes, palaces, and ships. Don't have one myself, but I'd be happy to take a look at your inventory."

"If I get back in one piece, of course."

She's about to respond when a clamorous rap on the door interrupts. There's a shadow on the other side of the glossy window. The shadow knocks again, harder. The voice of Shadir yells, "You in there, Rubias?"

Edia hollers, "You best stop that ruckus 'fore I come out there and knock you."

"Shush, child," Rubias says. "It's unlocked."

He jiggles the handle and rushes in on another level of anger. In our time together, I've never seen him this way. A vein throbs in his forehead as he demands, "Take us back to Krakau."

"The area will soon be crawling with Kingsguild and bounty hunting ships ready to try their luck with us."

"Then drop us off on a nearby shore where it's clear. We'll balloon back."

"Can't do that. Thought you of all people would want to go destroy what's in those ruins."

"Not at the risk of death or another curse on me. I'd wager your crew doesn't even know what they're looking for." That warps the captain's face a bit. There is some truth to what he said. She lied to her crew. He continues, "You've promised them treasure, haven't you? When will you tell them they won't be able to retrieve it?"

Edia ignores the remark. She either knows all the tricky details or doesn't care.

The captain, with eyes narrowed, looks the immortal man up and down. "I'm curious to know what would happen if you were to be cut into pieces and fed across the ocean to the sharks and koi. How immortal would you be then?"

"Is that a threat?" Shadir holds himself back, but his fists clench and the movement under his cheeks are teeth grinding. He's afraid. None of us know if he can come back from that kind of execution. And none of us, especially Shadir, want to find out.

The captain shrugs. "I suppose if we cannot find the Arwellian island, then the next best thing is to destroy the map so no one can find it."

"Pirates make me sick." He directed that at me. "If I won't tell you, what makes you think anyone else will pry it from me?"

"I'm not sure. But if that's true, why did Gilligan lock you in a chest?"

Shadir has no response except to purse his lips.

"Edia, do we torture people?" Rubias asks without taking her attention off Shadir.

"No, ma'am," the girl replies.

Back to Shadir, she says, "I have a code my people stand by. But other pirates do not. And other countries aren't much better. You might be tortured, and we have no way of knowing if you are susceptible to it. What if someone else comes along and pries it out with pain? Or worse, what if you decide to use your own knowledge for certain power?"

Edia adds, "Nobody wants a dim bulb in charge of lighting a room."

"Be respectful to guests," says Rubias. Hardly fazed, the girl shuffles pages around to focus on her work. "I don't want any of these possibilities to happen."

"What about Archie?" asks Shadir.

I say, "Perhaps you'll recall I was about to be charged with imbalance."

"Yeah, but—"

"I'm not happy to be in the company of pirates, but I've never hopped pebbles before. Seeing other islands might do me some good."

He gives up on all fronts. "This will not end well," he says as one last attempt to dissuade. "If Archie dies, or if you do something terrible I can't go along with, I'm done. I don't care if you threaten to kill me." She is about to accept that, but he forces another bargain into the deal. "After all this, when it's destroyed, I want safe passage for Archie and me directly back to the Port Ov Krakau. I want to live there in peace without your fleet bothering the entire archipelago ever again. Can you promise me that?"

"Of course. As I said before, I have a code. No quarrel with you means you don't have to worry about me stabbing you in the back in the end."

With finality, Shadir says, "Primeward to Kameya. That's when you'll get the next bit of the map." He storms out of the cabin.

I say, "I suppose you should show me around the ship."

Rubias smiles. "Not this ship. This is a satellite ship. We'll be on the *Prey Empress*."

THE PREY EMPRESS

The *Prey Mantas* is not Isadora Rubias's main ship. It was her first ship when she first became a pirate captain. When her fleet grew, she needed something bigger for her escapades. So she attained this, a manta-class warship. The belly of the beast holds dozens of compartments with weapons, distractions, and deterrents against the numerous creatures of the ocean. There are sixty gungills on each side with a cannon by each. A few smaller cannons and mortars were on the deck. Crewmates scurry across the beautiful red and brown wood. The ship is anchored by a nearby island while awaiting Rubias's return. A water wheel is on the rear of the ship underneath the raised stern. That would be powered by a steam engine somewhere within, and helps with the ship's speed along with the six masts. The front is a beak o' thorns for ramming. This is the *Prey Empress* I gaze upon, and it makes the other ship look like a trout next to a shark.

"How many bricks long is this?" I ask the captain, containing as much eagerness as possible.

She says, "We don't use bricklength out at sea. We use planklength. Each is a little over double your measurement. This beast is over fifty planks long, thirteen high from water to deck, and twenty wide."

I attempt to calculate the cargo capacity, but the exchange of measurements has me turned around in my head. I give up and simply admire the beauty as it is—a hulking swimmer of war ready to take down a fleet of ten smaller ships by itself. I've always had an interest in ships, and I actually admire Rubias more for commanding such a sea-brute. It requires a special kind of cognizance and valor.

We board and are greeted by a silent crewmate. He's scruffy with a metal foot swinging around on an ankle hinge. "This is Tango," Rubias tells us. "He's mute, but that doesn't keep him from being the best damn deck chief I've ever had."

It is customary for larger ships to have a second-in-command. Despite Rubias having such an air of authority, there is no way she could command over half the ship without another person to reliably relay orders to the whole crew. But a mute deck chief is an interesting choice. A large portion of this crew must know how to interpret his signing.

The deckhands shuffle about, wrangling ropes and cleaning the wood. I hear the thumps of moving crates by the hull crew underfoot. The eyes of the ship are the folks on the masts. They carry spyglasses and swing from ropes to secure lines, and prevent deterioration of the sails. An aroma of cooked fish pushes through the briny air. A chef is hard at work in the galley. There are two musicians near the captain's cabin—currently on a break. One tunes a banjola, and the other cleans some pipe instrument I've never seen before.

Rubias shuffles Shadir and I down the hatch to the hull. The smell of fish strengthens, churning rudders in my stomach. I haven't eaten all day. Rubias presses on beyond the crates, cannons, and barrels stacked so tightly that they made thin corridors in the hull. Stacks of timber are left around to quickly fix any damage. Turning a corner, I nearly bump into some figure in a suit of armor covered in spikes with deep, dark eyes. This being towers over me, but when it doesn't move I realize it's just mounted on a rack—empty.

Rubias says, "Be careful. Shark repelling diving suit. I wouldn't advise hugging it. This way, please." She's swift of foot, and turns every corner so assuredly that I'm convinced she could navigate this place blindfolded.

The corridor opens slightly to cramped sleeping quarters. Cots are stacked in twos. The delicious smell is replaced by a stench of sweat and salt. There are some private rooms and the infirmary, but the majority of the crew has their own cot here in the main room. At the foot of each is a personal chest for their belongings. Only a few are worth looking at.

"This will be where you stay while you're on board." Rubias points out two cots with rough linens. "Are these open?" she asks Tango. I didn't realize he is still behind us. Light-footed even with that metal foot.

Tango seems like the type to be perfectly organized. He knows off the top of his head which are available, and points them out.

I choose one and place my chest down at the foot of it. It feels strange. Where one's chest is makes that place home, and this is assuredly not homely.

As if sensing my thoughts, Shadir touches my shoulder, and says, "I'll get you back as quick as I can. I promise."

A slug of fear burrows into me because I'm not entirely sure I want to go home. Not if it means being a villein and dying in the Obitzu Bayou.

There is also something else nudging me to keep going—deep seeds growing into adventurous roots. Other islands. Arwellian ruins. *Treasure?* I'm caught in a conflicting ebb and flow like waves licking the shore.

Rubias interjects, "There will be a meal ready soon. The cooks on this ship are artists in their craft. I assure you it'll be delightful. And then we shall discuss our plan of action, and whatever jobs you may fulfill while on this ship." Then she leaves us.

A bell rings to call the first dining group. Shadir and I warily wander through the hull, following other hungry mates, to find the galley on the complete opposite end of the ship. Not all the crew members come. It's mostly hullards, Tango, and the two musicians. No more can fit around the galley's dining table, which is already surrounded by the stoves and cooking tools. The galley is in the center of the rear of the ship, so no portholes give us light. Instead, we're surrounded by frayed wires hooked to the walls and connected to some light bulbs. I never even thought about a ship being capable of having a generator on board, but I suppose a ship this large would benefit from it.

The white slices of fresh smoked koi are quickly passed around the room. Seats are occupied by people roaring hearty laughs at every crude remark. I step in line and a treenware plate is handed to me by Shadir. The chef, mustachioed and portly, double glances at the two of us.

A grisly voice rumbles from deep within him. "I don't serve stowaways." I hardly stammer an explanation before he cuts me off. "I'm only proddin' ye. New blubber, eh?"

I look to Shadir, but he only shrugs. For some reason, I keep looking to him for help with everything because he's older and well-traveled, but I forget he wasn't much older than myself when he was locked in the chest. In a way, he's still the same age as before, but with fifty years of extra trauma.

"I suppose," I say.

"I'll give ye both larger portions. A welcome gift. But don't be comin' round for seconds. We have fine-tuned rations 'tween pebbles." That one I understand. Hopping pebbles is a common expression for traveling between islands. He takes a spatula and slides the koi onto my plate. It comes with a side of blue-bleeding pickled beets. Finally, he slips me a very small vial. "Don't f'get your lemon juice. Good on the fish, but I drain it after the beets. Don't like beets myself, but there's no wastin' food in my galley. No exceptions."

Shadir and I eat in the corner next to a humming light. The fish goes down easy. The beets bleed through my teeth as I chew, but it isn't as bad as the cook says. It's actually some of the best prepared food I've ever had. Only Grifton's meals are better.

Grifton. The captain said she employed him to be there. Had he been a family friend because he was a pirate's spy, or did he actually care about us? Either way, I make myself nervous by thinking of confronting him someday. Him leading those pirates straight to me feels like betrayal, but I can't know for sure what happened. Things changed so drastically because I couldn't keep that chest to myself. Now I'm on a warship with pirates. What would my father think? He was afraid of everything beyond his own little world. It's the one thing I've never wanted to inherit from him.

The musicians finish their meals and are asked to sing a shanty. One of them strums and flicks the strings on her banjola. The other sings:

"They say the great sea washed away the Vulpine Beast.
"They say the giant Ape Queen will make us all a feast.
"They say the Onyx Pheonix may bury us in sand.
"They say the Star Koi will break apart the land.
"Oh, the ages pass us by and by,
"And the realm won't let us fly!
"Us it wants to kill and kill!
"Well we'd like to see it try!"

There are three verses, and everyone who knows it bellows the lyrics in unison with the musicians. When the song is over, the lot is replaced by the next group of starving crew. Rubias is the last to enter and take a plate. She eyes us and nods to the door. We follow her to the captain's cabin.

Rubias's personal quarters are not quite extravagant in the usual sense, but it still contains a sense of awe. It hints at the captain's personality. The walls are draped completely in the largest collection of flags. Doesn't matter what a flag stands for, if anything at all. The past and present collide on these walls in a flurry of cloth and colors. Neither friend nor enemy is spared—from the golds and greens of kings and queens to blacks and whites of pirate legends. Despite having windows and personal electric bulbs, she still prefers the subtle ambiance of glowfish in suspended orbs around the room. An armor rack dons a plated chest, scaly greaves, and two sets of high-collar bucklecoats of different leathers. It has a hook where she places her nickel-knuckles. Next to her armor is a knife with an ebony hilt. Finally, there is a small shelf with around a dozen books clamped in to keep from shifting.

My leg buckles beneath me as the boat lurches. Rubias says, "You'll get used to it. The sway of the ocean changes the way you walk. It imbues a kind of confidence in your stride."

Shadir cuts through the small talk. "I am still reeling from the idea of going back to that island. What has you so terrified of it? It's trapped there... I think."

The captain bites into the flesh of the koi. She washes it down with a dribble of whatever swirls in her bottle. She shuffles through her coat and reveals a journal. "This was my grandfather's."

"I recognize it," says Shadir. "He had his nose in it all the time when we first traveled to the ruin."

"He wrote down everything during your travels. You ripped out pages, didn't you?" She flips through the pages to show some missing.

"I did. I knew he could just write it down again, but I hoped to convince him not to. The path there is dangerous and out of the way. Not many would naturally stumble upon it."

"Except you and Gilligan and my grandfather did just that. By chance or not, it is still possible."

"Yes, but…" Shadir's voice slowly grows louder and faster. "What Desja knew—what we all knew—was that it is too dangerous for a world of people who seek power, money, or glory. That's why I—" He doesn't finish his statement, although it seems like it was about to be a confession.

"Did you kill him?" I ask.

"No," Shadir utters. "Not successfully. I thought I could, but I'm not that kind of person."

Rubias replies, "Well I thank you for being moral enough not to kill my grandfather. He told me all about his adventures when I was a kid. And he recorded some of it here." Rubias slides the volume into a gap on the bookshelf. "But there is nothing that shows the way to the island, unfortunately. He regretted not going back. He tried to but he wasn't much of a navigator."

"That's because Gilligan and I gained unfathomable abilities. Desja was jealous. Forget the gold we left behind, that touch of magic is the real treasure to those who don't realize it's a curse." The captain tries to interrupt, but he swipes her plea away. "No one but me knows the pain of being trapped in life. I suffered in that chest. Within the first few hours I ran out of air. I gasped and I gasped for days, or months—I can't know for sure. Eventually, my body was accustomed to the lack of oxygen. It got used to the hunger, the thirst, and the aches of being unable to move or sleep comfortably. The boredom, loneliness, and hate came in waves of endless torment. And my body endured it all.

"Don't talk about his regret. I regretted helping Gilligan. I regretted traveling to the island. And I still regret not killing your grandfather, because it was his incessant talking about what we agreed not to talk about that had Gilligan scared enough to lock me in a chest because I was the only one who could get there. Desja Rubias was power hungry. Either you are too or you're foolish enough to think you won't succumb to what dwells within those ruins."

Rubias nods and slurp down another piece of fish and beets. She wipes her mouth with a handkerchief and stands. A strong hand reaches out and shoves Shadir against the wall. Her fist is wrapped up in a swirl of his shirt. She doesn't need to reach for a pistol or knife or nick-knucks. Those yellow eyes threaten the man just fine.

"All three of you were cursed. My grandfather was a noble man who never sought power. If anything, he wanted to get rid of the power he had. He could see the future." Shadir's wide eyes narrow to a slivered glare. "It wasn't a bad thing at first. It was fairly helpful at times. We knew the best time to fish and grow crops. But as he got older, the past slipped away from him. The more he looked into the future, the more his memories disappeared. One day, the past was altogether gone from his mind. He couldn't take care of himself anymore. He never knew what he had for breakfast, but he could tell us what he'd be having for breakfast the next day. He rambled on about nothing, or what seemed like nothing to us. He told some people how they would die. He saw nothing but death in everything he saw, even his own family. He witnessed all our deaths like he was there, and couldn't prevent any of them. On his deathbed, he saw the planet's ages after ours. He saw ice and desert overtaking each other. Saw the death of all life. I believe what's on the island will cause that destruction. It will cause the end of us all."

"What is on the island?" I ask.

The captain's hand uncurls from Shadir's collar. She backs away.

Shadir answers with a notable change in his voice. Dry and nervous, but also somber. "It is a creature."

Rubias adds, "It is a creature we need to kill."

THE NEW COG IN THE MACHINE

It doesn't take long for the ship to feel like my cage. Without ever leaving the archipelago, it's easy to forget just how expansive the sea really is. There is nothing in sight but sky and water. Makes me restless. Even if I jump ship I can only tread water to my death. The nearest islands are leagues away. And Krakau folk are not the best of swimmers. Perhaps a diver from the Malla'ah Bay could make it with their strong lungs and raw instinct for direction, but I am nothing like them. I make chests—a useless trade here on this ship.

This thin cot is most uncomfortable. The wool is itchy, and the rickety frame feels like I might topple over the side if I suddenly lurch. Even now, my neck muscles tighten into knots to be kneaded later. Also, the stench of the crew baffles me. Every possible smell is somehow present when dozens of people sleep in the same area.

The sunlight bleeds through the portholes in the early morning, showing dusty sunbeams. The crew jumps to their feet at the ring of a bell, and proceeds to their respective stations. My bloodshot eyes find Shadir in the rush. He waves me over, and I follow his beckoning. We find the captain shouting orders, although the efficiency makes it clear the crew already knows the details of her commands.

"Telliot!" Rubias calls. A shirtless, furry-chested man scrubbing the planks jumps up and comes over. "Get these two a bandersheef." Telliot scurries off.

"Bandersheef?" I ask. Another nautical term I've never heard. It's as if they crafted their own language.

"Bandoleer pouch and sheath. If you're goin' to work on my ship, you'll need the proper equipage to last through the day." Telliot hurries back with two straps of pocketed leather, each with a built-in sheath. "The pouches'll have essentials: some rations in case you get stranded somewhere, any keys necessary for your rank, fishhooks, a needle, oc-pipe, pliers, minor medical supplies, some paper and a pencil. Just rummage through it and acquaint yourself with everything."

I sling the bandersheef over my head, from left shoulder to right hip, and tighten it around my chest. The snug leather strap has buttons and clasps across it for access to the different pockets. The knife in its sheath is over my heart, perfectly within my right arm's reach. The knife stays when I pull it. The sheath isn't just leather—it has bit of brass throughout, which leads me to assume there is a mechanism inside to grip the blade to keep it from slipping out. My spindly fingers crawl around it for the release until my middle finger finds a button on the side. Pressing it lets loose a small spring which gives the knife a boost into my palm, but not so much of a jump that it springs out of the sheath entirely. I wasn't aware springwork is so common outside of chests. I have seen bandoleers a few times on folks in my shop, but never did I think to ask about the mechanisms in them.

After rifling through the various pockets, Rubias gives me an assignment. I am to feed the glowfish and switch out their bowls, and Shadir is told to clean every porthole and window on the ship. She hands me a wooden box. Heavier than I expect. I swing the hinged top open to find dirt. Squirming through that dirt are glowworms—the natural prey for glowfish. Those orbs are located where electric bulbs or portholes are not.

I first shuffle down to the lowest level, the orlop deck, using the staircase by the galley. Only one other person is down here—Edia. The belly of the ship is a hazardous collection of barrels and boxes she hops across like stepping stones. She scribbles something down on paper.

"What is all this?" I ask.

Without taking eyes off her paper, she answers, "I'm cataloging the entire inventory down here for damages or unauthorized withdrawals."

"What kind of inventory?"

"Weaponry. Deterrents."

"Deterrents for what?"

"The use of weaponry."

She thinks I'm a simpleton. Although, her mannerisms make it clear she thinks everyone is, except her captain.

She points out a collection of barrels with red string around them. "That's chum. Attracts certain animals. There is squid ink in these with black string. Keeps those same animals away. Orange string is for gunpowder. Yellow for lemons. Blue for fresh water. Green—buoy bombs. White—extra harpoonguns."

She also shows me an assortment of experimental weapons I've never heard of: spiked cannonballs, mast stranglers, fletchette nets, gator wranglers, carapace drillers. Surely there's some metallurgist or weapon smith out in the world who is proud of this artisanal arsenal they have made.

"Are you going to continue wasting my time, or are you going to feed the fish?"

I fumble with the box, finally placing it down. My fingers drill into the dirt and search for a sacrifice. A thick selection is pried from the dirt and curls in my palm. I whip off the extra soil on my hand. Each orb is wrapped up in a lattice net with a stopper on the top. I pull the stopper carefully as to not spill the little water it has. I dangle the glowworm into the hole. As if it hasn't eaten for days, the fish devours the worm in seconds. I pull my fingers away in case it might mistake them for a second course. I take down the orb, replace the stopper, and hold it in both arms as I attempt to heave it into a bag. I shoulder the bag and carry the orb topside. Rubias also gave me a strainer to put over the orb. This allows me to pour out the old water without losing the fish. Then I lower the orb into a barrel of ocean water that was hoisted up earlier. The new, clean water flushes into the orb, and I replace the strainer with the stopper.

"That was fairly easy."

Startling me from behind, Rubias says, "There are twenty-five of those on board, and I expect it to be done before the first break. Those who fail to do their job well enough end up cleaning the ease-seats at the end of the day."

That is something to avoid at all costs. It's basically the ship's version of the communal outhouse back home. I rush back down with the orb, string it back up, and reach for the next one. I repeat twice more before realizing this task is inefficient. It isn't difficult by any means, but it just can't be done in the time frame she expects by one person. I know I can do it faster. In every chest, efficiency can be the difference between a good piece and a great one. I need a system. Perhaps two at a time. Why stop at two? Why not three or five at a time?

I end up rigging a pulley system with an empty barrel, a rope, and half a crate of cannonballs. There are two hatches leading to each level. One is a staircase, and the other is a large, square hole for moving large loads up and down each level. I choose these holes for my experiment. The stairs are far apart from each other, whereas the holes aren't, and they already had a pulley system to work off of.

Edia peers at me through the corner of her eye while I finish tying off the last of the rope around the barrel. They'll work as shoulder straps. I place a few orbs in the barrel, shoulder the ropes with the weight of the barrel in my back, and then grip another tether. Above me, teetering on the edge of the hatch, is the crate of cannonballs ready to plunge down into the lower level. One light tug of the tether loosens it. I wave to Edia who stopped scribbling to see what I'm up to. Then, I'm gone. The crate's weight heaves me and the barrel up with one swift motion. I hook my hand around a post and pull myself over.

At the next hatch I had set up a similar rig. All I have to do is attach myself and repeat the process. I grab and pull the tether to the side, flinging myself topside. I clean all the orbs and replace them in the dangling nests quicker than the previous routine could clean a single orb. Resetting the pulleys barely wastes any time. I finish the rest of them with plenty of time to spare before the first meal bell.

I stop to enjoy the musicians playing next to the captain's cabin. They sing a ballad that weaves their two instruments into a beautiful harmony. It's strange to hear music in the middle of nowhere. Music isn't much of a thing at home anymore. Charter barons convinced people the traditional arts are useless, brainwashing antics. My father disagreed, believing true art could be melded with utility, like with our chests. Along with the sounds, I appreciate the craftsmanship of the wooden instruments and their delicately carved etchings. And they're making use of their craft here in the middle of a vast ocean, entertaining the crew. Whereas I'm here giving clean water to fish.

The captain's voice hollers, "Light the tinder underfoot, Archie! I know you didn't choose this ride, but you still ain't ridin' for free!"

"I'm already done, captain," I say. Admittedly, it's a bit strange to call her by that title.

"Fantastic job, Archie," she says with an arched brow. The meal bell rings. "That's the fastest I've seen someone do that. Get yourself something to eat. Then you start your next assignment—catching the rats. If we kill a couple a day we keep the population down to a manageable amount."

All she gives me to achieve that task is a forked iron rod with a band of rubber and a pouch of stones—a slingshot. Not the easiest way to kill rats, but it's been a tactic for as long as ships have had rats.

I rush down to the galley to acquire my food. For the midday meal, the cook serves a hefty biscuit and canned fruits. The crew doesn't stick around in the galley like during supper meals. The cans allow them to slurp and chew on the job. They don't like being idle for too long.

The stormseer stays behind. He's an older man, perhaps the oldest in the crew. His job is to watch the skies and ocean for signs of storms. It's a gifted talent. "Reading the wind" some call it. Others might not feel the subtle shift in pressure that signals an incoming storm, but a stormseer trains to do just that. I don't receive his name. He just calls himself by his title. A sliver of fish on his finger goes to the furry bundle on his lap. This cat laps it up and rubs the back of its head against the stormseer's chest.

The stormseer says, "This is Ominix. He's quite the rat catcher. Good luck trying to beat him." A chuckle parts the old man's lip-curled smile.

It's a challenge I comfortably take, for I have the only shop in the Tyro Archipelago that rats would never come near. I've invented a contraption that'll help if I can find the parts. This ship will be free of the infestation within a few days.

I scarf down my lunch before venturing to find the engine room. I follow pipes and wiring until they all converge in one section in the hull near the rear. It should have engines, boilers, generators, and other various machinery. The heart of the ship. But this heart is behind a locked iron door. I rummage through the few keys in my pocket near my waist. None fit. Not sure why I tried. It's a vulnerable section and only engineers should have access.

The door swivels open from the other side. As if I too am built with a hinge, I pivot on one foot to match the swing of the door. Two women appear, each with smudged faces and a sheen of sweat along their bodies. They make their way to the galley for their biscuits. I'm able to slip inside the sweltering room before it shuts automatically. It is no wonder they are so damp. My pores open as soon as the heat hits me. The ventilation is poor. Must be a miserable place to work all day.

The engine for the propellers and electricity is at the center of this round room. The fiery mouth of the steam machine chews on black mounds of coal. It seems like anything not worth keeping is in here for potential burning. No use in sending something overboard when it could be used to power the ship for a bit. The heat feeds the boiler running the pistons. The pipes and copper wires run throughout the room and through the walls like arteries and veins. Near a set of pipes is a workbench with wrenches and hammers. Nearby that is a box of random parts: springs, frayed wires, cogs, wedges of wood, and nails.

I pick a few things out carefully, preferring not to get rustbite for a second time in my life. They have a doctor aboard the ship, but how much would a pirate doctor even know? Even doctors along the archipelago still recommended bayou leeches for many ailments.

With a bit of luck, I find enough pieces to craft two rat traps.

I'm not exactly sure how rats act on a ship, but I assume they're the same as on land. After crafting the spring-loaded traps, I place them near the galley when the last of the pirates leave to work again. I sprinkle crumbs from biscuits on the two traps and wait.

After a few hours of resetting traps, I go find Rubias. Outside of her cabin is a smaller shed. Next to it is an upside-down basket clasped to the boat. Underneath that is a box with the fabric that would turn that basket into an emergency air balloon. Rubias is checking it to make sure it's in working order when I interrupt her by dropping a bag with a dozen rats.

She gently kicks it with her foot to discern what's inside. Her eyes widen.

"You're pretty good with a slingshot."

"Didn't touch the slingshot. I made some traps. Did the same thing at my shop and it's been rat-free for a long time. There might be some left on board, but they'll be caught soon enough."

"I suppose you should leave some for the cat. Don't want it to get bored. You are quite something, aren't ya? Already paying for yourself. But if I'm not mistaken, you don't think much of pirates, do you?"

"My islands have not had much luck with your kind."

"My *kind*? Do you think I come from a sort of beastly lineage?"

"You are pirates, are you not?"

Her brows furrow. Her gaze, which I dodge expertly, is heated, but it will take much more to get her to do something drastic against me. After today, she has a high tolerance for me.

Arms folding, she asks, "Where did you get the parts for those traps?"

"I may have sourced them from the engine room."

"You've got a speck of gumption, I'll give you that. In fact, you've got a type of gumption I've not seen since my brother. You're different. You think different. More sensitive to the intricacies of the world around you."

"Shadir? What is he doing?"

She smirks. "Cleaning the ease-seats. He wasn't quick enough."

I cringe for him. "Do you have more work for me?"

"Nothing specific. For now, get more acquainted with the ship and crew. Ask someone if they need help. They'll appreciate it." She hands me a key. "That's for this shed here, should you ever need anything from it. It has tools, materials, whatever you might need. I'd rather you check here first before stealing from the engineers." She grins and returns to her work.

I peek inside the tool shed. There's barely enough room to fit inside, but it has nearly everything I need to continue crafting chests.

THE TOLL

"We don't have time for this," I hear Rubias grumble above me on the raised aft deck. She's talking to Tango.

A mast crawler up in the nest waves flags to give her a message. Tango retrieves his oc-pipe and looks out into the ocean. Something blocks our route.

"What is it?" I ask.

Rubias looks down at me and chews on her options. "We're in popular shipping lanes used by the Aronians. Usually, that doesn't pose a problem. But today, we're about to sail up to a toll privateer. And it's too late to go around once we've been spotted. We're already in their dragnet."

Overhearing this, Shadir steps up from behind me to ask, "How many of them?"

Tango signs something, and Rubias echoes what he said: "Looks like two galleons. There might be a barge nearby."

I ask, "What's a toll privateer?"

Rubias calls for Edia, and the girl comes sauntering out of the captain's cabin. Always looking for ways to test her pupil, Rubias says, "Tell Archie about toll privateers while we figure out how to deal with this."

Edia steps forward to inform me, although it's clear by the most exaggerated eye roll of all time that she doesn't want to waste her time with me. No matter how she feels about it, she obeys her captain.

"Toll privateers are vessels hired by countries who want to collect fees from random ships coming through an area. Most likely they have a barricade of explosive buoys to prevent faster ships from gliding right past them. The Aronian Kingdom likes to position them in strategic places as a way to lay claim to it and bring in extra income."

"That's absurd," I scoff. "You can't claim the ocean."

"Tell that to the Kingsguild navy. The fees they place on vessels can vary, but usually they'll try to squeeze the most they can out of you. They're basically pirates with fancier hats. And, mind you, I've seen pirate captains with quite the array of hats."

"What happens if the toll isn't paid?"

"The ship gets impounded. Either they take cargo from us until the toll is considered paid, or the crew works off the debt. We don't want either to happen."

All this seems to be leading to another fight, but is Rubias willing to risk that?

Splitting the horizon, the outlines of two waiting galleons sharpen as we approach, making this vague threat more tangible. I check the mast to see what colors we fly. There's nothing there at the moment. Rubias will have to make a decision on that soon. She's currently in a huddle with Tango and Shadir doing just that, but Shadir provides heated pushback on all her ideas.

"Just pay them the fee!" he argues. "You're trying to get treasure anyway. Won't that cover it?"

"You will never convince me to provide payment to a government currently hunting us down. Not to mention everything else they stand for."

"So getting us arrested or caught up in battle are the best options you have?"

Two galleons can't beat a warship and a quarvette that are as heavily armed as we are, but the win wouldn't be worth the scathing. The lives lost and repairs needed would be far more a toll than what they'll ask for. The risk outweighs the reward. That is an equation all pirates understand. But is that the kind of pirate Rubias is?

"Captain," says another crewmate. "The *Prey Mantas* is hailing us. They want to know what the plan is."

Rubias looks at all the faces on deck looking to her for an answer. When those piercing yellow eyes land on me, inspiration lights up her face. "Archie, do you know how to pick a lock?"

The question caught me off guard. It's a skill I haven't honed as much as crafting. But when you deal with locks on a daily basis, it becomes a necessity. I nod, hoping to get all these staring eyes away from me. My fingers look for the button on my cuff, but it's gone.

Shadir says, "What's he got to do with this? What are you planning?"

Rubias jumps up on the banister and grabs a ratline to hold steady. She announces to her crew, "Here's the plan. Tango, tell Hap to relay this plan to Mako. Now, listen up! We're not payin' these blaggards a single coin, but we're not wasting time fighting them either. This will require subterfuge. While Tango and I make a bureaucratic distraction, our esteemed chestmaker here will sneak aboard their ship, heist their coffers, and make it back here so that we may pay them with their own coin. And if there is anything left over… that's our bonus."

While the crew cheers on that insane plan, Shadir shouts, "Why would you volunteer him for something like that?"

Placing a halting hand on my friend's chest: "Please, Shadir, I can handle this myself." I step closer to the captain, and then snappishly hiss, "Why would you volunteer me for something like that?"

"I'm not taking suggestions for alternate plans at the moment." She jumps down from the banister, comes down from the aft, and grabs me by the shoulders. "You're perfect for the job. None of my crew can pick a lock, and most of them…" she purveys the brutish, unkempt pirates, "… will stand out on an Aronian ship. You're my only hope."

"Fine," I say, piling more strain upon Shadir. "Better than dodging cannonballs."

"Then I'm going too," he says, adjusting his bandersheef.

Although he's ready to fight for his inclusion, Rubias says, "I've no quarrel with that."

He clears his throat. "Oh, well, good then. Let's do it."

"Very well," says Rubias. "It's settled. Everyone, slow the ship to a halt as we near. Edia?" The girl nods. The captain rubs her hands together. "Any suggestions on colors? Perhaps Esperanian?"

Edia responds, "Why would an Esperanian trade ship be in this region? I suggest we also claim to be Aronian toll privateers. That'll muck things up enough to give more time for the two of 'em." She judges us a with side eye. "They'll need all the help they can get."

"Fine," the captain huffs. "I suppose I'll never get to try out my Esperanian accent."

Edia hops back into the captain's cabin to grab the flag. She brings out a bundle of orange in her small arms and hands it off to another crewmate to raise it on the mast.

"All right, spread to the crew that we are toll privateers. We need to get our story straight in case they start askin' questions. We used to be bounty hunters until switching to this for more stable employment." Those in the crew who heard that scurry off into the hull. Rubias turns to Tango, "I can't be the captain for this ruse. Are you up for it?"

Tango beams with excitement, and he wastes no time accepting that task.

"Excellent. I'll be your translator."

As we close in on the toll ships, I realize a vital lack of foresight which could dismantle this whole plan before it begins—my lockpicking set was left at home. I rush over to sift through random tools and materials in the shed to see if I can rustle up some kind of makeshift set. I fling nails and wrenches off to the side, trying to find something more delicate. It won't be much of a quiet theft if I bang off every lock with a hammer.

"You're running out of time," snaps an annoyed Edia. "Toll ships are hailing us. This whole plan revolves around you. Hurry it up."

Finally, I find a thin file to use as a pick, a jagged fishhook that might work as a rake in a pinch, as well as a bent woodworker's awl for a tension tool. It'll have to do.

After closing the shed, I walk to the beak of the ship where Shadir had tied two ropes for us. The idea is to wait until the rear of a toll ship is aligned with the front of the *Prey Empress*. These galleons have a balcony that goes into the captain's quarters. Ideally, we might find some chest in there to steal so we won't have to go deeper into the galleon's belly.

The *Prey Empress* halts a plank or two away from one galleon on our right side. The other idles at a distance, but close enough to provide backup if needed. Surrounding their ship would've been a hostile maneuver, so the *Prey Mantas* swims up to our left side.

Both toll ships are volt-class galleons. I've never seen one in person, as they are quite rare, but I've read about them. The orlop deck has a generator that can produce a high voltage through the copper plating of the hull and send it into the ocean—a machine meant to cripple enemies or jolt hostile sea creatures. Being next to one will be dangerous if this ploy doesn't work out for us. If they send out a current through the water, the conductive plating of our ship could pick up that electricity and fry our generator. We still have sails and a manual wheel for the propeller, but we'd be like fat frogs on a sandbar full of hungry gulls.

Shadir says, "Scale down the hull a brick or two before you swing over. Hold on tight. When you get to the balcony, tie the rope to something sturdy so you're able to use it to get back. Got it?"

"Yes. I need to get going. I don't want them to spot me climbing over. Shield me with your body."

He does so, but it's not as inconspicuous as he thinks. Rubias gives me a head nod, and I return it before climbing over the banister. I wait on the hull until some of their crew crosses the gangplank. Rubias welcomes them with faked heartiness, and guides them into her quarters. Shadir signals me, and I let go of the *Prey Empress*.

My stomach drops like an anchor. The rush of gravity is like ice in my veins. The galleon's balcony seems to be much too high and much too far until the upswing brings me perfectly level to it. My shaking hands reach out and hold on tight. Settled, I gather my wits and climb aboard.

As Shadir gets ready to follow me, I check the balcony doors. Unlocked. Luckily, this ship's captain isn't overly cautious. I get through without delay.

The captain's quarters are kept spotless and tidy. The first thing spotted worth checking is a wardrobe chest. I tie the rope to its handle before checking inside. No money there. Instead, as predicted by Edia, a lot of hats.

Shadir glides across the chasm and lands on the balcony much more smoothly than I did. He ties the rope to the banister. He enters, saying, "As of right now, Rubias is probably confusing their captain with some taxation jargon to give them the runaround. But she can only keep that up for so long. Let's work fast."

A quick scan of the rest of the cabin reveals no other chest, coffers, or places one might keep money. The drawers in the desk contain maps and documents. Rubias will have to keep it up because there is nothing in here worth sending back.

Checking the deck through the little window on the door, Shadir whispers his frustration, "Damn, we'll have to go find a treasury room in the hull."

But how to get down there without drawing attention to ourselves? I grab Shadir's attention and point at the one thing this ship has that the *Prey Empress* does not: a dumbwaiter. It's set between book shelves and likely goes straight down to the galley.

Shadir shakes his head, no.

I nod, yes.

He shakes vigorously.

I nod vigorously, and open the dumbwaiter door.

"Have you got salt for brains?" he asks. Looking inside the confined space freezes him. It would be a slightly tighter squeeze for his frame than for mine. His breathing grows more heavy and strained. "I'm not getting in there."

"But I will," I say, sticking my first leg in. "Besides, I need you to lower me down. Can't do it myself."

He nods and gulps. "Be careful. Whistle when you're ready to come back up."

There isn't much space inside. While in the fetal position, my lungs feel compressed. Ache quickly spreads across my legs and back. I can't imagine being stuck in something like this for more than a couple minutes let alone decades.

Shadir minds the wheel crank. The dumbwaiter squeaks as it lowers, unable to handle the full weight of a person. But I make it to the bottom without the pulley breaking.

Before opening the dumbwaiter door, I listen for any crew. One man is talking to another, but a moment later they are pulled away by a third. When the coast is clear, I open the door and slip out, minding my surroundings. There are bags of flour I can hide behind if necessary, but it doesn't look like anyone is coming inside the galley for a bit.

Now that I'm inside the hull, there is no reason for most crew here to think of me as suspicious. Walk with confidence—a natural, purposeful stride. If I do that, not many will stop to question me. I draw a long breath to steel my nerves, and exit the galley.

The toll ship's hullards scurry like rats, keeping busy. But there is something about it that bothers me. Many are shuffling crates and barrels and cannons around. Without preparing for a battle, what would be the reasoning for moving so many things? Was it boondoggling, or should we be worried about an attack?

The treasure is likely on this deck but on the other side of the ship, so I move through the gun deck. I pass thirty gungills before getting to the other end. I slip off to the side to hide in a crevice as two officers pass by.

One says to the other, "We received word via seagull to be on the lookout for pirates in this area. Captain Bucky told me to come back and tell you to prepare for impoundment. Possibly battle if they resist. Even if they are who they say they are, captain wants that warship for hisself."

They enter the din of the gun deck and I can no longer make out what they're saying, but I've heard enough. Change of plans. Even if I'm able to sneak some treasure out of here, we'll still be troubled.

There is a hatch nearby, likely going to the orlop deck where the conductor engine will be. It needs to be disabled for us to have a chance at getting away. However, like the engine room on the *Prey Empress*, this part of the ship is off limits to most crewmates. It will be locked, and I can't easily unlock it without being spotted. I need to make a distraction.

I hurry back to the galley, still empty. There is a pencil and paper in my bandersheef which I use to scribble down my new plan. I stick the message into the dumbwaiter and send up the shaft a sharp whistle. After that, the squeaky box wheels back up. That note will tell him to take this information back across immediately. Meanwhile, I'm going to take a page out of young Shadir's book and cause a disturbance. It's a plus that we have a whole deck separating us so he can't argue.

Leaving the galley again, I find shot lockers. The cannonballs are vertically held in place with a net covering the opening at the bottom. I pop the bandersheef knife out of its holder and make a small slice into the nets of the shot lockers. Cannonballs widen that slit and spill out across the floor of the gun deck. The motion of the ship rolls them every which way as the crew scrambles to gather them.

While they're all busy with that, I sprint to the other end again. With the commotion, no one is here to see me unlock the hatch door. I kneel by it, take out my makeshift set, and get to work. The fishhook rake doesn't work, so I switch it out for the file. But that's not working very well either.

Some of the cannonballs have nearly rolled all the way to me by now, which means I'm running out of time. Someone's going to come get those in a second. I keep working with the file, flicking pins and using the awl as a tension tool. I don't let the panic consume me. I have to stay patient and focused. Feeling that final click and turn floods me with relief. I open it and go down the steps before anyone takes notice.

The orlop deck, alight with electric bulbs, is like a metal cask. Occupying the whole middle space is a squat iron contraption with rods bolted to the keel of the ship like a heart with copper coil ribs. A faint vibration hums through the electric air. It is not yet ready for an attack, but it won't take much time to get it primed. Though I don't know much about a machine as complex as this, it won't take half as much effort to sabotage it as it would to repair it.

When reaching out to touch a gear, the electric beast nips at my finger with a small bolt of lightning. I shake off the pain. Surrounding the machine are several protective frames that are meant to ground a user. I make sure to have a body part touching one of those at all times from now on.

There is a safety release switch clearly marked. I flip it, but I can't rely on that alone. Whatever I do, it needs to be inconspicuous enough to pass whatever inspection they make before starting the machine up. I get to work studying the innards to find any potential weaknesses like that.

A waxy pitch coating is slathered onto the inner calibration ring as insulation. I take my awl and scrape away some of it. That might cause a problem, but probably nothing as immediate as what I need.

Time is running low. The talk between captains will soon turn sour, and then they'll send a shockwave to make the pirates vulnerable. After thinking for much too long, the best option I come up with is loosening pieces so the moving pieces might come undone as the spinning parts of the machine build momentum. As I do this, I discover a small ventilation shaft.

If seawater was funneled into that, it'd cause quite an issue that is hard to find. But that won't work. I have no water on me. Although, what about *in* me?

No that's ridiculous. I can't do that.

It would work pretty much the same, wouldn't it?

Sure, but that's undignified.

So undignified that it's worth letting people like this get away with robbing innocent traders and travelers?

I suppose not.

Then I've made up my mind.

After my business with the machine is done, I peek out the hatch to see if I can get out without being noticed. Voices shuffle closer, so I shut it and hide behind the stairs.

"I thought you said you locked this," one privateer says tumbling down the stairs. The one following behind grunts a reply. As they head to the machine, I slink up and out as quiet as a roach on a rowboat.

The shot locker issue has been dealt with, so all the crew is now preparing for a battle. Those men below are about to get that machine up and running. I hope I've caused enough problems with it so that it shuts down. That'll give Rubias's crew the advantage.

"Stop waitin' around and get to work!" an officer barks at me.

Keeping my head down, I answer, "Yes, sir," and move through the gun deck. I don't stop anywhere or return to the galley. I go straight up to the top deck and quickly glance across the gap to see if Shadir made it over. He's there, waiting by where the ropes are tied to the banister.

After spotting me, he mouths, "What are you doing?"

The doors to the *Prey Empress* cabin slam open, and the men from this ship exit in a rage, aiming for the gangplank. Who I presume to be Captain Bucky spits, "This is the most outlandish series of annoyances and misconduct I've ever been met with." He makes it across to this ship. Tango and Rubias stay behind. He yells back at them, "I'll no longer feed into this nonsense. In the name of the king, I demand your toll payment for two ships, or consider yourself—"

An explosion erupts from below, ripping through the gun deck and starting fires across the ship. Arcs of electricity squirm across the metal of the ship. The gangplank shudders and falls, leaving me stranded. Smoke coughs out from the hatches and portholes.

That was a little more than what I expected would happen.

Bucky yells, "What was that? Did they attack us?"

To scuttle that line of thinking, I yell out, "No, sir. That came from the orlop deck!"

He doesn't question my presence, or even look at my face.

Shadir is trying to get my attention. Rubias has already got her two ships drifting away.

"We'll leave you to this pressing matter, then," yells Rubias across the widening gap between the ships.

Bucky yells back, "Help us! We need hands! If you help us, your debt is paid."

Rubias pretends to have a discussion with Tango, stalling. Then, finally, she shrugs and answers, "No, I don't think that will be necessary. Good luck with it though. Hope things work out for you."

During that conversation, I snuck around Bucky and back into the captain's cabin. The rope I tied to the wardrobe chest is pulled taught as the *Prey Empress* swims away. The chest falls on its side and scrapes across the floor, out the doors, and across the balcony. I dash over the desk, spilling papers and ink across the floor, and grab hold of the rope as the wardrobe breaks through the balcony banisters. The knot is a loose one, so the rope unravels with all that weight, and the wardrobe tumbles down into the water. All of Captain Bucky's clothes and fancy hats flutter into the ocean while I swung back across.

A few strong arms in the crew ladle me up. I spill over the banister when I reach topside. A relieved Shadir leans against it and shakes his head in disbelief. As I lie sprawled out across the planks of a familiar ship, an impressed crew claps for me.

Shadir says, "Your note told me you were just going to disable their machine, not make it explode. What did you do to manage that?"

I shrug. "This and that. I'm not sure what did it in the end." True, although I could take a guess at what made the biggest impact.

"Impressive," says Rubias. "Though it's a shame we couldn't get some coin out of it for our troubles."

Edia says, "I got me some." She's smirking and twirling a tan pouch full of money.

The captain steps back. "From where?"

"While you so expertly distracted *Captain Bucky*, I sliced this off his belt. He was so emotional he didn't even notice."

Rubias let loose an uproarious laugh, and tousled the girl's hair. "Attagirl. Go put it in a safe place. Save it for something nice."

I look off to the toll ship getting farther and farther away. The second toll ship is already close enough to help them. They likely won't sink, but the damage is irreversible. It's quite unbelievable that I blew up a ship with my urine. That won't be shared with a single soul for as long as I live.

THE EXECUTION

With its one glowfish orb and no electricity or portholes, the brig is the darkest corner of the ship. Not much luxury necessary for the rare prisoner. While feeding the fish, I hear a slight shuffling in the cot inside the barred area. Holding the orb aloft to light the area, I see a figure behind the bars.

A familiar voice speaks: "Didn't think I'd see you here, lad." The figure moves closer—Aldrezier the mutineer. They must've moved him here from the *Prey Mantas* recently. "Find a good use for you, did they?"

"I'm not here against my will," I say to quell whatever he implies.

"Interesting. Not much use for you on that boondock island then, eh? The life of a pirate is more interesting."

"I'm not a rusted pirate, either. I'm here for now." I want to walk away but my feet are anchored in place. My eyes drift away from the dark reflective orbs in the cage.

"Seeking treasure perhaps? Going to get your cut?" There are gaps in his grin because he's missing so many teeth.

"There are things more valuable than gold."

Aldrezier scoffs. "Ain't nothin' more valuable than gold, save for jade perhaps. Or power. If you're lookin' for something valuable like that, I can help you."

I hang the glowfish orb up while saying, "Don't take me for a fool."

Finally breaking free of this moment of fear, I move toward the exit.

"She has an obsession, that Isadora Rubias." I stop and listen, but I don't turn for fear of him seeing me fidgeting with my cuff. "She's willing to do anything it takes to get to that island and complete her quest."

"Did she tell you what her quest is?"

"I know she wants to kill something, though I don't know what it is. I was only in it for the treasure. I don't believe there is anything else on that island. It's ramblings from her mad grandfather. Look at the journal if you can. You'll see. Rubias can't be trusted. She'll sacrifice *anyone*, and

">"

keep pushing forward."

I leave the brig. Maybe it was unwise to talk to him for so long.

The next room that happens to be on my list is the captain's cabin, and what Aldrezier said festers in my brain. *Look at the journal if you can.* It wouldn't cause anyone harm.

Since Rubias is not in her quarters, I first ask her for permission to enter. Even if it's a part of my job, manners are still important. She gives me a nod from a distance and I enter. The door is unlocked. The crew's quarters are open to everyone else, therefore why shouldn't her quarters be open to them? That's her reasoning for it, but also there isn't anything worth taking in here for someone else on the crew.

The colors of various draping flags are an aesthetic I always find pleasing. Makes for a cozy room over the wood and rust. The different fabrics, symbols, and weaves are a reminder of the different ways each of these places develop differently from one another.

The nickel-knuckles she usually carries on her person currently hang on a ring holder on her desk. A curious hand of mine takes the weapon off and tries them on. It gleams across my fingers. It's uncomfortable to wear, and I put them back.

The journal is there on the book shelf, but I don't go for it yet. First, I feed the fish as is my duty. The voice of another drowns out Aldrezier's presence: my father. Would the person I want to be break someone's trust, even if that someone is a pirate captain? Maybe there is a good reason for not knowing what's on that island. In the corner of my eye, that journal lingers.

I finish feeding the fish and rehang it in the netting. That's when something else interesting on the opposite side of the quarters nets my attention. There on the table by a porthole is a quaint little chest. I drift over to it and away from the troublesome journal. Always count on a chest to catch my eye over anything else.

It's a small thing, but with a stubborn weight to it. Must be the cast-iron filigree and escutcheon. Underneath is a beautiful but worn red wood. I flip open the unlocked lid. It's not what I expected to find inside.

"Tryin' to rob a pirate, are ya?" says the young spitfire voice of Edia. She has her pistol drawn on me. "Step away from it."

I hold up my hands and follow those instructions. "I thought it was Rubias's chest. I was curious. You can tell a lot about someone based on their chest. I was hoping to get something from it about her."

Edia lifts her chin in speculation. "Well, you had enough time. Without a second glance, tell me what you've got. *Who am I?*" Like a skeptic to a fortune-teller, she mocks me with this test.

"The red wood was likely imported from the Port Ov Imbaro. It's gorgeous but cheap. That, along with the metal suggest it comes from a family who wanted it to look nice but might not have the money for the best of the best. Even a pirate would shell out that kind of money for a chest, so you weren't always with Rubias." All of this I know to be accurate, but she's unimpressed so far. So, after a beat to think about it, I keep going. "There is a broken hinge. Easily fixed even without a chestmaker. It suggests sentimentality to keep it the way it is. And the contents, too. No money. Just nostalgic items. Personal letters. A doll. It's small, too. It used to be a funerary coffer, or was meant to be one. For your parents, I'd imagine."

The gun is placed back into her holster. The answer was sufficient. I don't know if Edia really planned on shooting me, but I'm glad I won't have to find out.

"Get out," she says. Brushing past her to the exit, she stops me first. "You were wrong about one thing." I wait to hear what it was. It feels right to want to know what I could be wrong about. "It's not a death chest for my parents. It was supposed to be for me." She closes the lid and caresses the metal.

<hr>

I can't trust what someone like Aldrezier says, but how exactly is Rubias any different? They're both pirates. I lay pondering this dilemma in my cot, fiddling with a rat trap. Shadir slumps in.

"Cleaned the ease-seats again?" I ask.

He falls into his cot and groans. It has become a daily job for him. No wonder he hates this journey more and more every day. I try to help him out when I can, but he usually refuses. I can't tell if it's a pride thing or if he's frustrated at me for how well I've been faring so far.

I give him a moment to settle before saying, "Aldrezier is in the brig."

"The one who shot me?" He takes out his bandersheef knife and starts carving something into one of the posts by him. "What are they are planning for him?"

"Does it matter?"

He shrugs, and blows wood shavings out of the 'GS' he carved in the post. I can't scrub the memory of his corpse from my mind. The slumped over body. Blood pooling around my knees. And that leads back to my father's mangled—

I can't keep thinking about this, but it doesn't go away. Perhaps there could be some solace on the next island. A place to stay and be of some value. I don't want to abandon Shadir, but there's nothing for me on a pirate ship.

After a long pause, I ask, "Does it hurt to die?"

He replies, "I got shot… in the head. Hardly felt a thing."

"The chest was worse?"

"Infinitely."

I sit up in my cot and put the rat trap away. "When did you first figure out you were cursed?"

Shadir saw other crewmates filtering into the quarters. He leaned in to not be overheard. "We were going home when our ship was attacked by pirates. While protecting Gilligan, I was stabbed in the stomach several times. Should've been a slow death after that, but it wasn't."

He fluffed the thin padding that passed for a pillow on this ship, and positioned himself away from me. That should be a good sign to end the conversation, but I needed to know one more thing. I get close enough to whisper over his shoulder.

"And the beast that cursed you… what is it? What are we going to find on the island?"

Shadir, frustrated, answers quietly, "It's all fuzzy, like I've said before. Like when I try to think about Gilligan's face. The more I try to remember, the more it disappears."

I suppose decades of being trapped in a box could corrode a memory like that.

~~~~~~~~~~~~~~~~~~~~~~~~~~~~~~~~~

Morning light is accompanied by Rubias's announcement of Aldrezier's execution. That's why he was moved. The crew gathers on deck where Tango and Rubias has the mutineer bound at the wrists and ankles. Aldrezier's demeanor is calm. He still has a prideful ego stuck to his face, as if there's still a way to get out of this.

"The waters have been chummed, captain," says someone in the crew.

Rubias guides Aldrezier to a part of the ship where there is no railing. A rope swing away from the *Prey Empress* is the *Prey Mantas* with Salmon Mako watching with his crew. In the gap between the two ships, the water below churns. The chum has attracted the ocean's teeth.

Loud enough for both crews to hear, Rubias shouts, "This man I once called a fine addition to my fleet has made his gold choice. His greed led him to have a lack of faith in me. Nearly destroyed over a decade of work. However, I am a reasonable woman. And I am your leader, not tyrant. Therefore, if the crew has more faith in him than me, speak up now. I will respect your decision."

No one says a thing. It isn't because they're afraid to speak their mind; it is because they trust their captain. They are loyal to her for various reasons that outweigh feeble mistakes she might make.

Over the water, meeting his demise face to face, everything calm and
~~~~~~~~~~~~~~~~~~~~~~~~~~~~~~~~~

collected about Aldrezier melts into cold panic. He backs into Rubias and Tango, begging, "Wait. Wait! Don't do this."

Rubias barely reacts. She pushes him back to the edge.

"I'm sorry! Please, I'm sorry! Shoot me. Just shoot me!"

Like him, I have a healthy fear of sharks. What an ancient lineage they have. Their toothy grins, long life spans, and keen senses have always been supernatural to me. Growing up, I saw several in the bay, menacingly waiting for a child to stray far out from the shore. There was a boy down the lane from our house who disappeared in the water one evening. I avoided the ocean as much as I could for the rest of that year. No matter how many leagues humans traverse, nor how many islands we conquer, the water will never be our domain.

Shadir, by my side, says, "This is disgusting. Feeding him alive to the sharks… I hate pirates."

"He shot you," I whisper, not wanting the crowd to turn their attention on us.

But Shadir is not as subtle when he remarks, "This is cruel."

Rubias spins, locking those fierce yellow eyes with Shadir. "Speak up!" she demands.

"You're a cruel witch!" Shadir shouts. He walks over to her. The crowd parts for him, uneasy about his outburst. "Make it quick. Shoot him. What's the point in making him suffer?"

Rubias grabs the pistol at her waist and offers it to him. "You do the honors, then. After all, he shot you. Return the favor."

Aldrezier is weeping now. Spit froths at his lips.

Shadir freezes looking down at the weapon. Furrowing his brows, he says, "No," and walks away. A second later, he flinches to the sound of a gunshot. He turns to see the smoking pistol pointed up to the sky next to the Aldrezier's head. Shadir continues down into the hull.

"I have made my decision," she says. "Take him back to the brig. We'll figure out what to do with him later."

She chose mercy. And I think she had always planned it that way.

THE ISLAND OF MERCHANTS

After several days of drifting through the ocean, and dozens of menial tasks completed, we're finally making port at Kameya Island—which will be the first time I've ever stepped foot on an island outside of the archipelago.

There are a few rules that come with warships because of their implication. An important one being they cannot casually sail into a civilian port or harbor without significant notice beforehand. Historically, it's been a declaration of war. That's partially why satellite ships accompany them.

A crewmember at the top of the foremast waves brightly colored flags to signal the *Prey Mantas*. The smaller quarvette makes its way to our ship, and a dozen of the crew, including Shadir and I, board it. The *Prey Mantas* swims over to the harbor of an island, which Captain Rubias calls the Port Ov Princip.

My hand eclipses the sun to lessen its blurring effect. The port looks nice from here. Less raggedy than home. A conch horn whines somewhere on the island, possibly signaling our incoming ship. Earlier, Rubias switched the flag out for a standard trading vessel flag to avoid trouble. A dinghy meets us halfway through the harbor to collect the port fee. From that I suspect it's a bustling city. Smaller islands need the tourism and coin of outsiders, so no fee enforced. I can only imagine the crowd of an island which demands a fee up front. The collector swings a small basket on the end of a large pole over to Rubias. She promptly drops in a small bag of coins. Once the *Prey Mantas* is properly moored in the wharf, we walk into town, passing under the arches of towering desalinating aqueducts.

We follow others through a seemingly random flow of the crowd. The lane opens up in the city, with multiple market squares across the island like a slapdash grid. This city harbors the most people I've ever seen in one place, all gathering in lines at vendors, stores, and bazaars that sold whatever I could've imagined—plus a lot of things I would have never imagined.

There are crafts of all kind here. Rug weavers. Glassblowers. Tailors. Metal smiths. Cobblers. Everyone here may be used to this sight, but it strikes me with awe. So many artisans haggling with an unending stream of people. With all these different kinds of folk around, I'd have no shortage of customers to make chests for. This is exactly what I've been looking for. Perhaps with the money I have, I can find a place to rent and get away from these pirates.

It is difficult weaving through the crowd while wanting to look at everything. Fishing rods. Baskets. Wine and ale. Fresh bread. And no one yelling at anyone else to clamp their tongues.

There is a stall I come upon. It draws me in by the rich aroma with a hint of smokiness. Barrels of freshly roasted coffee beans. They are scooped and sold in burlap sacks. Lightly burned in the sides of the sacks with a branding iron is a port symbol I am all too familiar with.

I pull on Shadir's sleeve and tell him to look. "It's Krakau coffee," I say.

He nods. "They sell it all over the place, don't they?"

"Yes, but…" My curiosity sours. "Do they know the cost of it?"

"They set the prices. Now come. We're going to lose the others."

"No, I mean the real cost of it."

Shadir is already gone when I say it. I wonder if the charter barons forced that girl into villeinage after we left. When I turn to follow my friend, he's gone. The crowd billows around me as I am left spinning to find him or anyone in the crew. They've all disappeared into the flow of buyers and sellers. There might not be any need to find them again. Rubias will leave with or without me to do what she needs to do.

I hover toward something in the corner of my eye. Cheese: crumbled in pouches, whole in wheels, sliced by thin wires, and almost tumbling off a pile. I have never tried cheese before, and only saw it once when traders brought it to Tyro. They claimed it was a rare delicacy for royalty only. Such stories gave me the assumption it's something I could never afford, but here it is piled in a large quantity for the masses to buy—and cheap, too. I have to try it.

I enter the line and wait for a long while, shuffling forward one step at a time. I hold my personal chest tight after seeing a few folk giving me a look-over. It must look strange to be carrying around even a small chest.

I pull out some tinstrips and coppercuts from the secret compartment and count them out when I make it to the front. The shopkeeper stops me, dead-eye serious. "We don't take that kind of stuff around 'ere. Go back to the slum island you came from.”

If there is one thing I hate the most, it’s being underestimated. My gold coins should have a different effect. Perhaps this change of currency will embarrass the merchant enough to apologize. I release the golden crowns from their slot and offer them. He looks them up and down, and then knocks my hand away. This sinks my smile.

“I want no coinage with your ancestors face on it,” he says.

I look at the golden crowned head on the coins. “It’s not my ancestor.”

“I don’t give a damn. Money like that’s no good ’ere on this island.”

“Then what do you take?”

“Gems, doubloons, triploons, coral clusters, CMT notes, any gold or silver that are *not crowns*.”

“It’s all I have.”

“Then you best get it exchanged at the Central Maritime Treasury.”

“That’s hundreds of leagues away.”

“Best o’ luck to ya.”

The next customer shoves me out of line.

Another man sees me walking away from the vendor. Loud enough for me to hear, he says, “Shoddy glittergrabbers. They’re everywhere now.”

As I wander off, I can’t keep that word out of my head. “Glittergrabber” spat through yellowed teeth over and over again. Such a spiteful remark used against the poor folk who kneel for every shiny glint on the ground in desperate hope for gold or coins. Sometimes I glittergrab when no one is around, but doesn’t everyone do that? I haven’t knelt since I arrived. He called me it all the same. Continuing my perusal, I hear other remarks like “fleahouse” and “wicker-snip”.

Why are they all so angry at me? I’ve done nothing, not even gotten in their way. Perhaps it’s because I haven’t bathed since leaving Krakau. There was no chance to on the ship. I’ll keep an eye out for a bathhouse.

I enter another curious store and wade through the apparel made of silk.

“Don’t touch the bone lace unless you buyin’,” says some seamstress with pearl-white teeth. She’s probably only a couple of years older than me. She’s smiling, but her tone is like a happy dagger. “I don’t want grime on my most expensive products, kid.”

“Not a kid,” I say. It is hardly standing up for myself with my eyes down and arms wrapped over my chest to close myself off from the world.

“Well I don’t see a man in front of me. Either way, keep your grubby hands off.”

“You don’t take crowns do you.” I don’t want any silk dress, but I also don’t want to look at the other trinkets without being able to buy them.

“You’d be hard-pressed in finding vendors on this island who do. Why?

You snatch something?"

Hastily leaving isn't the smartest thing to do without denying that accusation, but it is exactly what I did next. Makes me look guilty. I look over my shoulders to see her contacting some men nearby and pointing in my direction. I probably could've blended into the crowd and disappeared had I not tripped over and toppled a barrel of the Krakau coffee beans. The seller spits vile words at me, spurring me to take off, and the port guards follow.

They're big, to say the least. A full jump taller than myself and much more muscle. I bump into people while speeding up—a far cry from looking inconspicuous. They follow me through several lanes. I duck into the back alleys where the facade of the bustling port rips away.

Behind the affluent face of this island lays its foundation: derelict buildings and unkempt beggars. A scruffy dog chews on the bones of something that died there. A man approaches and holds out white necklaces that spill and tumble over his shaking bones.

"Wear what royalty wears," says the raggedy man. "They are made from the teeth of savages."

"I don't have anything." I open up my chest to show him it's empty.

Apparently, if I'm not a buyer, then I'm a thief. The man steps back and clutches his wares away from me. He drops one and shakily picks it up. If I did want them, it wouldn't take much to get them. The people back here are starved to skin and bones.

A palm presses my head down while three other hands swipe my chest to the ground and lock my arms behind my back. The necklace seller hastily pockets his items and sneaks off.

"What you doin', pocket-snatcher? You think you're clever? Bumpin' inta all those people, taking a coin here and there like no one'd notice."

The guards caught up to me.

"I wasn't doing that on purpose." I struggle in their arms to no avail—a bee bouncing around in a jar. Even if I could reach the bandersheef knife to sting them with, I can't imagine I would've gone through with it.

"Then let's take a look inside this box here." One of them flips open the chest with his foot. Finding nothing inside, they search me. All my coins are back in the secret compartment, so there's nothing for them to seize. "You some kind of magician, boy? I seen't a magician do coin tricks once." The other laughs. Was there a jest there I didn't get?

"Excuse me," says Shadir a couple paces away. "If you're lookin' for a fight, he's not the challenge."

"Oh, I see. You handed 'em off to this shiptipper." The thugs grin. A shiptipper is someone who is all talk and no fight. Damn. They're going to beat him to a pulp.

"I don't know him," I say, trying to save him. It doesn't work.

It's two against one. Shadir doesn't have enough arms to defend against both guards pummeling him. He hits the ground in seconds, but gets back up a moment later, completely unharmed. Two more guards were called over to enter the fray. Together, they beat Shadir to a point where most would die. They leave behind a battered and broken body when they decide necessary justice is given. My presence isn't even a concern anymore, like they expelled all their rage and forgot what they had come to do in the first place.

Shadir's gashes and bruises slowly return to unmarred skin, but the blood that remains dries on his shirt and clots in his hair. When he is strong enough to move, he leans on me for support back through town. No one stops to acknowledge us or offer support. Many don't even notice us, as if they see this kind of thing every day. They ignore it every day.

After returning to the *Prey Mantas*, he washes away the dried blood in a community wash bin. The only thing he can't heal is the memory of the pain. That torments him for a few hours afterward, but he doesn't want to talk much about it. I ask but he refuses to utter another word.

This ability of his is extraordinary, but I understand why he only sees it as a curse.

The night is quiet back on the *Prey Empress*. Even the sloshing waves seem to whisper rather than roar. The Aurora Tide is a little dim tonight. We're anchored nearby Kameya, and its lights squabble in the distance.

Sleep evades me, so I take in the cool, crisp air on deck while sitting on the guardrail with my legs through the ratline ropes. A hand slithers over my shoulder. Startling, but it's only Rubias staring into space.

She muses, "Imagine what it would be like to steer this ship up until we went there. There's a whole realm yet to be explored."

"I never thought of it as something to be explored. I always wondered what would happen if there was suddenly no more gravity. What if everything just fell off the planet?"

I can feel her side-eye boring into me.

"You're scared of a lot of things, aren't you?" she asks.

I nod. "Pirates. Anarchists. The sea. Sea creatures. And now apparently people on other islands I thought were peaceful."

"Oh?"

"The people on Kameya are violent. Hateful. And they wouldn't take my gold because they're crowns."

"Understandable mistake. Kameya fought to be free of monarchy, so of course they're a bit rusty about the whole thing."

"Gold is gold. I would've accepted it in a heartbeat. Anyone on my island would've."

"It's not about the gold itself. It's a pride thing."

Pride? I have pride in my work. If this is their version of that, I don't know if I want to be a part of it. In the end, it doesn't seem any better than Tyro. But Shadir, even after being beaten by guards, would probably rather have me stay. He wants me off this ship and out of danger.

I have to know: "Is it going to be like this everywhere?"

As if her piercing eyes could read what my true concerns are, Rubias says, "There are many other places I would choose to live over Kameya." With a huff, she steps up onto the guardrail, boots going with the grain of the wood, and a hand holding the ratlines. She scans the island. Lights dance as the bustle of the city remains steady. Her soothing voice cascades down to me. "To me, they aren't much better than the Aronians they proudly hate. A place where only commodity is worth a glance. Where you make unseemly profits on the backs of others. Subjugation of native tribalists. The whole island is steeped in a bloody history."

"Says the anarchist."

She looks down at me, but her eyes glimmer softly like one of the stars, so I don't feel the need to look away. "There you go again with that nonsense. Though, I understand." She hops down off the banister and leans against it. "Why do you have crowns, anyway? I thought Tyro wasn't a part of the kingdom."

I shiver a bit against a breeze and curl in on myself to warm up. I murmur, "Someone tried scamming me. Shadir helped. It's the reason why I employed him."

She gives me a hearty pat on the back, saying, "Try melting 'em down when you get the chance. People will still take clusters."

She leaves me alone to ponder.

THE CREW

As I sort through the tools and scraps of the shed, a sour stench surrounds me. A bulky shadow steals my light. A large man with silvery teeth breathes over me. Backing up into the shed rather than slipping out is my stupid mistake, but I reach for a hammer to defend myself if need be.

He's fuming, by the looks of it. Veins popping along his head and neck like pipes bursting with steam. I rattle my brain to come up with anything I had done recently to draw his ire. But there's nothing. I've done nothing. I don't even recognize him.

As he inspects me, I dig my nails into the wood handle of the hammer. I won't wield it until he makes his move.

With needles in my throat, I ask, "What do you want?"

"Heard you a chestmaker," he says.

I pivot my head. "I am."

"I love me a good chest."

"Were you… looking to commission one?"

"If you've got the time. Name's Wickit."

He juts out a steady hand that whips mine around like it's a dock rope. When he pulls away, a gold coin is left behind in my palm.

"Sure, but did I make you angry for something?"

"Wha—? Oh, no." He points at himself. "Just me face, I'm afraid."

The following belly laugh makes me jump. He steps back and I take that chance to squeeze out of the shed.

"Do you have any requests for the chest? Specifications?"

Rubbing his chin, he says, "Aye, can you engrave it for me. A message to my beloved. A gift when I get the chance to go home."

Home. Right. I suppose even pirates could have a home somewhere.

"Of course," I say, already planning something in my head. "I can craft something special for you."

He nods, eagerly, and rubs his hands together as we get started. After some questions, I sketch ideas on paper until we land on something he's satisfied with. It'll double as a music box. When opened, it will play a melody from a common song from his home island. I've never made one before, but I've seen enough of them to know how they work.

An immediate snag halts my progress. The shed has plenty of tools, but the other materials will need to be acquired. We've already departed Kameya, so I'll search the ship. On the back of the sketch paper, I make a list of items I'll need to find.

Delving into the hull, I try my best to avoid the pirates and stay out of their way. The scullery doesn't have much besides cutlery and cooking equipment. I don't want to rummage through the crew's personal effects, so that rules out the sleeping quarters. There are some items on my list I saw in the engine room. But based on what I've seen, those engineers don't trust anyone but themselves to go in there.

I'll have to sneak in again.

They aren't always in the engine room. It's easy to overheat and faint in there. Last time, I slipped through while they were leaving, but this time they're both already above deck getting fresh air.

I test the door first. Locked. I figured as much, and came prepared. From out of the lower pocket of my bandersheef, I retrieve the makeshift lockpicking set I assembled for the toll ship. A heavy *clunk* within the door lets me know I've succeeded. With one last look over my shoulder, I enter.

I'm a bit more familiar with the layout now, and can scavenge quickly. A hinge here. A latch there. Some of it will work in a pinch, but I definitely need more.

The pipes scream for a few seconds as the ship makes a sharp turn. I plug my ears until it stops. That shouldn't be happening like that. Although I've never been in an engine room like this before, I used to be obsessed with ship schematics when I was younger. The engineers are the experts here, but maybe they need an outsider's perspective.

Following the guts of this sea brute, I find an issue with the efficiency in the pipes. There's a choke point. Pressure builds at a critical juncture. It's obvious why it hasn't been changed. It would take a lot of delicate work. The engineers are either lazy or busy. Well, incompetent is also an option, but I'm hoping it's not that.

I glance between the exit and the pipes. It'll keep eating at me if I don't at least try to fix it. Hopefully Wickit isn't expecting a quick deadline.

I lose track of time working on it, and the ringing lunch bell shakes me loose from my focus. The engineers will be coming back soon. There is more I can do, but it'll have to wait. There will be other times to come back and make other adjustments. Hopefully, they don't notice until I have a chance to finish. I make the machinery and pipes look as normal as I can before slipping out of the engine room.

Looking down one way, I move the opposite direction—slamming into someone rushing over from that direction. Tango the deck chief. Our entangled arms hold each other steady, and then he peers over my shoulder to the engine room door closing shut behind me.

He makes a sign, but I don't understand.

"Please don't tell Rubias, or the engineers. I was looking for some materials for a chest for Wickit." I hold up the list of items I made earlier. "I swear that's all I did."

I am studied. Carefully. Up and down. He knows I was in there longer than needed for that. Being drenched in sweat pretty much gives it away.

I scrounge up the coin Wickit gave me for the chest and present to Tango. He's a pirate like the rest of them. Perhaps he can be bribed. "Please don't tell Rubias. She told me not to go in there, but the tool shed doesn't have everything I need."

Tango eyes the coin with knit brows. He doesn't reach for it, or check it to see if it's real like I'd expect. He nudges my arm away as a gentle declination. He retrieves a pencil from his bandersheef and scribbles something down on my paper next to the list.

Help the crew. Find all you need from them.

Someone passing by down the hall is waved over by Tango. The grease-marked man marches over for his orders. The deck chief points at me and makes some gestures to the crewmate.

"Him?" the man says with a strange accent upon his tongue. "All right then."

After he introduces himself as Oilm, Tango signs off with approval and leaves.

The smudgy-skinned Oilm guides me through the hull, and doesn't say much. Both of us avoid conversation as if it'll kill us. We enter one of the rooms for gun deck storage. There are stacks of round shot crates and barrels of gunpowder.

Oilm points at some dingy-looking crates. "Fix what you broke."

These are the ones I used for the pulley system for bringing the fish orbs up to the deck. Slamming them down repeatedly with cannonballs inside has an obvious side effect. They're dinged up, warped, and splintered.

Lifting one of them, I utter, "Right. Sorry."

Oilm doesn't acknowledge my apology. He huffs and inspects the inventory.

I had hoped to be of some value to the crew while here, but clearly I have been a nuisance. All the more reason to hop pebbles until I find a suitable place to stay.

The crates aren't in a dire state. There are a few pieces that can be repaired or replaced. As I start on that, Oilm grunts his way through chores, ignoring me.

I get a good look at him while he's distracted. The grease along his skin is actually ink splotched up and down his arms and neck. Tattoos most likely, but of what I couldn't say. They're often associated with sailors or island tribes, and so are rarely seen in Krakau.

Catching me gawking, Oilm huffs through his nose at me.

"I like the tattoos," I say in defense. And that is true. I could admire them as a craft like mine. But I'm not much of a conversationalist, so where to go from here is tricky. "I'm thinking about getting a skull somewhere around here." I point to my chest. That kind of works. It's enough to make him halt for a second and raise a brow. I need more, and continue to add to this lie. "Maybe with… octopus tentacles coming out and up here, wrapping around my throat. Like it's strangling me." I try to swallow the cannonball sized lump in my throat. With that stare, maybe he thinks I'm making fun of him. "I don't know. Just an idea."

There is a bent nail in the crate that I need to pry out, and focus all my attention on that, but Oilm is unrelenting. He hovers there in the corner of my eye, waiting, thinking. And finally releases, "That'd be shit, wouldn't it?" Then he lets out a guttural snicker. Not much, just enough for me to know he's got something akin to a sense of humor. "Doesn't fit a skinny squat like you."

"You're probably right about that."

Continuing with his chores, he wipes a cloth across the cannons, paying particular attention to crevices where dust and gunpowder builds up.

To keep loosening him up, I ask, "How long have you been with the crew?"

He shows no signs of thinking about it, so during the long pause I assume he has gone back to ignoring me. But eventually he says, "Fifteen years, on and off."

So he must also have a home somewhere. A place he goes back to every once in a while.

"Is that typical for a pirate?"

Shrugging, he says, "Only for those with a life outside of this crew." Oilm rips up one of his sleeves to reveal a splotchy face along the bicep. "That's my mum. I get back to her with money when I can."

"Very beautiful," I say, but can barely make out where her chin begins and her nose ends. I'm not going to question the artistic style of a permanent fixture on this pirate's body. Opting instead for a simple, "Where are you from?"

Another pause. Every answer from him is weighted. Calculated.

"Ever heard of Baloa?"

I shake my head, no. Geography was not one of my stronger interests back when my father was schooling me.

He twists the cloth in his hand like he's wringing a neck. "Small island. Knew no other life than the Baloa way, I did. Grew up there from only a babe. But because we weren't native to Baloa…"

Oilm decides not to finish, like he gave up too much and needs to retreat back into a shell. Like an exchange of goods, I tell more about myself and Krakau, but he doesn't ask too many follow-up questions.

After I fix the crates, we haul empty ones down to the orlop deck and replenish them with the shot locker inventory. He picks up a crate of cannonballs and makes for the stairs. I reach down and tug on a crate. There isn't even an inch of lift before I give up and leave it be.

My entertaining struggle manages to pry another little laugh from Oilm. "Thanks for the help, skinny, but you can leave this to me." He lugs them up, and then shows me a box of random parts from which I can take anything I need.

I knock a few things off the list, including a broken chest which I can use as a starting point. I'll still need wood. It would be best to use scraps so I'm not using up necessary materials.

After asking around, I meet two women named Gridda. One used to be a jester and carpenter. The other a playwright turned shipwright. When a hole is blown in the *Prey Empress*, they're in charge of making that hole disappear. They accept my help with sanding down and staining the wood that will be used to fix the banister blown to bits by the mortar fire from the Aronians.

There's no need to ask questions about them. They give it freely, hardly stopping for air. They were once a part of the Ilon Kingdom. It spans a few island on the opposite quadrant of the polar circle from Tyro.

The playwright Gridda says, "Statistically speaking, eighty percent of pirates from monarchies are women, y'know. They don't allow women in the navy and only two percent are allowed on tradin' ships, y'know."

"No one cares about the rusted statistics," the jester Gridda says. With a mocking tone, she shouts, "Now announcing First Lord Captain Admiralty Sovereign Lord Blah Blah of the Ilon Shitdom. Why would we want that ridiculous title anyway?"

I push my way into the conversation: "A title like that can be valuable. Right?"

She responds, "Value is in the eye of the beholder. Women aren't allowed any titles of authority in Ilon. Save for maybe the queen, but that's not somethin' we can aspire to be, now is it?"

Playwright Gridda adds, "Twist the laws out of peoples' favor, and Baldeva's revolution starts lookin' real nice, y'know."

"Cheers to that, my sister," jester Gridda says. The two clank pieces of wood together like glasses full of ale, and do the same with me.

After gaining scraps from them, I work with Noctis, who could take out his dagger, cut a throat, and sheath it again before the victim even knew what happened. He wants me to design a chest for him. What he describes is not a chest for his money, but for his collection of knives. It's an interesting challenge. I sketch on paper a design that opens like wings where each knife can be placed to display or closed back in to lock up.

When I get the chance, I ask him similar questions as the others. In his stilted and whispering voice, he returns, "Never had island home. Lived on pirate ship. But family was different. Violence most important. Trained me. Hurt me. Captain saved me. Destroyed them all. *Empress* home now."

I show him the sketch. He smiles and nods approval.

There are many anarchists, of course, as well as plenty of folk from monarch and democratic backgrounds. But in the minority are the tribalists, of which there are only three. The stormseer is one, another called Hap is a mast crawler, and the last one is the quartermaster Piston.

Piston tells me, "I find it funny people worship Baldeva like a folk hero for doing what my people have been doing our whole existence. Before they were the empire they are today, Aronians took my home island a hundred years before that man was born. Ever since, the native islanders have gone through waves of subjugation and revolution."

He made it on this ship through happenstance, and is gaining knowledge on the world to bring back to his home someday. The most shocking part about his life is how I've never heard of his home island and its struggles despite being so close to Tyro Archipelago. Their redwood forests are the source of the Aronian's lumber for ships. We're practically neighbors, and yet they are at constant war with the same kingdom who is our most significant trade partner.

I don't get the chef's name, but in talking to him I get the feeling he too is here because he identifies with these pirates. It's not because a galley position is steady employment or because he has nowhere else to go. Same with the two musicians, whom I receive help from to craft the cylinder that will play the melody in the music box. All three are here by choice to feed and entertain people who fight for free and open seas.

To speak of pirates and open seas in the same breath seems like a jest, but they believe it all the same. Same as the others. All are from places that forced them into piracy because there was no other way to live safely, comfortably, or fully.

These people are not marauders; they're refugees.

By the time everything on my list is scratched out, the day is dead. The next morning, before getting to work on Wickit's chest, I look for Rubias above deck. But before finding her, I nearly bump into someone else by the mast.

Aldrezier—unbound and out of the brig.

I reach for the knife in my bandersheef. His scrunched face makes no note of me. I'm of no threat to him.

A bucket lands next to me. The water sloshes over and wets the planks. It's from Rubias, who also hands over a brush. He grunts and accepts it.

Netting her attention as she walks away, I urgently ask, "What's he doing?"

With more confusion than she ought to have, she says, "Cleaning the deck. What does it look like?"

"He mutinied. And shot Shadir. You can't be serious about this."

"Why can't I be serious about this? He's starting from the bottom." She yells a command to Tango and heads toward the captain's cabin. Noticing me still following, she says, "Despite his arrogance, and that stupid mistake of his, he was also a very reliable captain at one time. It'd be a waste to get rid of him."

Keeping my voice out of earshot from the man, I say, "But I talked to him before your sham execution. He doesn't trust you. I don't think you should trust him, either."

She smiles. "So you noticed it was a sham, eh?" She looks over her shoulder and guides me over to the banister to look out into the ocean. She takes out her ocular-pipe—a small portable version of a spyglass—and studies the horizon. "I met the man when he was around your age. Caught him on the ship trying to steal food. Not weapons. Not money. Food. His island used to do things like feeding people to sharks. I wanted to give him a reminder of where he came from, and the second chance I gave him when he joined me."

On one hand, I don't like the man, but on the other... "That seems a bit excessive. He's not going to change. People don't change like that. He'll take his shot again once your back is turned."

"Perhaps. Perhaps not." The oc-pipe is put away, and she swivels to face me. She opens her hand for me to shake. "Shall we bet on it? Five gold?"

Squinting at her, I say, "Seems unfair if I can't end up collecting after I win."

"So sure of yourself," she says with a devilish half-smile. "If that happens to be the case, Edia will cover me. She's good for it."

I put my hand forward. "So be it."

"In other regards, you seem to be getting to know the crew. Do you understand it now? This is who I am, not the storybook menace your people talk about."

"I understand you think you're some kind of haven for the downtrodden. The cast-outs. Others like that."

"You're skeptical." She puts her hands behind her back.

"On the surface, you seem fair and certain of your goodness. However, I am curious who you attack."

"What do you mean?"

"You are pirates, right? It should be obvious what I mean. Who do you raid? What ships fall victim to your piracy?"

Her head tilts studiously. "I see. I won't say everything I've done has been for a just cause, or that all the people I've allied with would never cause harm to an innocent. But given the choice, I will always choose to target the systems that cause harm to average people."

Her smirk is one of pride. A held-up chin. A glance to the horizon as if picturing a better future. It is certainly an admirable trait. Other pirates would command through greed, violence, and brainwashing. But I don't think she isn't as selfless as she thinks. There is still a matter of this hidden agenda she doesn't share with her crew. The one embedded in that journal she carries around.

She continues, "That is a conviction which stems from my old captain. Grand Captain Dane Lurious. He felt it was our duty as pirates to target the ships and people who do great harm. The monarchs who attack sovereign islands. War ships and mercenaries. Profiteers and slavers. Even other pirates. And when choosing an island to raid, we do our best to limit civilian casualties."

"And there lies my skepticism," I say. "You think your piracy targets those who deserve it, but where do the ripples of your actions go?"

Her furrowed brows and shaking head indicate a wrestling of ideologies. I've lodged a pebble in her philosophical machine. She tries to strangle back control of the conversation by saying, "We are not liberators, Archie."

She stomps away to bark some orders at a crewmate, leaving me to overlook the sway of the ocean.

THE ANARCHISTS

I accepted the fact that I'd have to make chests for pirates a long time ago, whether I knew they were or not. It had to be done to make ends meet. That's something my father could never reconcile with. However, I never considered it would become a regular thing I do while living with them. But here we are.

Because I work in and around the shed, the crew has a chance to see me craft. Word gets around, and everyone wants to commission their own personal chest. Even Rubias acknowledges this as a morale booster and lightens my load for ship duties so that I might craft them.

Everyone I meet has ideas for gear-lock designs. Their enthusiasm is delightful, but some designs I'm given are insane. Like this one suggestion to make a chest that required a blood sacrifice. Needless to say, I declined to try and craft that. But overall, I was excited to try out most suggestions. There weren't very many days back in Krakau where I could be this creative.

After a few days of labor, the final touches are put into place for the music box chest. Wickit is in the crew's quarters at the end of the day playing cards with a couple others, all using empty barrels as seats. In the middle of their game, I place the chest down in front of him.

Wickit tosses his cards down, folding the hand, and admires the craftsmanship. I hand over the key. Nimbly, he unlocks the latch and opens it. Wound up earlier, the cylinder inside revolves. Pins along the mechanism strum a musical comb. The plucked melody is somber but sweet, reminding me of an old nursery rhyme someone used to sing to me. Wickit rubs a thumb over the engraving on the inside—a dedication to his better half back home.

"It's perfect," he says, holding back a quiver in his voice. The lid is gently closed, which stops the rotation of the cylinder. His giant hand slaps me on the back. "They're gonna call you the Artisan Pirate."

"Oh, I'm not—"

"You know how t'play Lanternkeeper, chestmaker?" he says, nodding to the game.

It's a game simulating the mythical soul ferryman. Must've played it hundreds of times with my father and Grifton. "I know the rules. Maybe played it once or twice." The first rule of a bluffing game is to not let them know how good you are at it.

"Join us!" shouts a woman across the table. She's a lean pirate with a bushy mohawk down the middle of a shiny head and a finger bone luck charm dangling from her neck. "We'd love to take some of your money."

The third person chimes in, "For the last time, we're not playing for money, Aljin." He wears what I can only describe as telescopic eyewear. The lenses magnify his irises so that at a certain angle he looks like a toad. "But we could use a fourth player. You can take Ominix's spot. He isn't very good at this."

He nods to the fourth seat with a hand of cards in front of the stormseer's cat—currently busy cleaning himself. A few weeks ago, I would have never considered playing a card game with pirates. But knowing this crew a little better now, it might be something I would actually enjoy. I shoo Ominix away and pull up the seat as they shuffle up a new game.

The game consists of one player being the Lanternkeeper, gathering as many cards as possible during the game without alerting the others. Those players are other divine entities with different tricks to be utilized against opponents. I'm not adept at lying, so everyone knows when I become the Lanternkeeper almost immediately. On the flip side, my analytical skills are good enough to win me a few games when I am not the titular character's avatar.

The toad-eye player, who I learn is Ellick the physician, has a tell I notice right away. Shifty eyes are easier to spot when they're magnified. Wickit is a bit harder to crack, but every once in a while he scratches an armpit before playing a good hand. The impenetrable fortress, however, is Aljin. She brags while winning or losing, and plays every hand as if it's royal gold. But confidence isn't necessarily a winning strategy in this game. It requires subtlety.

"You little bastard," Aljin says as I steal a win from her in the last second for the third hand in a row. Her cards are tossed up and they shower over Wickit and Ellick who are red in the face from laughter. Aljin grabs my neck and presses in. I brace to be strangled, but it becomes a light shake. It has been a long time since I shared this kind of joy with others. I miss it.

Shadir pops in as we settle down. Exhaustion has conquered the man. There are bags under his eyes so big one could store treasure in them.

I wave him over to join us. It would be good for him to take a load off.

He pores over the three others. "I can't. I have to go clean the ease-seats again."

There is no chance for me to come up with an argument before he's gone.

When he's out of earshot, Wickit says to me, "Your friend is having some difficulties here."

"Rubias is overworking him," I say. There is no fairness on the sea, but I think the captain could let up a little. Without him, her plan is dead in the water.

The cards need to be shuffled. I collect and organize them.

Ellick says, "Both of you have less work than most of us."

Aljin says, "He's just slow, the lazy bastard. Time is money."

Cards are dealt. Wickit leads, and says, "That ain't it. Somethin's wrong with the man. There's a storage room at the aft hull. Inside is that chest you brought with you."

"Chest?" I ask. "A runic chest?"

Wickit shrugs. "Don't know. I've walked past the room a couple times and saw him standing over itor kneeling by it. He spends a lot of time in there. Figured it was best not to pry. That's why he's always on ease-seat duty."

"Weird bloke," says Aljin. The card she plays is bold. There is an attempt to hide it behind conversation. "Heard Aldrezier shot him. Maybe that knocked a few screws loose. Hopefully, he isn't broken enough to get us to that island. Been a while since we've had a good treasure haul."

Ellick says, "Don't be so harsh. And did you think I wouldn't notice that?"

They slap down cards one after the other. I am unfocused, hiding behind my hand while they play on. Strategy slips away from me as my thoughts drift toward Shadir.

～～～～～～～～～～～～～～

The next day, I'm sneaking away from the engine room again when I hear Edia's voice near the timber planks. She sounds tense, irritated. I stay out of sight just around the corner. A crack through plank stacks allows me a peek.

From Edia to someone else, I hear, "Not a bit of them are without sporerot." Rubias comes into view and lifts planks to check the ones underneath. Three or four stacks of them are splotchy with a red mold. I saw sporerot once before back home. One person bought questionable lumber from a trader. After a month, the spores spread throughout the shack he built with it. It spread to his house, blighting it all bloody red. It had to be burned thoroughly to avoid contaminating the entire town.

Rubias snaps, "Just my shoddy luck," and kicks the planks. "I bought these from a reputable dealer."

"Apparently not," Edia says. "Should we take it to the engine furnace?"

"No, I don't want this filth anywhere near the rest of the ship. Get five of the crew to wrap it in a tarp and throw it overboard. Then I need several of them to scrub this entire area clean from top to bottom to get any lingering spores." Her eyes look straight toward me. It's a public area, so it's not really eavesdropping, but that stare still makes me stiffen every muscle. Only after she speaks do I realize I'm not spotted. "What are the next two islands?"

A deeper third voice speaks to the right of my sight. Shadir enters the foreground, blocking my view. "Koikin and then Kekume."

"I'm making a slight change of plans. First we head etherward to Carraca and Carcosa where I bought these planks. I have to pay the dealer a visit."

"I would rather we finish this in a timely manner so Archie and I may return home."

The captain's voice rises stern and harsh. "I am a grand captain. I will not be disrespected, especially on my home islands. I didn't get where I'm at today by shrugging off these kinds of violations."

And so, we travel a few days out of the way to Rubias's home. Growing up, I'd heard a great deal of stories about Carraca and Carcosa—the twin teeth islands of anarchy. Home of Baldeva's revolution and the birthplace of many pirates, including the most violent and legendary ones. Going to a place so infamous is unnerving.

Port Ov Taegot they call the harbor we settle into. Rubias is allowed to steer her warship near the port without an advance notice. It's a good-sized port but the *Prey Empress* is still too large for it to dock directly. Whoever goes will have to take the dinghy.

I picture cutthroats around every corner, or half the inhabitants as homeless, or even mass chaos and murder. How can that be sustainable? Why would anyone choose such a way of life? I want to find out, but tremble at the thought of getting off this ship. The harbor has this eerie silence to it, as if awaiting a victim.

Rubias notices my pale face. "Come ashore with me," she says. "I want to show you something. Don't worry. This is my home. No one messes with me or my crew. You'll be protected."

Shadir grabs her arm. "You bring him back in one piece."

"There is really nothing to worry about. I'm practically king of this rock. Which makes it all the more reason why I can't be disrespected by a *lumber dealer*, of all people." Rubias then walks over to the hull stairs and finds the deck chief. "Tango, come with me. I know that breaks protocol, but I need you with me on this one."

The deck chief smiles. It must be the first time he and Rubias disembarked together in a long time. He gets on the dinghy and sits next to me. His metal leg is cold against mine. Wickit also joins us—for intimidation, I imagine. He's one of the bulkiest on the crew.

A woman helps us latch our dinghy to the harbor docks. Rubias pays a small fee. Everything seems normal up to now. The main city is a bit farther inland past the port. Takes some time to walk there. Their farms are closer to the ocean. The fresh air has an aroma of spices. The irrigation along these farms is quite sophisticated—much more than I expected. The desalinating aqueducts suspended by giant arches are even more complex than those I saw on Kameya. They spread across the whole island as far as I can see. Truly amazing, I admit. Probably pre-revolution.

Rubias watches my intake of her home, attempting to piece together my thoughts. My avoidance keeps her in the dark for the time being.

We finally arrive at the nearest town. Netting my attention are beautiful parchment ribbons and painted ropes with colored lights. The houses and stores are not only intact and not ruins, but are also fairly large and exude a quaint fanciness—almost to the level of the charter baron mansion. The cobbled lanes have a frenzy of people dancing to a thick drum beat and whistling tunes. A festival. The anarchists are having a festival.

Tango holds out his hand to Rubias who graciously accepts. He pulls her into the fray and performs the same dance as the other citizens. Their moves are jagged and rough, but in a way that's meant to be. A holler of joy erupts from Rubias when Tango spins her in a circle. Then she sees someone she knows and they hug and talk for a moment. All while I stand with my mouth agape like a fool with fool's gold.

Rubias returns to me and tries to drag me in, but I am reluctant. She doesn't force me to dance, but the music is hypnotic. At one point I wish I could be a tortoise to hide in my shell, but that is momentary. My smile blooms when the citizens dance around me. Finally, the captain pulls me out on the other side, and we reconvene with Wickit. He had gone around and found a pile of fruit to eat from without payment.

Rubias says, "Is this the chaos you were expecting?"

Moving into a quieter area, I say, "I was told the twin teeth islands are a dangerous place full of pirates."

"It is. But not every second is a matter of life and death. People are more complex than you give them credit for, Archie. Most of these people are farmers and fishers and weavers. They are as normal as your own people."

"My people don't dance like that," I scoff.

"You don't celebrate Baldeva's Day?"

The infamous instigator of rebellion changed polar politics forever.

Uncomfortably, I answer, "Of course we acknowledge his importance in history. But we don't celebrate much of anything anymore. We're grateful someone was there to revolt against the monarchs, but he isn't our savior."

"Of course. I get it. Like I said, complex." She scans the area for a second to get her bearing straight. "Come along now. We have someone's face to break." She picks a lane and commits with a bounce to her stride.

We come across a storefront. Baylin's Arbor Lodge. A bell rings for our entrance. A man comes from the backroom. "Welcome to Baylin's. We've got—"

"I have a question, Baylin," says Rubias. He skitters to a stop. Her right hand slithers into an inner pocket and produces the nick-knucks. "Did you know those planks were rotten when you sold 'em to me?"

"Of course not, darlin'. I'd never do somethin' like that to you." There is a flickering smile on his lips. Not a very good liar, this one. "Mayhaps I did." He continues around the counter with a machete in hand. "Don't worry. I'm only gonna maim you."

This is more like I expected.

In a long, overhanded arch, he swings the machete. From a distance, it would look like Rubias catches that blade midair with her palm, but it's the nick-knucks stopping the blade. While the machete wavers above their heads, the captain retrieves her pistol with her free hand and shoves it into Baylin's cheek. The machete clatters to the floor. He backs up until there's no more room to spare. She follows, pressing the barrel deep past his teeth.

"So who's got the bounty on me?"

"Pé Dutanté," he whimpers. "A couple of his ships are here. They're expecting you."

Even though I don't know who that is, I know we're in immediate danger by the reactions of the others. Wickit wields his small bludgeon. Tango has his pistol, and he hides near the side of the door. Footsteps rumble across the deck outside. Two people bust through and let off a barrage of bullets. The captain is quick to take cover behind Baylin. He takes a couple rounds to the chest. Tango, hidden to the side of these men, raises his pistol. Upon firing, the perfectly angled shot takes down both of them, but more are outside.

I am windless, unsure of how to make myself safe. No piece of cover looks adequate. Tango notices and hobbles over to me before more pistols and rifles fire a wave of iron through the windows. He takes a bullet in his shoulder as his body covers me and pushes me down. Wickit barrels through the door when the barrage subsides. They're reloading when our hulking crewmate charges at them with his club.

While he dispatches the three outside, we three inside gather ourselves. Rubias raids Baylin's store chest before we leave. She informs us, "That was an ambush. He's probably stationed people all over the island. We must get back to the ship."

We disturb the festivities on our way back. After running through, they return to dancing. We maintain this pace to the port.

Shadir sees our rushed paddling in the dinghy and signals a few others.

"Ladle us up!" yells Rubias. She hooks dinghy to ship and we're hoisted on deck.

When aboard, Shadir asks, "What happened?"

I am the one to answer him while Tango and Rubias go to work commanding. "Some pirate put a bounty on Captain Rubias. It was an ambush."

"Rusted pirates!" Shadir yells before helping with the sails.

The crew hustles us back out to sea. I strip the wave of anxiety off layer by layer before being able to help with whatever is asked of me.

"Captain!" calls the person in the crow's nest. He peers through a spyglass. "They're not lettin' us go easy! They've sent a deepwater-class ironclad!"

I run to the stern of the ship and take out my oc-pipe. My untrained eyes would've never seen it on my own, even if I looked directly at it. All there is to see out in the water is a pipe sipping the air and lightly blowing smoke. It's probably wide enough for me to fit through, but I'm unsure at this angle and distance. Perhaps a bomb could be thrown in if close enough. The cannons certainly won't be able to strike it, and the water will absorb the momentum of the mortar rounds.

After taking a look for herself, Rubias commands the crew to prime the propellers and set the sails. "We'll have to outrun it," she tells me. "Ironclads are ship-killers. I didn't think Pé had one this close to us."

"What do we do?"

"We put squid ink in the water to obscure their main vision. They'll have to rely on a viewport which we can take out with a rifle." The captain turns to find Tango halfway across the ship. She whistles to get his attention, and yells, "Get the antichum ready to pour overboard! We're gonna blind 'em."

A series of snaps follow the crackle of gunfire. They fired a weapon, but none I have seen before. Several hooks chained to the ironclad fling up from under water. They break through the hull and grasp the wood like barbed fish hooks, slowing us down significantly.

"They're sending divers to board us." She catches Tango's attention again. "Forget the antichum! Gather the actual chum!" Tango rushes to the crew below to change the order he just sent down.

"You're going to attract the sharks?" I ask.

"Of course. They're sending over a feast." She grins.

Another crack of a cannon sends a hook up to the sail. The bladed iron tears down through the cloth. The edges of the gash flap wildly in the wind. Crewmates haul barrels up the hatch and roll them to the side of the ship. They lift them and dump the contents overboard. The air is choked with the nauseating smell of blood, fish, and brackish water. After a few minutes of silence, we see the fins closing in. Their backs rub against the ship. They swirl around the slimy remains to find the source of chum. Finally, the fins dive and are gone for a moment.

Two chains snap and whip off of the hull. I rush to the rear of the ship in time to see another snap back into the water and a fizzle of bubbles arise. The shark fins dip in and out. The divers crawling along the chains are forced to retreat as the sharks pick them off one by one. A few divers are lucky enough to get out and hang above the water by the chains, but they are easy to pick off with pistols.

Although we're holding them off well, an ironclad like that will have plenty of other tricks to reveal. It can still easily sink us, and then we'd be the ones picked off by sharks.

Another ship comes into view—Salmon Mako and the *Prey Mantas*. Backup. Someone on the crow's nest flaps two flags to communicate with the mate on our mast. After receiving the message, the quarvette stampedes perpendicular into the ironclad. Their metal ram glides over the underwater ship and cuts through its hull. Being a deepwater-class ship, it could've dove a bit to avoid the attack, but its focus was on us and the sharks. With water leaking in, it is forced to surface and face the onslaught of our dual artillery.

As the metal ship rises, and the ocean falls off it like a waterfall, Rubias orders the rear mortars to be loaded. They light and fire them, and projectiles rain from the sky to slay the ironclad. Remaining divers clinging to the side of it return to the water where they're pulled down into the sanguine depths. Shards of debris scatter across the water, and the ironclad slowly submerges, never to sip the air again.

The crew on both our ships let out a triumphant cheer, but I'm don't feel like joining in. Twice we've been attacked so far, and the journey isn't even half over. I'm beginning to worry I might not make it to the end.

THE RED FLAG

After ramming the ironclad, the hull of the *Prey Mantas* took too much damage. While we chartered a path back to our intended voyage, Salmon Mako sailed away from us to another port to find a shipyard for repairs. We'll have to be without a satellite ship for a while, but Shadir informed Mako of the next few islands on our voyage.

This other captain who Rubias has a conflict with got the best of her. Although, there is nothing to be done about it until this quest is settled. She's fuming at the ship's helm over it. The crew don't dare get caught dawdling by those yellow eyes in a moment like this. They keep their heads down and work.

After a few leagues of distance from the ironclad, we come across red water. The scarlet color is splayed out in front of us for as far as we can see, even through my oc-pipe.

"It's a red flag," grumbles one of the musicians coming up beside me. I believe his name is Arginon, and his speaking voice is not nearly as pleasant as his singing voice.

The other musician hears it and rushes over to us on the left side of the *Prey Empress*. Her name is Pelica. "Tha's a good omen, for sure," she says. "Stunning!"

"*That's* a red flag?" I ask, bewildered. "I'd heard they were large, but I didn't expect them to spread across so many leagues."

The fleshy, flat invertebrate floats along the ocean surface. It's the largest animal in the sea, and the most magnificent thing one could ever witness in this world. Its surface flows with the waves like an aimlessly floating sheet. All kinds of marine life live collectively in the billowing folds beneath, and in the algae and seaweed growth on top. A manta ray, with a wingspan twice my size, rests near a cluster of crabs. There is a grey spot no bigger than a human head. I see more as we keep gliding over it.

Must be dead spots akin to blanched coral. Some of the other animals feed off of those dead parts and help it regenerate. It's a completely self-sustained ecosystem. Every entity within helps maintain real equilibrium.

More folk on the ship want to look at it. They halt all their work. Shadir climbs down from the mast where he was helping with the torn sail.

"Now that's a sight," Shadir says, as awestruck as the rest of us. It's not a creature many get a chance to see.

Arginon says, "I've always wished I was born early enough to see the great whales when they reigned, but this beast just might make up for that."

Rubias interjects, "Light the tinder underfoot, lads and ladies! We're not here to sight-see."

The crew breaks and returns to their tasks.

Before backing away, I ask the musicians, "Will we harm it by sailing over?"

Pelica answers, "Don't imagine so. You don't get to be 'undreds of years old by being that weak."

The two return to their instruments, and an original song springs from newfound inspiration.

Shadir is about to continue assisting with the sail when Rubias commands, "Shadir! The mast crawlers can handle that. The ease-seats need a once-over."

Throwing down a bundle of ropes, he yells back, "Are you prodding me? You've got a rusted mutineer right there who's ripe for the job!" He flails a gesture toward Aldrezier who finished cleaning the deck and is dumping the bucket overboard.

"He pulls the weight he is asked to pull."

"Perhaps it'd be best if I jump ship and leave you with nothing." Shadir paces closer to her position at the helm. "What say you to that?" He's now at the first of the steps that curve up to her. The crew can't help but watch when something as dramatic as insubordination happens in front of them. "No, a better idea. Maybe I challenge you to a fight. Winner is captain. You'll win the first bout, but what about the second? Or the third? Or fourth? You know I can't be—"

A tight grip on his shoulder stops the immortal man halfway up the stairs. It's Tango. Nothing but a threat to his crew brings out this side of him. But he's not going to harm Shadir. Rather, he makes a quick suggestion with some signs.

Rubias translates, "Tango has agreed to take on this task for you. Thank your deck chief for this generous offer."

Shaking loose of the hold, Shadir whips out a peeved, "Thank you, Tango," and then returns to the mast without returning a glance to the woman leering at him from above.

I meander over to voice my opinion on the matter. "Don't you think you're being a little harsh on him?"

"That man's been snipping at my seams since he got here. I'm just snipping back."

"He's your guide. Without him, you'd be getting nowhere," I remind her.

"In my mind, young Archie, he's less trustworthy than Aldrezier."

I could piece together why it was that way in her mind. The failed mutineer has nowhere to go but up. Shadir has nowhere to go but out. He has no dedication to the ship or the captain. And without that kind of commitment, there is no actual motivation to ever get these pirates to this mysterious island.

What if he isn't taking us anywhere? For all I know, for all the captain knows, we could be hopping pebbles until Shadir gets his chance to disappear. This whole rusted journey could be a farce.

We're nearly all the way across the red flag when the stormseer yells, "Captain!" while holding his cat like a baby. "Fogkrill over portward. It's billowing this way. Probably following the air current we're in."

Rubias hustles to the side of the ship and pulls out her oc-pipe. Many of us do the same. In the distance is a cloud of white, much like fog descending over the ocean. It's a kind of krill as light as air billowing together, feeding on dead marine life floating on the surface. Seems harmless from this distance.

Shadir yells, "I've never seen a cloud of fogkrill that big before!" It blocks a large portion of the portward horizon. "The red flag must be a treasure trove of food."

"Are fogkrill dangerous?" asks a nearby Ellick.

Pelica says, "There are stories for everything. Some say they get to feeding right away on your eyes. Then breath 'em in and they'll get your lungs."

The captain says, "I'd rather not find out what myths are true the hard way. Make some hard turns! Get us goin' nautward!" The ship pushes forward at a high speed. The captain calls to me. "Archie!"

Before I have a chance to respond, a groan from the ship comes from a strain in the ship. From nearly full speed, we stop completely. Many of us are thrown to our knees. I hear yelling from the hullards as they're troubled with things being flung around below.

Rubias commands Edia, "Run down to the engine room and see what's goin' on!" The girl scurries along to do that. She comes back with the two engineer women. "Dalia, what happened down there. Why did we lurch?"

Dalia—tall, muscular, with red burns across her skin—replies, "We looked all around. Found some strange things out of place. Someone's been messing with the engine."

The captain's face smolders with anger as her eyes descend on the several subjects at her command. But I know it was none of them. I wonder if she'd risk Shadir's scorn by punishing me. My father's words flood my head again. He was always willing to take the fall for the mistakes he made. I have to do the same.

"It was me," I say, more of a whimper than I wanted.

The other engineer hisses, "You've been messing with our steam, boy?"

"Your engine room was a mess. Your steam flow goes everywhere. You lose half of the steam before it's even put to use. I made it more efficient." It's more of a plea to the captain than to convince the engineers. They'll hate me either way.

"You're not supposed to be in there. It's locked for a reason," Rubias says.

"Captain, I assure you my meddling is not the cause of this lurch. That was a full stop, meaning something is lodged in the propeller. Manually turn it with the wheel and you'll see."

The captain turns to a few crewmates and points at the manual propeller push wheel near the aft of the ship; which is only used when the engine is halted for maintenance. They attempt turning the wheel, but it's lodged. They try the other way to see if it can be unclogged, but it's still stuck. After a long bout of pushing, it groans again.

"Stop," I yell. "A propeller is harder to fix than nearly anything else."

Rubias says, "The fogkrill is coming this way, and we still might have Pé's ships tailing us."

She steps down from the stern and tells Tango something. He descends into the hull and returns with Wickit and Oilm hauling the spiked armor. They set the two shark-repellent diving suits down in front of the engineers.

"Put these on and go fix the propeller," the captain commands.

"I can't even fit in that metal corset," says Dalia. It is quite a thin suit. Few of the crewmates could fit in it comfortably.

"There are sharks down there," protests the other. "No matter how spiked this is, I can't be expected to go down in shark-infested waters."

Although we're a league or two away from our previous battle, some chum had clung to our hull. Sharks will follow even a hint of blood for leagues. We won't be rid of them for at least a couple of days.

"You're the only ones who can," says Rubias. She keeps looking over her shoulder toward the fogkrill.

The stormseer says, "I can say with certainty it's coming toward us."

"I'll go," my voice croaks. I'm nearly as surprised about my words as they are.

Shadir is getting ready to climb back up to help stitch the sail, but hears me volunteer. "Excuse me," he says, dropping his tools. "You are doing no such thing."

Rubias gives me a raised eyebrow. "I'll allow it, but you've got to convince him first."

I say, "I'm the only one who knows how to get that thing working again. No offense to the engineers, of course. Their job is the engine, not the propeller. I'd wager the captain gets outside help for a job like that. I have experience with this. Not of this size, but it's the same principle. Something's down there that just needs to be pried out. It's easy."

Shadir looks at the fogkrill. "Fine. I'll take the other suit."

Rubias nods in agreement.

Piece by piece we are suited up. Each spiked plate of shark armor is like having a bucket of water tied to my limbs. As the spiked gauntlets are put on last, I feel safe. Impervious. With the whole suit on, I know I can take on those ancient beasts.

Barely able to move in these, the crew needs to hoist us up like flags. They lower us down off the side of the ship with an air tether on our heads and an emergency rope wrapped around us. After my waist is in the water, the load lightens. The porthole on my helmet fills with bubbles before clearing and revealing the great expanse of the underwater realm.

The edge of the red flag we passed over was pushed deep asunder by the force of our ship's sudden stop. In that direction, it's like a billowing red wall marbled with streams of sunlight. However, everywhere else I survey is as beautiful as it is terrifying. I am a weightless speck of flesh in a blue void. Without the tethers I would sink and drown before finding the bottom.

My breathing becomes erratic when I spot the first shark. It's as colossal as I imagined. These deep ocean sharks are two or three times the size of sharks that hang around the shores of Tyro. I hope they cannot sense me. I'd rather this be quick, easy, and painless.

A knock on my back sends a shiver down my spine. I'm about to turn and punch with my spiked fist before seeing the eyeless, skeletal suit that entombs Shadir. I can't see into his porthole unless a rare beam of light pierces right through it. His floating presence is eerie, almost lifeless until he speaks. Our air tubes are connected a few bricks above us, so we can speak but have to yell. I hear his distant voice telling me to hurry, and so I do.

We traverse the rusted rails along the belly of the ship. The rudder is a few planks away. Something rubs against Shadir and I, pushing us against the wood. I glance back and briefly spot a fin. More have come to greet us, and this one tests our docility. A second one attempts a pass. Shadir pushes his luck by giving it a sting with his knuckle spikes. It swims away, flashing teeth.

We curve up the backside rudder with propellers on either side.

They're much bigger than ones I've seen at home, but not much more complicated. The steam engine feeds gears with movement that churns these hulking screw-like mechanisms. I'm beyond glad we aren't on the whiptail-class *Prey Mantas*. The propulsion on that is far superior and beyond my knowledge.

Wading around the left propeller, a quick investigation yields no result. The corkscrew blades twitch, but nothing prevents them from moving. I check where the water comes in and out.

"Anything?" yells Shadir, looking out for sharks.

"Not yet. I'll check the other one."

Moving on to the right propeller, there is something noticeably off about it. One blade has a slightly bent edge. I swim over to that spot to get a closer look. A piece of thin metal is wedged there. Although it was warped and stretched by the propeller before halting, I can tell it's one of those hooks from the ironclad. It was hooked somewhere to the belly of the ship for a while before getting sucked into the propeller.

I point at it and ask for the pry bar. Shadir unclasps it from his waist and hands it over. If it was any deeper into this propeller, we'd be out of luck. I could fit inside, but once the mechanism is free to move again, I could end up being that hook. I jam the pry bar into a place where I might get enough leverage. With every jab and pull the metal loosens, but then the propeller moves and tightens it again.

"*Damn rusted bloody thing.*" My cursing gets longer with each failed attempt.

"Archie?" Shadir says, but I ignore it. "Careful!"

If I lean a shoulder against the propeller blade and pry at the same time, this could work. There is framework inside which I can grab and hold onto for better support. I give the metal one final twist and the propeller churns again faster than I anticipated, taking the pry bar and my arm with it.

The vambrace of the diving suit has latches which break off, and the edge of it bends inward. It's a pinch at first, just below my elbow. Then the pain increases and my own scream punctures my ears, but I can't hold it in. Shadir squirms in the water to get to me, but the force of the blade crunches my bone in seconds. After that, tearing the rest away is easy for it. It chews up my arm and spits it out the other side. A bloody current gushes from me as Shadir grabs hold and pulls me back along the rails.

The reinvigorated sharks prowl after sensing fresh blood. A toothy grin wraps around my head, but that shark swims away after getting a mouthful of spikes. They're smart. It'll only take a minute to figure out how to consume us safely. They don't even need to eat us. All the beasts have to do is clamp down on our tethers and we'd float to the depths and drown.

The pain is disappearing. That can't be good for me.

Shadir pulls on the safety rope. Bells toll above. He swats at sharks. The crew reels us up. A tight grip on me. We surface, dripping water. Blood. Fins circle below. I reach for Rubias. Arm gone.

Dark now. A muffled voice. Then nothing.

THE RECOVERY

Home. I want to visit my father's spot at the cemetower. I want to eat at the Brewed Bay, and finally retreat to my den to work on my chests. I want to go back to my bed, and leave these lumpy cots behind. I want to swim home, but it's so far away. So strong is the urge to jump ship.

I dive, straight into the water, no hesitation. Rubias and Shadir call to me. I'm not fooling myself. It's obvious that this isn't real. It's my death creating dreams to ease me into nothingness, but I keep going. Leagues upon leagues until Tyro Archipelago is in sight. And before I can make it to shore, I am ripped under the water by the maw of a shark. Others come to feed as well. But my body reshapes after every bite. It takes form again and again as if I have stolen Shadir's restorative immortality.

It is a curse, as he says. I keep swimming toward home. The sharks tear me apart, and I keep healing and swimming. Biting, healing, swimming. Chomping, healing, swimming. Hoping it ends one way or another.

Then I recall the moments before being taken on this voyage. The charter barons. The villein contracts. The people who used to care about things until it all came crumbling down. The Port Ov Krakau isn't my home anymore. It hasn't been for a long time.

And then I sink, and encounter a long span of darkness.

***

Finally, a blurry light from a porthole pushes through. It shines on a face hovering above me. A rough outline of Shadir. He touches my cheek.

"Can you hear me?" he asks. I try to nod but instead blink slowly. "How are you feeling?"

A groan is the only thing I can muster, but my thoughts are coherent. Behind the numbness is a faint sting below my elbow. I've been stitched up by the physician and given medicine. My locked-up memories unravel: the sharks, the propeller, the pain in my arm. It's all too vivid now. Finally, Shadir confirms it.

"I don't know how much you remember, but I need you to know you lost your arm just below the elbow. You're currently in the infirmary room." He clears his throat. "I'm so very sorry, Archie. I didn't want anything like this to happen to you. You don't deserve it."

He stays with me for a bit, holding my left hand—the one that remains.

When the grogginess clears, and I can communicate, I ask, "What kind of medicine did Ellick give me?" I smack my tongue against the roof of my mouth. There's a rancid slime in the back of my mouth.

Shadir rotates a jar on a nearby medical table. "Some kind of anesthetic seaweed. Honestly, the doc here seems to know what he's doing despite being a pirate."

Pushing myself up, I say, "He used to be a surgeon in the Kaima Cluster before a volcanic eruption displaced him."

"*Hm.*" Shadir fiddles with his hands, and then peers out the porthole. "You've gotten to know some of these people well, haven't you?"

I return one lazy head bob.

"Listen, Archie… Rubias will come to check up on you soon. Before she does, I need to warn you."

Here we go. I lost an arm. My stomach feels like something ferments inside me. A headache is about to hack through my brain. And this is the time he chooses to drive a wedge between the captain and me.

Seeing the exasperation overcome me, he says, "No, listen. This is important. She's using you. I don't know what she'll do or say, but she's going to try and convince you to stay aboard the ship. I'm trying to get you dropped off somewhere to recover."

Fine. I'll bite. "Why would she try to convince me of this? She knows what shape I'm in."

He tones down his voice and leans in. "Because she knows I'm only sticking around because of you. If it had just been me from the start, I could've scrammed at any opportune moment. Or I might've killed her if I had to. But I can't do anything if you're in the way."

"So now I'm in the way?"

He scrunches his face. "You know what I mean. This is for everyone's benefit, not just yours."

I move to rub out the growing ache behind my eyes, but forgot that hand is gone.

Seeing the pain setting in, Shadir says, "I'll find the doc," and reaches for the door.

"Wait." He does. "Are you actually taking us in the right direction?"

"Thus far… yes."

The door creaks as Rubias pushes her way through, nearly banging the door against Shadir's face.

"Oh, Shadir…" she says. "Ease-seats need cleaning." His sour face prompts her to add, "Only proddin'. May we have the room?"

"I was just leaving." Shadir gives me one final look of warning before snapping the door shut behind him.

"Can't take a jest, that one," Rubias says as she takes a seat next to my cot. "I'm sorry to bother your rest, Archie. I wanted to thank you for helping. The fogkrill just missed us because of you. I want to give this to you." She ruffles around in her bandersheef for a key, and wraps my fingers around it. "It's goes to the engine room. There are only five on board. I'm giving one to you. Dalia reluctantly admitted that your changes in there have made the ship's steam consumption more efficient. It's impressive, but there is still work to be done. So I'll allow you to keep tinkering without having to sneak in. Understood?"

I only nod.

"Get better. We'll need you on deck."

I stare at the key in my shaking palm after she leaves. Only five on board. This isn't just a key; it's a sign of trust. But is it really what she wants, or is this as Shadir said? She gave me a token to embolden me to stay as his anchor. These two are playing games using me. One is going all in, and the other is looking for the perfect place to fold. It frustrates me to no end that I'm nothing more than a convenient trump card to them.

I am trapped in this infirmary cot for days, relearning how to accomplish simple tasks. Eating. Washing. Using the ease-seats. I instinctively reach for things with the wrong arm. My balance is off. Even sleeping is different. Phantom pains taunt me at every step of this new reality.

At one point, Oilm came in with a broken rat trap for me to fix. With one hand, I fiddle with the springs and the plank of wood, but it doesn't do what I want it to do. It doesn't set the way it needs to set. My dexterity is ruined. My fingers shake like an old codger whose body can no longer keep up with his hard-earned skills.

"Why did it have to be my dominant arm?" I say to myself, gritting my teeth. A premature snap sends delicate bits of metal and springs fall to the floor. "Rust it all!"

I toss the junk away.

Ellick is busy, so Tango comes later to change my bandages.

I tell him, "I was just beginning to learn some of your signing. But now..."

With his hands busy, he doesn't speak, but there is an inquiry in that raised eyebrow.

"What I mean is that I could learn some to understand you, but I can never sign back to you now."

He huffs, and tightens the bandage before stepping back. With a single hand, he signs what would be a long-winded lecture if spoken aloud; either proper rope-knotting etiquette or something about the mast. Hard to tell exactly, but a lecture is a lecture.

"Great, thanks for that," I say, lying back in my cot.

Tango tries to say something else, but I'm in no mood to be attentive.

〰〰〰〰〰〰〰〰〰〰

Wickit and Aljin come to play card games. The latter of the two convinces me to play for money. Of course, she knows I'll lose while in my current state. Aljin may be the only true pirate on this ship, but it's money well spent for the distraction. After the game, she escapes with her earnings and Wickit brings out the music box chest I made for him.

"Don't be mad," he says, "but I may have broken part of the mechanism when I was fiddling with it earlier. Think you could...?"

My remaining trembling hand clenches.

"I don't—"

He sticks the chest down on the table, scattering the cards.

It's not going to work. I know it's not. I'll make it even worse, most likely. But I take a look anyways. Perhaps I can tell him how to fix it himself.

Inside, the musical cylinder doesn't move. I stick my hand in a crevice of the mechanism to see what I can deduce. "Did you crank it the wrong way?" I ask.

He shrugs. He definitely did. There is a tiny piece here that snapped. It shouldn't be a problem. All I have to do is—

A stitch tightens when I reach forward with my right arm, shooting pain across my body. It feels like I've been ripped in half, and lasts a lifetime.

I curse under my breath. The wincing Wickit holds his hand up in anticipation of my needs, but I lean away from his touch.

After all these years of crafting and building up my skills, everything went down the drain because I made one rusted mistake. Many years ago, my father taught me proper safety practices for things like engines and mills and the like. "Don't go stickin' your hands in a pinch!" I hammered that into my brain when I was young. However, when the adrenaline was pumping through me down under the ship, and my wits were carved out because of the sharks, I finally disregarded everything I knew and stuck something somewhere it doesn't belong.

"I can't do it," I say, snapping the lid shut.

"Archie—"

"Leave me alone." I bury my head in the pillow. "I'm getting dizzy."

Picking up the chest, Wickit says, "Right, I shouldn't have asked that of you." He places the chest in the corner of the room. "But in case you get bored…"

The rest of what he says drifts past me.

〜〜〜〜〜〜〜〜〜〜〜〜〜〜

It's infected. An ooze dribbles out of the stitches. My face boils with fever. Breathing becomes a chore. I'm going to die here, I know it. No matter how good Ellick is, there is nothing he can do about this.

The stormseer, adorned with Ominix upon his shoulder, informs me of our next destination. Apparently an upcoming island has miraculous medicinal supplies which can help my healing. But all I can think about is what Shadir and Rubias are thinking. They're gauging my reaction, seeing if I want to stop somewhere—to *stay* somewhere.

When we dock in the port, Ellick and Shadir help me off the ship. I wonder why we were able to dock with a warship, but it makes sense after we go ashore. This pebble is small compared to most, and there isn't much of a society at all. There are no businesses or crowds. I can barely even see any homes at all. A cottage here and there in the distance, but nothing else. It's a peaceful place, with a meadow of herbs and flowers making waves in the wind.

But I can't enjoy the view. Throbbing echoes across my body.

There are three paths splitting through these fields. The bug-eyed Ellick inspects each and chooses the one in the center. Every step is torture. Shadir and Ellick are practically dragging me by the end. The winding path leads us to a strange arboreal hut, wherein multiple figures with reed-woven masks kneel and hum in harmony.

"I don't know if I like this," I mutter.

"Quiet," whispers Shadir. "These are the Mystics of Cartos Haven."

Ellick says, "They are healers. They will help you."

As we approach, the figures—thirteen in total—step out of their trance and move towards us. With those sheer white garbs hanging off them, and how they glide across the ground, it feels like we're being surrounded by spirits.

The Mystics peel me away from Ellick and Shadir and lay me down inside the arboreal hut. The stone floor is warm, relaxing. Wisps of white garbs surround me. The bandage unwraps by nimble fingers. Bodies moved around, gathering herbs of all kinds blending them. Despite being watched by so many, I don't feel overwhelmed by their presence like I do with others. Truly dreamlike.

But then a sting at the base of my arm stump tears me back into focus. They touched it… or took a sample… or stung me with I don't know what. Now I am aware of everything and everyone under a tinge of pricked anger.

After a span of this to and fro of Mystics, finally one of them emerges with a conch cup. Hands come from behind and lift my head for me while the Mystic tilts the cup against my lips. The concoction curls my tongue and coats my throat with bitterness.

Nothing, at first. Then, a heat simmers inside my stomach, and boils over into my nervous system. For eons it feels like my body rejects my mind. I know I'm convulsing but I cannot stop it. Foam builds upon my lips, and everything goes dark.

I awake on a cushioned wicker chair overlooking a field of lavender. The world is more clear now, as if my insides have been taken out like the gears of a chest and cleaned of all grime and grease. Remembering why I came here, I inspect my arm. The seams where the skin was folded over and stitched are there, but they look healthier than before. Cleaned up and somehow almost completely healed.

"How is that possible?" I say aloud.

A feminine voice responds, "The body is easy to repair."

Beside me, the Mystic who spoke is kneeling, facing out toward the field of lavender as I am.

Shadir's immortality comes to mind, and I ask, "Is this magic of some kind?"

"Only to those who don't understand it."

Similar to my chests in a way. So many can't conceive of the inner design, so from the outside it seems much more amazing than it is.

"What's the price? I've got gold back on the ship. I can go get it."

"This is nothing gold can buy," says the Mystic. I don't like the sound of that, because a service like this can't be free. She continues, "Someday, you shall be asked a favor. Accept the call when it comes to you, and your debt is paid."

"What if I wanted the whole thing back?"

The front of the reed-woven mask angles toward me. "You wish to be whole again?" She pauses for a while, taking in the waves of the field. "That is not a price you are able to pay."

***

Back in the infirmary, I lie in the cot. Despite the miraculous medicinal arts of the Mystics, Ellick doesn't want me to strain myself too much yet.

And so I wait there, staring at the chest Wickit left in the corner.

No one but a chestmaker thinks of the small pieces it takes to make the whole. What happens when a small but important component breaks? The entire thing is ruined. All of it. Of course, when something breaks in a chest, it can be replaced by a good chestmaker. It is not devoid of all value yet. But if the chestmaker is broken…

I have no home to go back to. I'm of no practical use to anyone. And now, how can I ever be a chestmaker without a complete set of the most basic tools? My life has been thoroughly scuttled, and that brings the sea to my eyes.

The door creaks open, and I wipe away tears hastily. This time, it's Edia who enters. She presents me with two salted meat sticks and a cup of water.

"Eat."

I try sitting up using my missing arm and fall to the floor. There's a gnawing hunch I might never get used to this. Maybe I should be dropped off somewhere. What use am I? I am of no value to myself or this ship. Better yet, throw me overboard and let the ocean's teeth finish me off. Like father, like son.

Tears drip from my face and splatter on the chalky planks.

"Get up," Edia demands.

I mumble, "I can't."

"Get up! You're not missing two arms."

My hand grips the cot. Weak muscles barely heave me back to the cot, with a bit of help from the impatient girl behind me. The meat sticks are tossed into my lap, and the drink is shoved into my fumbling fingers.

As she leaves, I beg, "Wait."

"I've got work to do."

"Just wait, please."

She scoffs. "Fine." Then scoots the stool over and sits. "Maybe I should lose an arm so I can get a day off."

I peer at her, not meaning for my eyes to appear so angry, but she takes it as such.

"I'm sorry. Captain's been running me ragged recently."

"Would I make a mistake by staying here? Should I let them drop me off on some random island?"

She rolls her eyes. "It would be nonsense to tell you your destiny is on this ship. But I think the captain needs you for whatever reason. She sees something in you that she thinks is more valuable than gold."

"But what does that mean? I met a pirate a long time ago. One who raided my home. Told me someone worth fighting for is more valuable than gold. How do I be that person that everyone wants me to be?"

Edia explores that question before shrugging. "No idea. But let me tell you a story. The twin teeth islands produce some of the most notorious pirates in the world. Isadora Rubias grew up around them and their culture. She and her brother didn't want to live the short pirate life. They wanted to grow a fishing business into a fishing empire to prove they had a choice in the matter. So they bought a boat and were successful for a while, until her brother drowned in an accident. He was the savvy one of the two, and the business crumbled without his expertise.

"Rubias knew she was bound to become a pirate to survive. If she were to become a pirate, she promised to become the greatest pirate to ever swim this blue planet. After acquiring the *Mantas*, she found herself employed by Dane Lurious, grand captain of the Seathorns. Shortly after, Pé Dutanté orchestrated the very first successful mass mutiny against a grand captain. Kept over eighty percent of the fleet intact. Never been done before. Rubias was furious, and vowed to commit as much vengeance as she could against him.

"Over the next couple years, as she built her own fleet, she made sure to annoy Dutanté every chance she got. It was mostly small things at first, like making sure his ships couldn't complete their assignments. Then, as her fleet grew, she stole some of his best crew members, luring them with offers of more money and freedoms they couldn't have under Dutanté. Finally, she was powerful enough to wage a pirate war against the man. Although it wasn't much of a war, just a few skirmishes, but it was enough to distract her foe from his raids."

Edia takes a bite out of one of my meat sticks—a tax for wasting her time. Then, kicking up her feet, she continues, "She also wrote a book called *The Art of Piracy*. Have you ever heard of it?"

"I think I have."

There's a book considered to be like a guide to piracy, but I had no idea Rubias authored it.

"She kept the printing to a limited amount, so the secrets within would seem more rare and special. I'm going to tell you something that mustn't leave this room, not even to those on this ship. It's all lies. People to this day still study that book to be a good pirate or to learn how to counteract piracy. Only the smart ones know that the secrets within *The Art of Piracy* are misleading. Following it like it's gospel is the first grave mistake a wannabe pirate can make. There are twelve pirate fleets with twelve grand captains. That book accompanying her tenacity has helped her host the second largest of all those fleets, just behind Pé Dutanté. Someday, she'll dethrone him."

"I knew she was clever, but I had no idea she was such a force as that. She basically has her own small navy."

"Yes, but that's not all. She did it twice. Under a false name, Captain Corvarulius, she wrote a second book called *On Justice and Defense* to counteract that first book. This was more widespread, and certain islands have built entire penal systems around it as if it were some manifesto or constitution. Rubias herself has told me it was supposed to be satire." Edia gives off an earsplitting cackle. I've never seen her so joyous before. It's nice to see this girl as just a girl, and not some sarcasm-spitting pirate ward.

"I think my father had a copy of that," I recall. I can picture the markings on its red cover. "He thought he could stop a pirate with that book." Awash with memories, I crack a smile, and eventually laugh with Edia. "She is one of a kind."

"So now you see the point of my story. She is someone worth fighting for, don't you think? And when d'ya think that happened? When did she become someone worth talking about? At what point did she become valuable?"

I shrug.

"All the way from the beginning, her brother thought she was worth fighting for. Before his death, before the piracy, before the treasure and infamy… before all that, she was just Isadora. Clever Isadora who was loved by her family and friends. She didn't need to become who people wanted her to be. She already was. Forget your arm. It's gone, but your mind is not. You're clever like the captain, and myself. You'll figure out a way around this. I know you will."

Although her words sometime sting like an urchin, she's also one of the most truthful people I've ever met.

When Edia gets up to leave, she proudly says to herself, "Nailed that advice, didn't I?"

What a fool I've been. So many of the crew had come by to check up on me. Oilm gave me the rat trap to give me something to do. Aljin and Wickit played cards with me. Tango even tried to help and I pushed him away. No one forced any of them to bring fresh food and water, or to make sure I was comfortable, or to entertain me when boredom struck. None demanded that I pull my weight, or finish the chests they've asked for. They hoped for my swift recovery.

They didn't give up on me. Why should I?

I move the chest to the center of the room and open it. The music box component needs to come out. After retrieving my tools, I take out the screws that keep it in place. Extracting each tiny element is like an operation. I lay out the pieces across the floorboard like a skeleton. It's a slow process with one hand, but I find a way. Behind the ear can hold tools. My mouth can hold a nail or screw. My feet can keep things from rolling away.

After an hour of focus, the broken component is replaced. The puzzle of putting it all back together again comes next. And that's my favorite part.

I find Wickit on deck replacing frayed ropes along the ratlines. His face lights up when he notices me.

"You did it!" Tossing down his work, he barrels over and lifts the chest out from under my armpit, nearly taking me up with it. After opening it and hearing the chime, he grabs my shoulder and shakes me harder than a ship in a storm. "Now this is the famous craftsmanship I've come to know from the Artisan Pirate. And all that one-handed… Amazing."

After taking it back down to the crew's quarters for him, I make my way back out to the captain's quarters. Naturally, I reach up to knock with my bandaged stub. Someday I'll get used to that. My left fist finishes the knock.

"Come in," says Rubias.

"No, don't come in," Shadir demands. "We're busy."

I open the door to the exasperation of Shadir, but he calms down after seeing me.

"Shouldn't you—" Rubias starts.

"I've rested enough. I'm here to settle this issue we have."

"Look at that." She backhands Shadir's chest. "He's got more grit under his fingernails than you've got in your whole body."

Shadir's face turns red with both fury and embarrassment. "I promised to return to the island with you. I would just like him to be out of harm's way first."

"I understand," says Rubias. "But I'm not willing to turn back. The Kingsguild and bounty hunters of all types are scouring the seas looking for me because of that scum Dutanté. If he so desires, I'll drop Archie off at the next island with a good chunk of change and we will pick him up again on our return."

"What if we don't return?"

I interject, "I will not sit idly by on an island while you two go on some grand adventure. I'm staying aboard."

She makes a gesture to say the matter is settled.

Shadir says, "You can't just shut your mouth for your own good, can you?" and storms out.

I tag along, saying, "You're not my father."

Without slowing down for me: "No. I'm a friend trying to help you."

"I'm trying to help *her*. I think we can trust her."

He pulls me away from the earshot of some crewmates. But they're respectful and stay out of it. "I'm not looking to become a pirate, Archie. You shouldn't either."

118

I am surprised at how offended I am, and react defensively. "I'm not trying to become a pirate. There is something we have to kill so I'm ready to go kill it. I'm obviously scared about this whole thing, but watching the captain makes me believe everything will be okay." His eyes wander down my arm as if to say everything is already not okay. "This was not her doing. This is my fault."

"Fine, but if you impress her enough, she'll want you here all the time. When that happens, just remember what choice is right for you. Don't get caught up in the moment."

With that as a final statement, he returns to his duties.

I'm eager to get back to work and help the crew, but it's not time yet. Despite the Mystic's healing, Ellick warned me my arm isn't completely ready for strenuous work. There is something I can do in the meantime.

I need to make myself an arm.

THE ATTACK

I don't know who the best one-armed whittler on the planet is, but I think I have some claim to the title. On the workbench below me is an arm. Not an arm of flesh and bone, of course. It's made of ebony wood I bought during a stop on the Port Ov Cinder. I bought multiple logs in case I messed up the first carving. It cost me a fair bit of gold, but the final product makes the purchase worth it—and finally someone accepted the crowns I had.

Stepping out of the tool shed, I slip my stump in the hollowed arm, and latch the harness around my torso. In the palm is a hook that can swivel in and out for easy access, and along the wrist are a few compartments with other useful tools which can be attached.

"Ah, so you've finally finished it?" Shadir says while I'm adjusting the bandersheef.

"Just about. It'll work for now, but I should put a lacquer finish over it."

"How does it feel?"

"It can't feel anything," I jest. "It's wood."

Shadir chuckles awkwardly, but then waits for the real answer.

"It feels good. Like I'm balanced again." I swing it around to test the mobility.

"Good. Now you should probably get back to work or Rubias is going to hang it on her flag wall as punishment."

"She'd never." But he's right. It's time to go help the crew. I've been out of commission long enough.

I leave the shed to a chilly wind that soaks the bones. We've hit a cold spell as we get closer to the pole. The sun remains on the horizon in a perpetual state of dusk, and the Aurora Tide colors the sky and sea almost at all times.

The crew is running around in a fervor they've maintained for days now. Rubias has been pushing them with very little rest. A momentum fueled by impatience. She wants to get to the Arwellian ruin as quick as possible. They do to, I suppose, so few complain despite being on the brink of exhaustion.

"You've finished it, lad," comes the slithering voice of Aldrezier walking past with a rope. I instinctively reach for the knife on my bandersheef. "Why don't you give me a hand," he says, and chuckles. Whatever he needs help with, I leave him to it.

I've been keeping an eye on him for a while. Someday he'll try to sabotage something, or strike at the captain when she's unsuspecting. I want to trust Rubias's decision to give him a second chance, but it's harder than I thought.

The *Prey Mantas* has yet to catch up with us, and Rubias expressed her annoyance with that. It's a fast ship, and we've been leaving messages behind at each port. Tango has tried to suggest the hull damage was probably much worse than we thought, and that they must've dry docked for extensive repairs, but the captain thinks some other ship may have gotten the best of them.

"I'll assume the worst and accept reality later," she had stated. A little bit rash, I'd say.

At midday, I see something on the horizon—an incoming ship. Others notice it too. Oc-pipes are pulled out to spy on it. It's not the *Prey Mantas*. Nor is it from the Kingsguild as far as I can tell. The flag is barely visible, but not enough to discern anything more. I would not have known this ship is attacking if Rubias didn't holler it a moment later. "Stations at the ready!" is echoed down through the hull. So much time at sea has altered their way of thinking. They see tactics in a ship's movement imperceptible to a novice like me.

The crew scrambles to battle positions. I am unsure where my place is now. We haven't been in a scrape like this since the ironclad, so I remain stationary, staring at the enemy vessel.

The captain sees my frustration. "Archie! Go below to the gungills. Help light the cannons on my mark."

With the adrenaline, I jog to the hatch with the stairs to the hull.

A crackle from a mortar reaches us. They shot first. There is something about being in front of a ship's weapon. A feeling of helplessness. There's no place one can truly run. No way to tell whether the shot will land near me or completely miss. Every thunderous explosion rattles me, makes me wince. I could turn into pink mist at any—

The deck explodes right in front of me, obliterating planks where I am about to be. I fall down to the next level, completely missing the stairs. When I land, it's on my back. Pain spreads around my neck, groin, and gut. I expel a hideous groan and squirm.

I have enough sight left to witness a cannonball skewer through one of the portholes and hit someone's shoulder. It was Dalia running to assist from the engine room. She's flung to the wall, dead on impact.

"Fire!" I faintly hear from above. Tango tumbles down the stairs and repeats the command with hand signs. Others are already lighting the powder and firing the line of cannons. I stumble to my feet and find a lighter to help. There's a wick on a stick already glowing red which my good hand grips. I peer through the gungill hole before pressing the lighter against the powder in the hole. It fizzles for a second and the cannonball lunges to find its prey. Every blast is like thunder in this enclosed space. Ears ringing from the blast, I light a couple more. Oilm reloads and resets them behind me.

After firing ten, I realize I might have hit more than the ship. My hand and the wick tremble. What if I've just killed someone like Dalia. It makes me freeze and stare out the gungill at the vessel across from us. Cannonballs are crumbling their planks, and only one of their cannons fire back. Tango runs over to me and points at my chest, and then makes a fist.

"Strong heart?" I ask.

He nods and continues relaying the captain's orders.

"Keep a strong heart," I repeat to myself. I'm defending myself and other people I care about now. This is survival whether I like it or not. My lighter finds its way into another cannon. Then another. Another. Another. Blow after blow hits them, but is it helping? Are we actually winning? It's hard to tell down here.

Not very many of their shots have hit us so far. Why aren't they firing as much as we are? Looking out again at the enemy, I don't see many people. They would need much more crew than what I see to sail such a vessel.

Because they're preserving our ship!

I hand the lighter to Oilm and rush upstairs despite Tango signing after me to get back to my post. I sprint to the side opposite of the battle. Dripping hands wrap around the railing next to grapple hooks. They've used some brilliant tactic to get in a surprise attack.

I yell to the captain, "They flanked us! Coming over this side!"

She places nick-knucks over her fingers. Her knife gleams in the sunlight after popping out of her bandersheef. "They're boarding us!" she howls. "Ship combat!"

The crew goes to war. The enemies hop over the ledge, knives and bludgeons swinging. Pistols fire every once in a while, but it's mostly a brawl. I pop the knife out of my bandersheef, and plunge the point toward someone still climbing over the ledge. She snatches my weak wrist, stopping my attack. My wooden arm whacks the side of her head when I swing it, loosening her grip enough for me to back away. She's completely on the ship now and coming after me. Her eyes a deep blue, hair blond, and skin dotted with sunspots. Beautiful in a mangy way. I would've been nervous talking to her in another situation. A warrior spirit within compels her to grab and toss me farther than I can jump. As she prepares to finish me off, a pistol shot from the captain takes her down.

In a daze, I watch Hap climb up the mast. Two of the intruders climb after him. Multiple shots from somewhere else topple both to the deck. Several planks away is the playwright Gridda with two smoking pistols.

"Archie," yells Rubias. She kicks over a pistol dropped by someone else. Her fists return to pounding a man's teeth out. I try to retrieve the weapon, but another foot knocks it out of my reach.

Rubias dodges a dagger and slashes with her own. Nearby, Aldrezier picks up the pistol kicked away from me, checks to see if it is loaded, and points it at Rubias.

"No!" I yell, pulling myself to my feet. "Aldrezier!"

Distracted, the mutineer spots me and puts up a defensive hand before I ram my shoulder into his gut, tackling him to the deck. "You fool!" he yells. "I was trying to help the captain!"

I spin to see what he's talking about. There is a man atop the stern behind her. He jumps down and lands on her with his full weight. He holds down her flailing body, nick-knucks barely missing the man's chin. Aldrezier goes to retrieve the pistol again, but he can't fire without the risk of hitting Rubias. Running to assist, I entangle myself in the burly arms of another. Grimy hands slither around my throat.

Those not among the dead stop fighting. Our crew knows we're outmatched. The entire crew is bunched together on our knees. The shame on the captain's face is apparent. She remains calm, but can't hide the glimmer of failure in her yellow eyes.

How did it come to this? The whole crew apprehended, and by whom?

"Amazing," says the confident, wispy voice of the enemy captain as she boards the ship. The bucklecoat draped around her is so long that it brushes her feet. After removing a tricorn hat, black fingernails scratch at a bald head that bounces the sunlight. "This had better be worth it, Krack," she says to their deck chief. "We nearly let them sink our satellite ship with that maneuver."

"Aye, captain, I have faith it will be," says Krack, whose boot is now pressing down on Rubias's nick-knuck hand. He wears the traditional striped and baggy clothing of the folk from Port Ov Lamau.

A bullet shot from the crow's nest splits wood by this enemy captain's foot. She retaliates with a blind shot up the mast. Shadir and Hap are up top. They duck, though the shot never comes near them. Shadir reloads and points the pistol down.

"You shoot like a bird shits," yells their captain. The barrel of her gun turns on us, indiscriminately aiming. "I've got plenty of target practice here. You're in no position to be taking shots. My name is Decker Pard. Come down here, I just want to talk. I've got a proposition."

There is no good to be made of this. I know it. The crew knows it. Shadir and Hap have no choice but to climb down and surrender.

Rubias looks up from her sulk and stares straight into the cold eyes of this pirate who bested her.

"Captain Isadora Rubias, it's nice to finally meet you," says Decker.

With a hollow glare: "I've never heard of you." It may be the truth, but between pirate captains it's a grave-digging insult.

"No, not many have. Not yet. But I've got quite the plan to change that. You're gunna help me."

Rubias waits to respond. She studies every aspect of her predicament. Any lesser person would've given in right away, and anyone stubborn enough to immediately decline would've made a foolish mistake. She is level-headed, weighs every option, and listens before speaking.

Decker continues, "Do you know what's in that direction?" A finger pokes out to a specific spot on the horizon. Starward, I think, but I have yet to perfect my inner compass.

Rubias doesn't look. "I know where I am at all times."

"I want something hidden within. You're gunna fetch it for me."

"Are you feigning anchor?" Rubias says, baffled by the notion. "It can't be done."

"Captain?" I ask, but a gun barrel touches the back of my head before I can say anything else.

"Quiet, lad." Decker kneels by Rubias. "But go ahead and tell them."

With a lilted head to address us, she says, "She wants us to heist the Central Maritime Treasury."

A murmur ripples through the crew. The CMT controls the flow and value of every currency in the polar circle—from crown to jade. The only way to heist it is to sack their island with an entire army. No pirate, king, queen, or other has dared to do that, because waging war on the CMT means waging war with every other island relying on its services. It has no army, but can employ the services of other nations at a moment's notice.

"You're insane," says Rubias. The lot of us want to express the same thing, but in this situation we aren't allowed as much gumption.

"Aye, always have been."

"It wouldn't be worth the risk. Also, as I mentioned before, it *can't* be done."

"Do you know where gold came from? Some think it came from space— meteoric impacts long before we existed. Melted into the cracks of the planet. But there is a solid nugget out there called the Goddess Doubloon.

So big, you'd need a ship to transport it." Decker says this while sticking a greasy pinky into her nostril.

"You think the CMT has a giant chunk of gold just sitting around, waiting to be plucked from their grasp?" A snort punctuates Rubias's short laugh.

"I do. They keep it as a sort of decoration, I s'pose. They don't factor it into their gold stash. So taking it won't do anything to the value of gold."

"Unless they change the value out of spite."

"They couldn't do that for long. Not without pitting major islands against them. Trust me, I've done all the calculations. Krack here is an excellent mathematician."

The captain asks, "How good is he about weights and measurements?" Krack is about to speak on his own behalf, but Rubias continues, "Because the risk outweighs the reward. And I measure that neither your crew nor mine has the grit to commit."

Decker laughs, clearly exaggerated for offense. "There will be no risk for me. You see, if your crew fails, or refuses, then I'll give you up to the great Pé Dutanté. I hear he has quite the bounty on you. That'll most certainly be a death sentence for you and your entire crew. Plus, I'll get this beautiful ship." She taps her heel on the *Prey Empress*. "A win for me either way. But only one path for you leads to freedom. If your team brings me the Goddess Doubloon, I'll let you all go with your ship intact. That's a win for both of us."

"What if I get caught or killed? Your plan crumbles."

"Oh, you're not going inside. You'll be right here with me. So I hope you got a trustworthy crew, because they're gunna be without your famous wit and intuition."

Her fist, with dirt in every ridge, unfurls in front of Rubias. With no other choice, our captain puts forth her own hand and shakes. They lock eyes for a long while until Decker's face turns red. Decker pulls her squeezed hand out and rubs the pain away. Rubias unleashes her half smile. She may not have the upper hand, but she has the stronger one and wants this bloody trickster to know it.

THE HEIST

The CMT is a castle—difficult to siege even with an army. I'd say hundreds of planks tall from base to tip of the spires, and made entirely of stone masonry. It's a small, self-governed island, with the CMT taking up most of the inner space. The surrounding outside is grassy land leading to windswept cliffs on one side and one gravelly beach on the other. There are no homes or shops since no one lives here except for bankers working for the treasury who have living quarters inside.

There are only two places for ships to enter. The main harbor is on that beach side. The entrance on the other side is only for the employee trade ships. They enter through a waterway passage in the cliffs guarded by cannons all the way through. It's a straight shot into the castle's inner bay. Ramparts are alongside the cliffs to further inhibit an attack. According to Krack, we have to infiltrate that inner bay.

It is early morning when we gather around a table in the captain's cabin to discuss the plan and those best suited to get it done. Krack lays out a map of the CMT. It shows a rough estimate on the innards of the castle. They're not sure where the gold is—or if it exists at all.

Tango takes the lead as deck chief. Wickit and Aljin were also chosen. Well, actually Aljin volunteered. With that golden glint in her eyes, it's obvious why. Shadir, although pessimistically involved, volunteered to go considering he could take a hit and keep going. That was going to be the full team at first.

Decker flicks a curious eye over my wooden arm. "Great craftsmanship on that. Make that yourself, didja?" she asks.

Aljin jumps in, "You're lookin' at the finest chestmaker in the world. He'll be known far and wide as the Artisan Pirate." She then gave me a wink, as if saying that was doing me a favor.

Shadir scrunches his eyes at this. Explaining it to him isn't going to go over well.

Decker says, "Well, chestmaker, you familiar with picking locks?"

Krack says, "No way he can. You need two hands for that."

Another rusted pirate underestimating me. I've had enough of that. When designing my arm, I incorporated many tools I might need, including a tension tool that comes out of the wooden pinky. Holding tension with that, I can pick with my left hand. Even though I've never actually tried it yet, I show that to them and explain how it could work as if I've done it a thousand times.

Tango signals Rubias. I didn't catch what it was, but he did end it by pointing at me.

Rubias asks, "Are you feeling up to the task, Archie?"

And only then do I realize what I've done. There could be plenty of locked doors the heist team have to get through. No one else in the crew can, as established with the toll privateers. I just offered myself up.

Shadir speaks for me. "No, he's not ready. Are you trying to get him killed?"

"You best clamp your tongue," the captain snaps. "To be honest, I trust him with this more than I trust you. I wouldn't even let you go if it weren't for—" Rubias looks to Decker and Krack waiting beside them. She lies, "For your persistence."

I finally answer, "I can do it."

Shadir leans in to my ear. "I'm tired of defending you just to fail at it."

Impatiently, Decker says, "Are we settled?" The rest of us share a reluctant nod. She steps toward the door. "Then we begin."

The preparations are easy. Decker already took control of a CMT sixgill-class galley earlier in the year. It's significantly smaller than the pirate ships, and can fit through that cliffside waterway. Apparently she's been planning this for quite some time. The infiltration team, along with a member from Decker's crew, boards it.

The waterway is dauntingly narrow. The ship's wall is a bricklength away from the rough cliff on either side. Every move by our crew is deliberate and slow to avoid any scraping. Decker's crewmate, Grimmel, tells us to be out of sight. They've studied the incoming and outgoing traffic for a while. Apparently these CMT ships have almost no crew on deck and barely any cargo.

We're waiting in the hull when Grimmel's scratchy voice yells from the helm, "When we boarded this ship to take it, there were only five on board, an' none of 'em claimed to be capt'n! Like a ghost ship! Creepy, init?"

How the treasury functions has always been a complete mystery. No one who has ever worked inside this castle has ever come out. No quitter or retirees. No one taking a vacation or visiting home. No stories about the insides of this place have ever been spilled. Rumors are all we have.

I peek out the hull up through the hatch and see cannons aimed straight down at us through the ramparts above, following us like the eyes of a painting. They could tear us apart at any moment. Perhaps we're sailing over a ship graveyard at the bottom of this trench.

Three gates bar our path. With each, Grimmel gives a password through flag signals. We pass through the final gate into a cavern, which opens up into the inner bay of the CMT. We aren't just inside the treasury. We're inside a highly restricted area. Making a single wrong move will be dire for us. Do they have a prison? A trial system? Or is it a quick execution for trespassers? We have to be on guard at all times.

Grimmel says, "This is as far as my knowledge goes. When we make port, we'll take out whoever comes to meet us. Then your team'll sneak off the ship and find the gold."

We're in a miniature harbor within the castle, fairly bright and warm with so many lit braziers. The mooring zone has stone jetties, and tethered to them are other ships exactly like ours. By the jetties are neatly piled stacks of crates, extra oars, planks, and ropes. At the far end of every direction is a wall with evenly spaced doors, but they're the smallest doors I've ever seen. It's odd, but not as odd as the silence. Hardly any people are walking around, and the few unloaders we see are as quiet as a roach on a rowboat. They don't even make conversation with one another. The map we looked over earlier must've been drafted from faulty information, for it is of no help to us in this strange layout.

We glide to an empty area, looking out for anyone who might alert guards. After we dock, a few bankers come from the corresponding door. Grimmel lowers the docking ramp and lets them come up. From where I'm hidden in the hull, I can see a sliver of what is happening. They walk synchronized with such uniformity, and wear identical brown, roughspun clothes.

Grimmel greets them. "How's it goin', mates?" They're like sentinels, standing in orderly silence. I ready a crowbar to use as a weapon. "I'm fairly new at this so you might not remember me," he lies. When they don't answer, continues, "Well, anyway, it's the usual down in the hull if you wanna help me get it."

"It knows you're coming," they say in unison.

"Does it now?" Grimmel says, pulling his pistol on them.

Their eyes drift to the hatch where we wait.

"It knows all of you. It awaits you. Leave here."

Grimmel retorts, "Well we ain't doing that. Come out. They know you're down there."

We ascend to the deck and subdue the two with no resistance. There is no brig to stash them in. Instead, Wickit and Tango tie them to a post in the hull.

Shadir seems perturbed. When I ask why, he says, "Did you see how they looked at us? Something's not right with this place."

To rationalize everything, I affirm, "The CMT has always been a mystery."

"A mystery is different than an oddity."

Grimmel shouts down the hatch, "I hope you haven't changed your minds down there. I'll have to do something drastic. Get up 'ere."

On deck, we search for hints. No sign of gold, nor anything of value. The only possible thing we can do is go through one of the doors and see where it leads. But we have no idea what could be behind them. Perhaps hundreds of workers going through what we assume to be a maze of small corridors. There would be nowhere to hide with no knowledge of where to go.

Wickit says, "Maybe if we just act like we belong, no one will question it."

"What if the Goddess Doubloon doesn't exist?" asks Aljin.

Grimmel scoffs. "You better hope it exists."

With his hand on my shoulder, Shadir asks, "Archie, if you were to move a giant boulder of gold to a higher floor, how would you do it?"

I know of only one way. I had utilized it on the *Prey Empress*. "A pulley system." When I realize what that entails, my eyes trail up to the ceiling. Above, in the center of the harbor, is a rather large hole covered with wooden lattices. If anything large were to go up or down, that's the way to do it. "But something tells me they're not going to let us set up a pulley system to gently let it down."

Tango taps on my shoulder and performs a motion. His fist breaks through several layers of his other hand, and finally ends in a cupped hand. He wants to drop the gold into the ship through the latticework.

Grimmel adds, "I'll wait for some time 'fore I sail this ship into place. Hope the thing isn't goin' to crack it like a rock to an egg. Then shimmy as fast as possible. I ain't breaking a clock for you. Ain't dishonor to scram if the water gets chummed."

I look to Wickit for a translation of that last part. He says, "We get back down quick or he won't hesitate to leave us behind."

Aljin replies, "First we have to figure out how to get up."

We try not to draw attention to ourselves as we get off the ship and scurry across the stone docks. Few are around, and those few are too far away to notice us. Our first task is to look inside one of the doors. We crack one open enough for Shadir to look in.

He announces, "It's just a thin corridor with lanterns. I see no bankers."

"We go now, or not at all," Wickit says.

Shadir enters first, followed by me, then Wickit, Aljin, and Tango.

The walls are stone bricks. Between them is enough space for two to walk abreast, and our heads hover just beneath the ceiling. We can't see very far. The corridor is not as well-lit as the bay.

"Are those stairs?" Aljin asks as we turn a corner.

Shadir confirms it's a winding staircase, but still no sign of bankers. These tight corridors could make for a difficult scuffle if we meet any. But even as we move on to the next level there is no one to be seen.

We find no electricity in the entire castle. Every corridor and chamber is either too dark to see, has lanterns, or lit naturally from barred windows. Strange to think anyone works in such conditions. Bankers are an odd breed. Few people decide to be a banker. They sever all ties from their former lives to live within the CMT, and are never seen again.

Somewhere on the second floor, we stumble upon the first treasure. A whole floor of jade. The green stone and statuettes are piled high inside hollowed out cubic chambers in the wall. We all stop in our tracks to look over the most wealth any of us has ever seen. Jade is especially rare. It was the defining currency of the ages before gold was in circulation. Some of these pieces might predate the flooding of the world.

Shadir tethers us back to reality by saying, "Wipe your drool. We don't have much time. Let's go."

Aljin is the last to pull her fixation off the mounds of green stone.

The next floor boasts stacks of silver. Upon this discovery, I say, "Each level is dedicated to a different currency. We should keep going up until we find gold."

The others agree and we move along.

The next floor is the gold level. There is significantly more of this than the other two floors. Each chamber is dedicated to the coins of different major governments. Elsewhere there are bricks of it stacked against the wall. And there are buckets of trinkets or jewelry next to a smelter to be melted down and repurposed.

Aljin gives off a squeaky utterance when she sees this. Disregarding any following protestations, she takes a bucket and tries to stuff extra in her pockets. Upon seeing us all staring, she responds, "Just in case."

As we search for any signs of a giant hunk of gold, Tango and I enter a secondary room filled with machinery designed to create different currencies. There is nothing else of importance.

We all gather around the entrance of another room. Because there is no switch, we enter this dark place under complete silence. Wickit grabs a lantern off a hook and brings it in. Our shuffling feet halt as the light reveals cots against the walls. I hold my breath. There are at least twenty of them—each occupied. Bodies lie around us, all sleeping face up with arms to their sides and without covers or pillows.

We're in the bankers' sleeping quarters.

Wickit pivots with his finger against his lips. Then he gestures for us to get out. We creep back out of the room where we wait for him. Still inside, he points to the back wall which is still in darkness. He wants to ensure the Goddess Doubloon is not here. He plunges into the dark, lantern extended. At the end of it, there is no gold. He huffs and turns back to see each of the bankers rising off of their cots. The quick-witted pirate extinguishes the lantern, and is enveloped in darkness. As soon as he rushes out the door, we sprint to another corridor we haven't explored before.

"Put the bucket down," yells Shadir to Aljin.

She says, "Shut up. Just go!"

As they run off, Tango pulls on my sleeve and looks back at the door to the sleeping quarters. The ragged tunic-clad men and women who pour out are synchronous. Their shuffling is like a performed habit—like marching sleepwalkers. Besides the dead-tired eyes, they don't look to have just woken up. They go straight to work without any speaking or eating.

We catch up to the others in one of the antechambers with the lattice grate over a hole. Looking down, we see through to the bay below where Grimmel will soon be. Looking up, we see at least three more floors. Luckily, at the corner of the room is an access shaft with a ladder which can get us to each of them. That will also be our easy way down to the jade floor when we need to go. We hurry up the access ladder—which is believably difficult without two arms, but I press on.

I can differentiate the floors as this: the stone harbor where we made port, the jade floor, silver, gold, and then copper, gemstones, lesser metals like tin and nickel, and finally miscellaneous supplies at the top. This topmost floor is where we rest because it's the most inactive tier. The other floors have bankers who must've woken up around the same time as the gold workers. Being a level for storage, this area doesn't need upkeep or bankers. It's like a dusty attic littered with ripped tarpaulins and empty crates. We look down through the lattice to workers below. Hanging from the ceiling is a web of ropes. Probably a dismantled pulley system.

Shadir pulls me out of earshot from the others. He whispers, "Let's go. There's a corridor over there. We can make our way back down and find an alternate route to get us back into an area of the bank where customers are allowed." He pulls a handful of gold out of his pocket. "We use this to bribe our way onto a ship doing business here. From there, we figure out a way home."

"Have you been drinkin' seawater?" I say, exasperated.

"Keep your voice down. Look at where we're at. Breaking into the CMT for something that clearly doesn't exist. As soon as we return without it, Rubias will be sold as bounty. And who knows what will happen to us."

Wickit waves us over to see something. I hold up a finger.

I say, "I'm not giving up on this. I'm not giving up on the captain."

I move toward Wickit and the others, but Shadir pulls me back by my wooden arm.

"The *captain*? So she's your captain now, eh? Willin' to die for her?"

I swipe his hand off me. "That's not what I'm saying. You… you don't understand."

"Then help me understand!"

"What is there for me at Tyro? Charter Barons? Villeinage? The gators of the bayou ready to eat what's left of me? I am of no value there."

"You have value whether they recognize it or not."

"You keep trying to drag me back. I know you've been trying to get back home all this time. I know that's all you've wanted for so long. It's been out of your reach and I hurt for you. I do. But when you were suffocating inside that chest, I was suffocating too. It's not a home for me anymore."

"Then you go and make it a home."

"I cannot change an entire island, Shadir! I am not a liberator."

Where have I got that from? Rubias… She said that to me. I'm using the same excuse.

"Everything all right?" asks Aljin. Our voices had gone above whispers by the end.

Shadir's lip quivers like he wants to say something else, but I pull away and join the others.

There is something in the corner of the room covered in a wilted fabric. Wickit whips it off, revealing the thing we so desperately seek. The boulder of gold said to have come from the sky is real, and it's here. The Goddess Doubloon.

Tango mouths silently what Aljin repeats out loud: "Bloody Baldeva."

"What a snare," says Wickit. "I can't believe it exists. And it's huge."

It's more egg shaped than I thought, if an egg was dented and porous like coral. It's double my height, and it'd take three together to wrap their arms all the way around it. The shine is dull and marred with black spots. Holding it in place are wedges along the bottom. They don't have it on a pedestal or locked away. Nor is it used as decoration. It has been collecting dust for generations here in a corner of a castle that no one can enter.

"Fine. Help me move this lattice," Shadir says, and whispers something irate under his breath.

Aljin places her bucket down by it to help. We all encircle the piece of wood and quietly lift it out of the way.

"Bloodied waters," curses Wickit. "The next level has crates all over it. This thing might not break all the way through if it doesn't get the proper momentum."

Shadir says, "I'll go down to the next level and clear the way. Tango, will you assist me?"

Tango agrees and moves toward the ladder.

"You three stay here and get the gold over to the hole. After it goes down, go down the ladder and jump into the water by the ship. That'll be our quickest escape."

Shadir follows Tango while the rest of us try to figure out which wedge to displace first. Wickit kicks one away. He and Aljin press bulging arms and shoulders against it to control its path. The gold boulder, severely unevenly weighted, wobbles out of place and rolls wherever it wants. I will never forget the scraping sound—like two bricks rubbing together. They have to let it go, and we all dodge its crushing, meandering path. When it finally settles, Aljin and Wickit set about rolling it as best they can. I squat next to the hole to survey the floor below. Shadir and Tango have reached it.

The bankers are still like mindless beings. Shadir mimics them—a combination of stiffness and sharp turns. The bankers ignore him while stacking and unstacking boxes in a manner I can't comprehend. It's as if each has a specific, simple job and can't deviate from it. They can't complete anything more complex than what they were assigned. Shadir and Tango try to do the same while clearing the lattice framework.

I lean in. Half of my body hovers over the hole. One of the drones looks at Shadir. Still working, but watching suspiciously. I wave to get Shadir's attention, but he can't see me. I hook my foot around the heavy bucket of gold to keep myself from falling. I slap the bricks and wave my hands.

"Archie!" shouts Wickit. I didn't notice the scraping was so close to me. I swivel, see the boulder a brick away from me, and trip on the bucket of gold. My hand instinctively reaches out for the vine-like tangle of pulley ropes, but as I flail downward they entangle my body and neck. The bucket slaps hard on the wood below, and the coins shower down through each level of the CMT to the harbor below. My good arm is stuck. I wrestle and spasm to get loose, but this tightens the rope around my neck. The blood pools in my face and feels like my head might burst.

As I hang above them, Shadir and Tango scramble to get the rest of the crates. The bankers take notice of them. Down on the other levels are faces of other bankers staring up through the lattices. Every banker has stopped what they were doing—their deadened eyes wait for something else to happen. The bankers on Shadir's floor grab at him. They rip him away but he pushes back. His fists smack against unresponsive skin. Their untrimmed fingernails cut into him.

There is a tug at my leg. One of the bankers is hanging on my leg. My noose tightens. Looking up, the boulder moves into place, ready to come crushing down. Below, guards with pistols charge into the room. Death has come for me on all sides.

But Tango—the mad lad wrestles a pistol away from a guard. I can't see much as my vision darkens, but I can see a faint silhouette of Tango knocking the guards to their backs. Shadir frees himself from the bankers after his stomach is half ripped open. He limps away, waiting for it to heal. A few shots ring out, but the darkness has fully enveloped me.

The chunk of gold falls, severing all the ropes that have me constricted.

I don't know where I am, or what is happening.

I am floating, spinning...

Pressure against my body...

And then nothing but pain.

Vision returns as spotty images. The boulder of fortune is in front of me, crashed straight into the center of the ship like we wanted. One leg of mine is off to the side. My right leg. Broken, I think... No, that's not where the pain is. It's my other leg causing the agony. A weak hand traces my torso down my pelvis and thigh. Below the knee, I feel the boulder's gritty surface. It has crushed my leg.

The others have climbed down to the lowest level and are dropping into the water next to the ship. Despite the pain, I crane my head to see them climbing over the banister. Most of the bankers in the harbor are unresponsive, as if all puppeteering is being delegated to a few individuals. As Aljin climbs aboard, three shots from the harbor pass through her with no resistance. She falls limp backward into the water. Wickit screams for her, but there is nothing he can do. She's already gone.

Shadir finds me pinned to the ship and runs over. He holds my top half in his arms.

Grimmel hoists the anchor and guides us back through the channel. The gates are open, and the cannons aren't firing down on us. They don't want the gold to sink into the water where it will be irretrievable. In our haste, we scrape against some of the jagged walls on the way out.

"Salt in the belly!" yells Grimmel. "Bale the water out. Bale it!"

Shadir, Wickit, and Tango grab buckets and flee to the depths of the ship to bale the water.

Through pain and tears, I yell, "Land us on the beach side of the island."

Grimmel says, "I know ye dying, lad, but that is mad talk. They've got gunners and guards far more resilient than this driftwood."

"Trust me...." The rest is a gurgle of spit and hollering anguish.

Around the cliffs we sail, sinking bit by bit. But when we arrive at the shore the sinking matters little. The belly of the boat scrapes against the sand bank and remains in a state between floating and sinking. Shadir and Tango come topside.

"What have you done?" Shadir yells.

"It was your lad that told me to do it," Grimmel says.

I groan, "They don't want to lose their gold. They won't fire on us."

"Maybe not, but now it's beached here for the taking. Look over there." Shadir nods to the CMT. Some bankers are amassed outside and waiting for others. Their cannons are kept at bay for the moment.

Grimmel says, "Aye, but there's the *Prey Empress* coming our way. They must've eyed us floundering."

"How are you holding up, Archie?"

"Everything below my waist… is throbbing like a jellyfish's cuddle. Can you see my leg below deck?"

What Shadir expresses next is like a disgusted groan. "Ugh. It's hanging by a thread. You're going to lose it."

After some time, and when in such pain all time seems infinite, the *Prey Empress* and all its faculties graze as close as possible to the sand bank on which we are perched.

Decker swings over by rope. When she sees me, she says, "That's a gruesome sight. How'd this happen? Never mind that. We can use the tug lines to pull in the gold. You'll need to push loose from this sand bank first and scuttle this so we can get it closer to the *Empress*."

Grimmel yells, "They've amassed a boarding party. The bankers are coming." The mindless drones scurry like ants down the beach and charge into the waves without any rowboats. Someone lets down the sails. The wind dislodges the ship with a crack and rumble. The entire rudder breaks off, opening a gaping hole much too large to consider baling. Grimmel sails the sinking ship closer to the *Prey Empress*. The crew aboard the bigger ship flings the tug lines down to us. Decker, Wickit, and a few others place the hooks in the grooves and holes of the gold to secure it. The crew then works the winch to raise the gold up. Wickit rides it up to keep it secure.

I cry out as the searing, salty air meets my fresh dismemberment. I still can't move. What's left of my flesh is still impaled by the shattered planks.

Decker says, "Everyone in the rowboat." She points at one still tethered halfway down the side of the *Prey Empress*.

"What about Archie?" asks Shadir.

"Shame to lose a gifted chestmaker, but he's a dead lad."

Any of Decker's crew on this ship enter the rowboat. Tango and Shadir stay put.

The boat tips as it capsizes. Rust it all. After everything I've been through lately, I'm going to drown. What dreaded luck to be buried alive at sea—choked by the world itself. I'm not going to let that be my death. Not yet.

"Throw me a knife!" I reach out to the rowboat.

Tango makes frantic signs which, under the circumstances, I assume translates to: *what are you going to do?*

Decker shrugs, and throws one over out of curiosity. It slides over the deck and Shadir stops it with his foot. He places it in my palm and wraps my fingers around the hilt. Then he says to Tango, "You go. I've got him."

Tango nods and flees to the rowboat.

"Push me up," I say after failing to sit up myself. He gives me the boost. I clench my teeth and stab down into my left shin. Hurts less than I thought, but then again I'm not sure it is possible to feel more pain. I saw at bits of flesh around the plank shards until I come loose. Shadir holds me by my torso and motions for a line to be thrown. Someone throws down a hook and rope on which Shadir and I hang when the ship beneath us sinks.

"Ladle us up!" Decker hollers, and we're all tugged aboard.

Decker comes to me while I'm bloody and dying. She holds out a grimy hand for the knife. I give it up. She says, "That's a daring sailor if I've ever seen one, and I've seen aplenty. If you weren't so mangled, I'd ask you to join my crew."

Even under duress I can't help but spew a retort. "If I were right-minded… I'd still decline."

Rubias and Shadir ask for a blanket and stretcher to take me to the infirmary. Surprisingly, Decker offers to let her own physician help out in saving me. Must've made a favorable impression. It could double my chances, but even in my state I know it'll take a miracle. And I don't believe in miracles.

While I'm carried away, someone shouts as the bankers board. They're quick blaggards. They've already swam that gap and scaled the *Prey Empress*. Before being taken down the hatch, I see Decker, Krack, Tango, Rubias, Shadir, and everyone else firing upon these invaders.

Then, with so much blood lost, I feel very tired and close my eyes.

THE JOURNAL

"You dead yet?" Edia teases as she enters the infirmary, which has basically become my personal quarters as I have recovered the past month. She finds me peering out the porthole at the endless blue ocean. "I guess not. What kind o' peg leg you want?"

"What?" I ask. Turning to face her, the room spins. Ellick has been upping the dosage of anesthetic seaweed as I've been building up a tolerance to it. But there are gross side effects, such as nausea and occasionally throwing up a greenish-blue sludge.

She repeats and emphasizes each word. "What kind of peg leg do you want?"

"What kind?"

"Yes, you driftwood. I've got a bunch down in storage. Birch, ebony, spruce, even bone. Or are you goin' to hop everywhere and look like a rusted fool?"

It is time to start walking on my own again after so long being cooped up in this room. It's agonizing not being useful, passing the time counting ocean swells while the crew are out there working hard.

"Ebony, I suppose." It'll pair well with the arm. Luckily, it hadn't been damaged back when I was crushed by the Goddess Doubloon. Otherwise I'd have to start from scratch.

She leaves to get it. As I wait, the room closes in on me. Chokes me. I stare at my blood stains on the floorboards that wouldn't scrub out. It's hard to believe I survived it all, even with the leftover medicine Ellick purchased from the Mystics. Unbelievable pain. Blood loss. Infection. And I wish they hadn't told me about the maggots. I squirm at the thought of it. Ellick told me stories of my feverish sleep. As harrowing as those stories are, I don't remember much of it, which is a blessing.

Edia returns to lean the wooden leg against the door. Before she's able to leave, I ask her to wait without anything to actually ask or talk about. After a span of waiting on me to say something further, Edia says, "Sorry, driftwood. I can't wait for you to overcome your awkwardness. I've got to get back to things. Captain's been prickly lately." She's off in a blink.

Truth is, it has been lonely and painfully boring. The islands come and go through the porthole with a rare stop here and there. There weren't as many visitations compared to losing my arm. The crew has been busy, and Shadir avoids me. In order to keep my sanity, I focused on ideas for chests. I couldn't work on them, but I drew diagrams in a sketchbook.

I flip through the pages. Each day is marked with a fresh page and a new idea. Hidden keyholes. Extra drawers. A spherical puzzle. Ornamental designs utilizing shark teeth. Some are more practical than others. With the boredom getting to me, I designed more absurd things with miniature generators, catapults, food, and on a particularly bad day I may have designed one with a sacrificial element. But all that was good practice for my left hand. My handwriting and diagram drawing got better over time.

Putting aside the sketchbook, I finally try the leg on. It has a kind of harness to slip the nub of my leg into, and then tightens with lace. Finally, it has a strap kind of like suspenders to clip onto my clothing. It's secure, although it'll need some adjustments for comfort. And the peg's going to need some sanding down. But it'll do.

Walking on it is more difficult than I imagined. Right below the knee is where they stitched everything up. That knee isn't used to taking on so much pressure and weight, causing aches. I practice by walking out of the infirmary into the crew's quarters. Wickit is there, hunched over the chest I made for him.

"Archie," he says, greeting me with a sad smile. His puffy eyes reveal the same exhaustion that I have seen in other crewmates as of late. "Good to see you up and movin' again."

I am genuinely worried about his health. The few times I've seen him lately, he hasn't been his old jovial self. "Aljin still on your mind?"

He eases out a long sigh, heavy with the decisions of life. "Before coming aboard again for this cycle, I wondered how many more years of this I could bare. Here we are, running from navies, bounty hunters, and even other pirates. Nowhere safe to land. And then we lose mates and the captain barely gives us the time to mourn before we're off again."

I was out of commission during the funeral ceremony for Aljin, Dalia, and the others lost during Decker's attack, but I heard it wasn't as long of a service as it normally would be. There was no celebration of life. Just counting the losses and moving on. No wonder Wickit would feel dejected when it could all be ended so suddenly and without fanfare or purpose.

He continues, "I am now more convinced than ever to quit piracy after this final score that Rubias promised us. She said it'll be our biggest yet. I'll take my share home, get a normal, respectable job. Finally settle down with the love of my life. No more leaving."

"That sounds like a good idea," I say. He's one of the few people here who has that choice. Might as well take it while he can. But it makes me more concerned about whether or not there is treasure to be claimed and distributed. Shadir once said we won't be able to. It's time I figured out why.

"I better get back to it before Rubias finds out I snuck down here for a quick lull." Wickit put his chest at the foot of his cot, nodded at me, and returned to his station.

As I stumble around the ship trying to get the hang of this leg, Tango takes notice of me. He generously offers his free time to help me get used to it. Although it was only his foot, he went through something similar when he was younger. At the start, he tells me learning to walk again takes someone to lean on. Over the coming days, he helps me find the techniques and balance to get me walking straight and upright. I steadily gain a confidence in my stride.

During one of these sessions, I ask, "Do you know what it is we are looking for on this faraway island Rubias is obsessed with?"

A little confused, he signs, *Treasure.*

Tango is one of the people Rubias trusts most in the world. It would make sense if he knew something more about this island. Trying to pry something out of him, I press on, "But what about the other thing she's looking for?"

I don't know about…

I don't fully understand all of his signs yet, but I get the gist of what he's saying. Even Tango doesn't truly know what Rubias is up to. She really believes this information is dangerous.

"Do you think there really is treasure there?"

He pulls out a piece of paper and writes, *I don't care about treasure. Haven't touched a flake of it in my life.*

An exaggeration, surely. How can a pirate go through life without caring for money?

The final dinner bell rings, and Tango assists me with my walk to the galley. From the chef I receive a treenware bowl of nutmalt with cinnamon.

The chef informs me, "Food supply's runnin' low. All we got left."

I take a seat and shovel the soupy substance into my mouth. It tastes better than I thought, but it won't sustain anyone for long. The crew around me looks sullen and hungry. Oilm in the corner looks like he's about to fall asleep face first into his bowl. Our meals over the weeks had gone from full course, to stew, to singular potatoes, and finally to this. It's hardly a dinner for me, let alone the crewmates with stomachs bigger than my head.

Tango waits for everyone else to get a bowl first before he gets his and takes a seat next to me. He's not the kind of person I'd expect to be a pirate. It's clear he's passionate about this ship and crew, but couldn't he get that same sense of satisfaction from sailing with a trader ship?

While we eat, he draws on a piece of paper. A triangular design. Inside is a rudimentary depiction of a boot. What a strange thing to sketch.

Feeling the need to pry, I ask, "What are you drawing?"

He answers underneath the drawing, *My flag for when I become captain.*

"Not a Blackscabbard flag?"

Need both. Customary. Below Blackscabbard flag will be triangle flag designed by new captain.

Then he points to himself before slurping a spoonful of nutmalt. It makes sense to have one flag with the association to a whole fleet, and then a smaller one which identifies the specific ship and captain. I don't remember the one for the *Prey Mantas*, but I suppose Mako would have designed a new one once he took over from Aldrezier.

With a point to the image, I write, "Why a boot?"

Special boot, he writes.

Not much of a clarification. "Will that happen soon? Becoming a captain, I mean?"

He responds with a shrug first, then writes, *Long overdue.*

The next day I feel healthy enough to go above deck on my own and finally finish the layers of varnish on my arm. I amble around deck with a proud grin and fresh clothes—a sailor's sweater, baggy trousers, hemp belt, and a single boot.

Rubias smiles at me when I pass by her cabin. She comes out saying, "You're already looking more like a veteran pirate than me."

"I'm thinking about getting an eye patch next."

"Our course is nautward to one last stop before we enter uncharted waters."

"Are you running out of funds for supplies?" I ask on behalf of my empty stomach.

"We haven't done any actual pirating since getting word from Grifton. We have been scraping the bottom of our coffers. But I've got a plan for that."

For a moment, I'm worried she's going to say she's found a target to raid. But all she says is, "The Tontine Isle."

"Tontine Isle?"

"A unique place. A tontine is a pact. Every member puts money into a fund every year until there is one left. The remainder gets the whole fortune. These people have made an entire economic system based around it."

"Wouldn't that be chaotic?"

"Sounds like it should be, most certainly, but murder there is still illegal. The system and accompanying laws force the wisest and most cunning to survive and top the political mast."

"I can't even begin to wrap my head around how that works," I say while holding myself to get warm. It's not often the wind on the sea chills to the bone, but this day is especially bad. But soon, we'll be going above the polar line where the heat will be unrelenting.

Rubias waves me over to her cabin. "It's annoyingly complicated. But disregarding that, I would like to speak with you inside. I've got some of the last of my coffee brewing to help heat you up."

"You don't want me to get back to work? I think I'm feeling up to it now."

Although I can't do it as fast as before, getting back to feeding the glowfish will be a nice change of pace.

"Not yet. Come."

We head inside where the smell of the bitter beans envelops us. She hands me a conch. It warms me from the inside. Been a while since I drank coffee. Reminds me of Grifton. My eyes wander over the flags and furniture and land on the shelf of black and brown books. There on the end is her grandfather's journal with all his secrets and insights contained within. Would it be wrong for me to—

"Assuming we all survive this, I want you to stay with us," Rubias says.

I almost choke on a sip of coffee. "What? I can't. Look at me. I've lost an arm and a leg already. I don't think I could survive much longer out here."

"I admit it's been a more butchered quest than I prefer, but I see potential in you. Not just as a crewmate, but perhaps someday as a captain. I've got a whole fleet needing leadership. I can prepare you for it. Show you the ropes like I do with Edia."

"I'm not a—"

"A pirate. Aye, as you've made clear in the past." She fiddles with her nick-knucks. "But have you been having doubts about what you believe in?"

I nod, and feel for my chestmaker sketchbook tucked under my sweater.

"You see, very few of us actually expected to be pirates. I myself wanted a fishing empire with my brother Taegot."

In a casual motion, I walk by the shelf to observe the spines, and then ask, "If I say yes, will you tell me more about the island before we get there?"

She gives a quick laugh at my audacity. "Unfortunately, that's not a strong enough promise. It's dangerous information until we destroy what's there. Imagine if someone like Decker got wind of it."

Finishing my coffee, I say, "Hard to imagine what I don't fully know. Can you not describe to me what this thing is that you are trying to kill?"

Her mouth opens to speak, but in place of answering she takes my empty conch. As she goes to clean it out with a rag by the coffee brewer, I pluck the journal off the shelf and stuff it under my shirt, adjusting my bandersheef to hide the bulge. Then I stick my sketchbook in the gap. Ideally I can get back in here during my rounds of changing out the fish orb water and switch them again before she notices.

She puts the conch back in a cabinet and looks back at me. I'm aware of how awkward my smile must look. To hide behind conversation, I say, "Tango's an interesting fellow. He'd be a great captain."

Rubias is happy to talk about him. It's easy to see they are dear friends. "He's one of the best people I've known. Grew up on this tiny island that, as far as I know, doesn't even have a name. He grew up mute, terribly impoverished, and living off scarce land. They have no currency, no government, no system of any kind. You can't even call them anarchists. It's more like a bunch of people marooned on the same island. He has never told me about what happened to his foot, but I suspect the worst. They didn't have much… to sustain themselves."

Food. She means food. I suppose I was lucky to have as much as I did, even if it was a dainty, little store. I barely made enough to get by, but at least I had something.

"That sounds horrible."

"Through a series of events, I convinced him to join my crew, and he rose through the ranks quickly. Strange man, though. Never touches a single gold coin or drop of alcohol. He lives on the bare minimum, and makes sure everyone else gets their fair share."

"Strange way to be for a pirate."

"I tried to offer him some money when we first met, but he wouldn't except it. He's so afraid of having wealth. I think something happened to his island. A history of greed or something that destroyed them. So instead I offered him one of my boots, and he gladly accepted it."

That explains the boot flag. Symbolic of a gift that changed his life.

Rubias continues, "I know he wants to be a captain. I don't have the heart to tell him he can't. Not as a mute. A captain needs to be able to communicate in an instant. And I'm not so sure his signing can cut it."

"I'm disappointed, Rubias."

Taken aback, she scrunches her brows at me. "At what?"

"At you." I move toward the door, but leave her with the following contemplation. "If you think I'm capable of being a captain and he's not, then I'll have to reject your offer."

<hr>

During my chores, I take a moment for myself to get a look at Desja Rubias's journal. I pull off to the side of the corridor in a nook where no one really needs to go often. Page one would probably be the best place to start. I hold it next to the glowfish orb. Skimming it, I find a lot of description of the journey to the island, but not much more than that. After skipping a few pages, I find a short rambling passage about mounds of gold.

A mound a hill a mountain of it, growing when I close my eyes. It breathes I swear it breathes. Coins and not coins. Treasure and not treasure. A mouth biting chewing. Shine shine always shining in the dark. It crawls. Squirms. Not rats. Bugs perhaps? Was that it just now squirming in my brain? The gold talks. Whispers through the cracks. Drips into the floorboards. Don't touch it. Don't count it. If you count it, it counts you back. Eyes in the puddles. Don't drink. Don't drink the water. O it's in my teeth now. I can feel them.

What was it Aldrezier said that one time when he was in the brig? Something about ramblings from the captain's grandfather. I need to keep reading to find out for sure, but if this is all there is…

A storage closet door opens nearby. Out comes Shadir. "Archie?" he says, noticing me curled in the dark with an orb. I quickly stash the journal.

I stammer about a chest idea which I needed to stop and write down before forgetting it.

When I finally stop, he says, "But are you feeling well?"

"Well enough," I say. This is the first time I have spoken with him in a while. It feels like the edges of our words are frayed. I always hated social dynamics. The tension. People not saying what they need to say. It's like a puzzle box, but not as fun solving.

He says, "I want to yell at you, but I know that won't be good for your health. Just know I'm disappointed. You've been lucky surviving all this. I don't think you'll stay lucky."

"I don't need your protection. You can leave anytime you want. No need to stay on my account."

He's not very good at hiding the hurt this causes him.

"Fine. I hope you have fun with your adventure." Said with more salt than sugar.

He leaves me be, and I take a peek inside the storage room. Inside is the chest I found months ago that sent me on this journey—the runic chest Shadir was locked inside for decades. He's still spending too much time with this thing. It's like he never left it.

He's still trapped.

THE TONTINE ISLE

Port Ov Soha on the Tontine Isle is a large and lively wharf. What stands out the most is their massive, spiraled dome structures that look like multi-colored onions. They aren't homes or cemetowers. I ask Edia and she mentions something about places of worship. Apparently they worship some kind of deities related to money and law. And besides their strange economic values, Rubias says they are well known for their fried foods and fireworks. I can smell both in the wind as we make anchor.

After getting into the port town, Rubias guides us to the yellow-painted home of one named Sal Momentés. His wrinkled, sun-burnt face cracks a grin when he discovers Edia and the captain at his doorstep.

"My darlings. What luck to see you on this day. Isadora, good mornin' to you." He greets each of us with hardy and fast handshakes as we pass through his threshold one by one. "Edia, you young thing, look how much you've sprouted. And who are these strapping lads?"

"Shadir and Archie," the captain answers.

"Friends they shall be," says Sal. "Come in. Come in."

His place is no small shack like some we saw elsewhere. It's a place of strong foundation and even stronger perfumes. There are vibrant colors and decor, and every piece of furniture is cushioned wicker. Outside, I saw a gardener trimming his bushes. And inside are a couple servants.

We follow Sal to a living room where he flips on bright bulbs with hardly a flicker. His generator must be a good one. Along one wall is a great woven tapestry. In the red fibers are black threads branching out in all different directions. A family tree detailing every member of the Momentés family and extended family going back several generations. On the wall near that is a giant shelf of books and journals of every sort.

"Please, take a seat, all. What brings you back here? Not that I'm complaining. Would anyone want a conch o' tea?" The old man fires several questions at once without waiting for an answer to any. "How long has it been again?" With a handkerchief he dabs at spittle in the corner of lips. "And what brings you here?"

Rubias interjects before he asks another question. "Only a year. We're on a quest. This is our last stop before going into uncharted waters."

"Uncharted waters? Very curious. What are you doing that for?"

"I'm afraid I cannot give details beyond that. But we don't have the necessary funds to get us there. I'm here to ask for a loan."

"A loan, you say?"

"A loan of supplies, specifically. If it helps, I've brought collateral." She searches her pockets for a piece of paper.

I clear my throat. Sal looks to me. I ask, "I don't mean to interrupt, but I'm very curious about your island. How do you all keep peace with such an economy?"

He silently pieces together a lecture, and responds, "The main thing you have to remember is that we trust in the value of currency, and we must also trust that anarchy will not be the most efficient way to exchange goods, no offense to present company. It is really all a complicated matter." He points to the tapestry. "It is tradition to keep track of each tontine to remain vigilant and knowledgeable. These tapestries along with our personal journals mark the history of every tontine, every nuance in society, and every noticeable change. It is because of this that suspicion is always high, but the wise survive."

There are hundreds of journals on those shelves. Must be the same in every household. If so, it's possible the Tontine Isle has the most well-documented history of any island. An investigation into murder could be so efficiently conducted with everyone's personal viewpoint. Any obvious deception would be uncovered, and true murder would need to be a matter of mastered subterfuge and mind games. This culture is a labyrinth, and only the smartest make their way to the center to be the leaders for the next generation.

I ask, "So who does the manual labor?"

Sal nods. "I see you've picked up on my fortune. A couple of my family, including myself, have won our tontines. There are other families who have won so many that they become the richest on the island. Unfortunately, not all families have the same luck or skill. There are some families who win a tontine often enough to survive. Others have to do manual labor because they're families have rarely or never won. And some get absorbed into other families. It isn't the most pleasant way to live. With such a hostile social structure, those without much are treated as inferior. I've made it part of my life to extend hospitality and charity to those in need."

"But could things be changed?"

"Changed in what way?"

Shadir, wide-eyed, knows what I'm doing, and shakes his head at me. But I press on. Curiosity gets the best of me.

"To help the people who need help instead of relying on your charity."

"Change here is quite slow. To have such a rapid shift would require such an upheaval. If you are interested, please take a look at my shelf. There are plenty of books there on Tontinian economic theory and law." He waves his hand to a section of the shelf.

Rubias says, "Pé Dutanté is from here," and hands Sal the paper she patiently held.

Putting on spectacles, Sal says, "Yes. Unfortunately the wise and patient aren't the only ones to win their tontines. The most ruthless can be very successful." He skims the page. His shaking hands can barely keep the thing still enough to read. "This is a letter to you. What's it for?"

"Look at who wrote it."

Eyes dart to the bottom signature. He forms several words with his lips but express none. Instead, he weeps—slow at first, but the sea soon comes forth. Rubias places a steady hand on his shoulder.

"What's wrong?" Shadir asks. "What's on the letter?"

Rubias answers, "Pé wrote me that letter."

Sal says behind croaking moans, "There were three left in his tontine: my daughter Piña, Pé, and another boy named Achea. Achea and Piña fell in love. It has happened before. Generations ago, the lawmakers made it possible for two in the same tontine to consolidate their win through marriage if they were the final two. That was the plan. But..." Another wave of tears stops Sal from speaking.

Rubias finishes, "That bastard arranged a murder to look like a suicide pact. With that, Pé won his tontine. He even wrote suicide notes in each of their personal journals. No link to Pé was ever found."

Sal's voice rages, "I know he did it! I knew that handwriting was not my daughter's handwriting. All of us knew. But I had no way to prove it without a sample of Pé's writing. But he conveniently hid or destroyed all of his journals in the years leading up to that night. Then he funded his pirating with that money. What a disgrace—present company excluded."

Edia says excitedly, "You can get him with that letter, right? Compare it."

"I shall, bright girl. I shall." He retrieves a journal from the shelf. His finger flips to a marked page, but he can't wipe his tears away fast enough to accurately compare the two.

Shadir puts up his hands. "Let me. I studied cartography a long time ago. I'm good with lines."

"Thank you." Sal hands over the notes.

Edia, Rubias, and I get close and squeeze our eyeballs into the folds of that journal. I notice some changes, but nothing that can't be written off as the nervous scratching of an agitated or distraught person. Shadir doesn't blink as he investigates the ink.

He mumbles, "'Appear', 'age', 'tontine'. A and E."

"What's that?" asks Sal.

"I've got it. Look at the A's and the E's here in these words. They have an eccentricity to them that the writer may have overlooked when trying to write plainly. It matches the eccentricities in the letter by Pé." He flips through previous pages. "I can't seem to find any instances of it in the earlier writings. This woman—your daughter, I mean—would not have been teaching herself that kind of flourish to her penmanship if she meant to kill herself moments later. It is very possible you have a case against Pé if they accept this."

I say, "He's a pirate. Shouldn't that be enough?"

Edia smacks the back of my head.

Sal says, "The council doesn't care about his wrongdoings off the island. Especially because he brings in imports and valuables. They don't like him, no one does, but they overlook his fraudulent behavior and pirating because it helps them more than harms them. But the law is the law. They won't overlook this. At the very least, I can bring him to trial. But I don't think I would win, unfortunately."

"What would happen if you did win?" Edia wonders. "Would you get reimbursement? Would he be executed?"

"Probably expelled off the island, but that wouldn't be much of a punishment. As for the tontine funds, I don't know. For the past couple years there has been philosophical and legal debates on the ownership of a tontine. This may exacerbate those talks. Executed or not, they would discuss whether the money belongs to a tontine remainder—which is the family line of the winners—or if it should be absorbed into the government. What knot this will cause. I don't need the money, but I would like Achea's family to have it. They have had many losses in recent generations, and the elders in their family have nearly dried up their funds. They're old and can't do labor, so they've had a hard time as of late. Perhaps I could convince the council that their family deserves it." He dabs at his frothing lips again.

Edia scoffs, "He wouldn't cough up a single flake of gold if his life depended on it. That's why they call him the infamous treasure hoarder."

Rubias says, "Don't forget I'm the only person besides him who knows where his stash is hidden. I'm the only person to have ever stolen from his hoard." The captain chuckles. "I reckon he still has no idea I've done so. Perhaps I can bring that in and donate it to them. Your government has no right to keep donated money."

Sal smiles again at Rubias. "You're so kindhearted. You must be a terrible pirate."

"As of late, it doesn't feel like I'm much of a pirate at all. But if it makes you feel better, I won't donate all of it." She sneaks him a wink.

He chuckles, and says, "This alone is worth the risk of giving a pirate a loan." He goes off into another part of the house to bring back a satchel with money and a loan agreement for Rubias to sign. Once all the ink has been dried and wax stamped, Sal says, "Stay a while if you wish. My servants will cook you something nice. Have a look around. I have to go to the council now. Pé is expected to return in two days. I must make preparations." Sal clasps each of them on the shoulders as a formal farewell. He takes his leave with the letter and journals.

Shadir says, "I'm going to take a stroll around the island. Anyone care to join?" His eyes dart straight to me, but I decline. He goes by himself. Rubias and Edia leave to start the resupply.

This leaves me alone in a stranger's lavish house. I reach for the stolen journal digging into my back to continue reading it. I skimmed it earlier, and couldn't really find anything noteworthy. I peel through the pages to find critical information, but there isn't much left to his pre-insanity journaling. Shadir thoroughly ripped out all the good bits back then. But there are still bits I can gather.

Apparently, the animals are ghastly. Desja Rubias mentions lizards of enormous size, some with feathers and others with camouflaging scales. The apes are described as monstrous howlers. Snakes fall from the trees. Things akin to crocodiles hide in the mud. It's infested with lurchpurrs and sapstabbers. Yet with all those described at length, I find nothing about a beast needing to be killed or destroyed.

Scribbled throughout the back half are ramblings interlaced with memories. There was something Rubias mentioned early in our voyage. Her grandfather was cursed to see the future. Perhaps these ramblings are some of those visions. But I can't make out what they mean. Receding waters, plains of ice, wars in deserts and jungles, and the planet itself cracking like an egg. I can't piece together what came before and what will come after. But there is one tidbit that intrigues me.

"I feel the Goldsire. It is always everywhere," I read aloud. If Shadir wasn't with us to corroborate the story, I'd think the island is the mythical compilations of a madman.

I put the journal down on a shelf and scour the tomes documenting Tontinian history. I pick out one with a lavish binding—a dot of pearl with intricate green script. It describes complicated connections between a few houses. A man had been murdered. Members of his own house were accused of tontine gerrymandering. Flipping forward a few months gets me to some house feud being waged. Bored of it, I put the journal back.

There are normal books along with those journals. I don't recognize most. I follow my finger along the spines, brushing over *Tontine Economic Theory*, *Ethics of the Tontine Council*, *Sanctions and Gerrymandering From a Modern Perspective*, and *Hostility Appeasement*. I even chuckle a bit when I find *On Justice and Defense* by a Captain Corvarulius. I'm curious if Sal knows about its origin.

The History of Arwellian Ruins nets my attention. I pull it out and read for the next hour. There are drawings of ruins with pillars larger than cemetowers. Some depict rusted machinery for uses I could never guess. The author detailed each account of discovery down to the smallest totem, cairn, and grain of art. It was from them we descended, and yet we lost so much knowledge. We held on to some about electricity and machinery, but they had it perfected. They had mechanical suits that spewed fire. Their farms were vast—covering swaths of flat land with the ocean nowhere in sight. Their lives were twice as long and probably twice as rich with experience. But the world was indifferent as the sea swallow those farms and valleys.

I flip through a chunk of the book to a drawing of a man with a blade like an elegantly curved machete. It's a cutlass. Turning the page reveals rapiers and sabres and scimitars. Swords like these were used after the flood for a little while, but were phased out with the popularity of other weapons. Machetes, hatchets, and daggers are easier to make, and firearms are more convenient. Rumors say some islands have kept the sword crafting tradition alive, but I've never seen one in person.

Flipping through pages, I find lists and images of animals that used to exist. Beasts of burden. Pack animals. Pets. Rodents. And, of course, the whales—archaic kings of the ocean before the flood.

To my surprise, there's a whole chapter dedicated to the beginning of piracy. The first pirates started off as explorers—finding treasures long forgotten. As ruins were sufficiently plundered, they were hired as privateers by other governments. Finally, that took the shape of modern-day piracy. Interesting. Earlier, Rubias said she hasn't felt like a pirate lately, but in reality she isn't too far off from its origins.

I didn't see Shadir return, but his voice breaks my concentration. "Food is ready."

I close my eyes to help store each new piece of information, and then go to the kitchen where Rubias and the others are already getting supper around a large dining table. We eat roasted pheasants, buttered bread, and other dishes I can't name. Each of us get goblets of fresh water without a speck of dirt in it. It's the most food I've ever seen in my entire life. I hold myself back from stuffing everything into my mouth.

When there is a lull in the conversation, Rubias looks at Shadir.

Although enjoying himself with the feast, his mood turns sour when he realizes she's about to ask something. I slow down my chewing to prepare for the incoming query.

She says, "I need you to make a map. The *Prey Mantas* might be right behind us. With no more known islands to reach, they'll need a way to follow us."

Shadir washes down whatever he has in his mouth with his cup. "That would be unwise." He wants to leave it at that, but Rubias won't let that happen.

I say, "Perhaps this is best to—"

As if I never started speaking at all, Rubias says, "We can leave it in Sal's possession. He'll hand it off to Mako as soon as they make port. It'll be partial. From here to the island. No other markings or indicators to what the map is for. It'll be useless for anyone else. We won't even tell Sal—"

Shadir pushes back his wicker chair and gets up. He uses a hand towel to wipe the juices off his hands and face and throws it on the table. Then his finger sticks out threateningly to Rubias. "I already told you, you get it piece by piece. I don't even know if I could accurately remake it from scratch."

Through clenched teeth, the captain says, "I insist." She doesn't want to make a scene with Sal's servants nearby.

"After I do, I essentially become useless to you. What will happen to me then? In fact, what will happen to me after all of this?"

"I'm taking you and Archie home."

"Whether we succeed or not, how can I trust you'll follow through with that? You've still got that chest. Still hopin' to use it if things don't go your way, *hm*?"

Shadir storms out before she could answer any of those questions.

"Are you?" I ask. She looks to me, astonished at the accusation coming from me. "Is that why you still have it?"

It lost its magical properties, but perhaps she'll trap him inside and chain it closed. Or is that why she wants me around? Perhaps to figure out how to make it usable again.

"The chest could prove to be very valuable. I don't know what to do with it yet. But truly, I need my satellite ship back. We'll need the backup."

Having the *Prey Mantas* around did make things easier. It's been difficult docking on every island we've been to with just a warship. For example, we're currently anchored near a beach away from the wharf. We had to paddle the dinghy all the way over, and then walk the rest of the way.

Edia wipes pheasant juice off her hands and grabs a roll. With a full mouth, she asks, "Can't we wait for them here?"

"Not with Pé Dutanté expected to be here in two days. As much as I'd like to surprise him, now is not the time for that kind of confrontation. For many reasons."

My appetite disappears with all this going on. I look at the remains of my food like I've lost a battle. "He's planning on leaving," I tell them. Maybe it's a betrayal. Maybe not. But if I can stop the worst from happening, that is what I need to do. "You know he was only still with us because of me, but I told him not to worry about me anymore. He tried to get me to leave many times, including at the CMT. But I refused."

Rubias stands and leans over the table. "Bloody Baldeva, I knew I should've had him locked up. He's probably out there right now looking for a ride to hijack." She makes for the door, but nearly bolts right into Sal returning from his errands.

He grabs her by the shoulders, and says, "Well, young lass, take it easy. It seems I've stumbled into a spat of some kind. Is it something I can assist with? Is it about that other fellow?"

Trying to get past him, Rubias says, "It's none of your concern, Sal."

I say, "Something else needs to be done. Would it not be better to offer your hand to him than to put his in shackles?"

Sal took my lead and added his own wisdom: "Right you are. An extension of good will and trust. As the old adage goes, 'More cost efficient to build a ship for trade than one for war.'"

Edia speaks up, "They're probably right, captain. If my opinion means anything to you, I believe it would be best to show him we can be trusted. Though I've no idea how.

Calming herself down, Rubias looks around the room to each of us. A nod of agreement eases the tension, and after a moment of consideration, she says, "Come with me. I have an idea."

***

With the Aurora Tide dancing across the night sky, Rubias and I are on the beach where we came ashore on the dinghy. My bare feet squirm around in the sand. Lights twinkle on the *Prey Empress* anchored far out in the water.

"Now what do you want," Shadir says coming up from behind. He's being guided by Edia who retrieved him.

Rubias, with a blazing torch in hand, gets closer to the object we've brought to the beach. On a bed of sticks and leaves is the runic chest.

Shadir says, "You'll have to shoot me in the head and stuff me in there if that's what you want. I'm not getting in on my own volition."

The captain says, "You're not very trusting, are you?" She gets closer to him. He flinches, but stays still. "Here." She holds the torch up. He slowly wraps his fingers around it, and she let's go. "Destroy it."

Shadir looks at me. I nod.

Rubias says, "I have freed people from shackles before, but only you can free yourself from this one. Burn your burden."

Shadir approaches the chest, slowly at first, but then with more confidence. He swallows. Holds the torch over the chest, drops it on the bed of sticks, and stands there as the fire grows.

"Step away from it," Edia says. "Come back here by us."

He steps back without taking his eyes off the flames. It spreads and spits, warps the metal, makes the ivory runes glow. It engulfs the chest and chars the wood. The flames eat away at the letters 'GS' carved into the side until they are removed from this world. The lid bursts open with a series of colorful, crackling explosions. Shadir and I both jump back like we were shot at, while Edia and Rubias cackle.

Shadir screams, "What was that?"

"The Tontine Isle loves their fireworks," the captain answers, and grins. They hadn't told me they were going to add that.

I laugh when Shadir laughs. Finally, for the first time since we've gone on this quest, I'm able to witness his joy. And the next morning, without being asked again, he makes the map to the best his ability.

THE UNCHARTED WATERS

To avoid a giant fishing cage, we pass over a coral reef on our way out of the Tontine Isle. Not much of a sight alone, but frothing around in it are coral koi—as large as sharks but much friendlier. The multi-colored scales glimmer in the water while they swim and play with one another. Such smart animals. They'll drop a rock from the surface and watch as it tumbles down the coral landscape. There are also bloatkoi farther out. They can expand like an air balloon. Sometimes one would expand while the others bounce it around under the water. If there are rules to these games, no human will ever know them. More secrets I may never understand.

Not all creatures of the deep are as playful as the koi. Not evil, just hungry. Rubias warns us about them as we pass the polar boundaries into uncharted waters. This portion of the ocean is heated and poisoned by the fumes of volcanic vents—habitable for the most dangerous of ocean life and not much else. We have to be on guard every bit of the day, especially since we don't yet have a satellite ship to back us up.

Temperatures rise significantly as we travel in the direction of the equator—which Shadir says is north after we switched from polar to cardinal directions. Weather changes drastically—from hot and humid to powerful storms within minutes. Night comes with its own difficulties since we no longer have the Aurora Tide to give us some light. After the sun goes down, our world becomes pitch black. We have a couple spotlights mounted, but the weak bulbs are about as useful as a lit candle in a rainstorm. None on the crew are gifted star navigators, so we have to anchor at night, wasting precious traveling time.

Instead of sleeping, I wormed my hand under my cot to grab Desja's journal. While everyone else is resting or working somewhere else, I can sneak another reading by lantern light. There must be something in it I have missed.

As I pull it out, Wickit lifts his head from his cot nearby and whispers, "What are you sneakin'?"

By reflex, I shove it back under, making him all the more suspicious. Curiosity wafts him from his cot over to me.

"Promise I won't say nothin'."

I don't know if it's because I couldn't stop him if I tried or if I did actually trust him, but I bring the book back out. Perhaps he won't have any clue as to what it is. I hand it over.

"*The History of Arwellian Ruins*?" he says aloud, reading from the gold lettering stamped on the spine.

My heart sinks. I grabbed the wrong book.

"What're you being so sly about this for?" He flips through it, but there isn't much to see without more light.

I develop an answer that is not totally untrue. "Because I stole it when we were at the Tontine Isle. I was embarrassed."

Wickit grins, and gives the book back. "Now you're stealin', are you? Exactly the kind of treasure I'd expect the Artisan Pirate to plunder."

When he turns to go back to his cot, my palm strikes my forehead as if to unburden myself of all stupidity. Perhaps we can return to the Tontine Isle after our quest is complete, but that means revealing to Rubias what I've done. What would she do once she knows I've betrayed her trust?

Before sinking too deep into this anxiety, the ship moves unusually. The cots sway. Wickit leans against a support beam for balance. "What d'ya suppose that was?" he asks.

Trying not to wake anyone else, we make haste to the deck to see if the waves were picking up. Ellick is also here. He had come topside for some fresh air when he saw something in the water. He's swiveling the spotlight when we approach.

"You see somethin'?" Wickit asks, looking out into the dark sea.

"Thought so," Ellick says, bug-eyes blinking rapidly. "Although it could be my imagination."

He puts a hand on the physician's shoulder. "You never had a good imagination, my friend."

We peer over the banister, unaware of something coming up from the other side of the ship until I feel a hairy appendage swipe my neck. I turn to swat at it, but it's gone.

"What's wrong?" Wickit asks.

I utter, "Why do I have the feeling like I've just been… tasted?"

The *Prey Empress* lurches to the side, flinging us to our knees. We exchange glances, all of us knowing how large a creature must be to do such a thing. Moments later, the crew scurries out of the hull like ants.

158

The spotlights are manned, but the beams of light only catch glimpses of whatever is out there. I see shelled skin and mandibles, but nothing more than that.

There are bursts of light from fired cannons followed by a screeching of the beast and groaning of the ship. Somewhere in the darkness, Rubias calls for a raised anchor. Wickit pulls me toward the anchor winch, but I fall behind, limping on my peg leg.

"Anchor here! Anchor here!" he screams out to lure others to him. "Anchor—"

A shadow swipes across the darkness in front of me. I can hear no more shouting from Wickit. Approaching the anchor winch, the man is nowhere to be seen. He's gone. The stars are unevenly blacked out by the presence of this beast which now presumably looks down on us... if it has eyes.

I flee as fast as I can manage, but I can't see where I'm going. By memory, I navigate the ship, dodging other crewmates and the mast and the hull hatch until I get to the tool shed. I swing open the door as something thuds on the deck behind me. I can't stop to see what, or who, it was. I close the shed door and sink down, cradling my knees. The sounds of the battle and crew are not drowned out by these thin wooden walls. One of the masts cracks and falls like a hacked tree.

The distant voice of Shadir calls out, "Someone come help me! I need help!"

I ignore it. Someone else will go. Someone far more capable than me. I can't. I don't belong here. There is nothing I can do.

The ship is bumped and careens. This beast may capsize us, and then we'll be food. So close to our final destination. So close to—I try to net a breath, but my chest constricts.

Behind the tool shed is the emergency air balloon. If I prepare it now, maybe I can save some crew. We can get away and meet back with Mako and the *Prey Mantas.* I exit the shed, find the nearby basket, and reach for the clasps.

"Please, someone follow my voice. I can get it away from us." Shadir again. But what can we do? These kinds of creatures thrive here. It was a foolish mistake coming here.

I hear his voice again, but this time he calls to me directly. "Archie! I need you!"

That above all else breaks through the thick armor of fear. Cursing myself, I clench my shaking hand and back away from the basket. Why am I afraid of this when I've already faced far worse? Every day, normal people face monsters. Kings turning into tyrants. Feuds to war. Famine and disease. People with far more to lose face that every day. Rust it all, I've already lost an arm and a leg. I'm not going to add to that the people I care about the most.

I blindly rush toward the plea for help. A floating lantern helps me find his exact location. "What do you need?" I ask.

"Oh, Archie, there you are," Shadir gasps. He brings me over to the banister. "Do you hear that?" I don't hear anything except for the chaos around me. "It's the sound of maelstrom piranha. We came across some last time. They swim in a circle fast enough to create a whirlpool which sucks in anything nearby. And then they feast. Nasty things, but we can lead this creature to them."

A voice nearby says, "I hear it. But how do you know where it's at?" It's Aldrezier. I didn't notice him only a couple paces away. That's the extent of this darkness.

"No damn clue where it's at, but I'm going to do something extremely dumb to find out. I'll need you two to lower me down into the water. I'm going to feel where the current pulls me. Then I need you, Archie, to relay that information to Rubias so we can steer the ship."

I can't help but imagine him getting sucked into that whirlpool of piranha. "What happens when you find it?"

"I reckon they'd strip the flesh off my bone. Ideally, you'll pull me up before that."

The sea creature picks off stragglers on deck. Meanwhile, we lower Shadir down with rope tethers. A minute later, he yells a command, which Aldrezier repeats. I stumble over to Rubias and relay the information and our reasoning. She echoes the command into the darkness toward the rudder wheel. Sluggishly, we drift to the right with the beast still grappling us. Shadir alters his original command, so we let the sails down and shut down the hind rudders to do what he needs. After two more commands, Shadir yells, "Pull me up! It's getting close!"

I hobble to the rope to help the Aldrezier pull him up. The beast screeches—no, not the beast. It's quiet, hidden underneath the growing roar of the incoming whirlpool. That horrid sound is coming from Shadir. We pull faster, but the current grips him tight. Aldrezier sticks a foot up on the banister for leverage. Employment of a few more arms is needed. I call for help, and Tango sprints from the darkness to us. When we're able to pull Shadir free from the water, the load is significantly lighter than before. Shadir has gone still and quiet—maybe dead or passed out from the piranhas' feasting. With each tug of the ship's yarn I plunge deeper into sorrow for my friend.

I mumble, "He's not dead," over and over again.

The body squelches over the banister. I bring over a lantern to assess the damage. All I see is blood before Tango pulls me away to avoid seeing the rest. He makes the sign for the infirmary. He and Aldrezier cover Shadir with something and take him away.

With one final lurch of the ship, the sea creature slithers away. Shadir saved us all. The maelstrom piranha had feasted on the thing and scared it off. The crew sails us away before either can do us further harm.

There is too much time between then and the morning light. In a way, the wait for something to happen becomes worse than what actually happened. No one can sleep. I can't even blink. The few images I can conjure of the beast stains the inside of my eyelids. And Wickit is nowhere to be seen.

No one can say how big the whole creature was. At times it seemed bigger than the ship, wrapping appendages of unknown length around us, blocking out the stars. Other times it seemed to be multiple things at once—a family of horrors from the same world as ours, and yet also from another.

The dawn comes to rescue us from our own minds filling in the blanks.

I am the first to acknowledge the extensive damage to the engine room and the rudders. The mast is a little more obvious. It'll take days before we can get it up and running again. Rubias is going to hate that.

They don't let me see Shadir, but they inform me he will recover. If it were anyone else, it wouldn't have been possible. However, despite his miraculous ability, I know how much pain he's in. I wouldn't wish it upon anyone.

Wickit is never found. Not a body or anything. Four others were also not recovered. Two were. The shipwright Gridda is found bawling over the body of the carpenter Gridda. Something had slammed into her during the fray. The two used to be inseparable. The other was Oilm—found at the bottom of the hull steps. The tattooed man from Baloa was dropped from a height none can determine.

Rubias refuses to hold a funeral ceremony. She demands we press forward. To make up for the losses, all nonstandard crew members, such as the musicians and the chef, are called into action beyond their normal tasks. Maybe she's right about it being too dangerous to remain here for long, but the crew is tired and in mourning. It's too much too soon.

Despite being pushed onward, I sneak down to the crew's quarters and search for the music box chest I made for Wickit. It's at the foot of his cot with all his other belongings—soon to be absorbed by the rest of the crew. I open it and listen to the tinkling ballad. The song always sounded familiar, but now I know why. It is the same melody as an old folk song I heard when I was a kid. Back when Krakau had festivities and people played music. My eyes well up with tears.

I claim the chest before anyone else can. Because where one's chest is makes that place home. On the island Wickit called home, someone awaits his return. They don't know yet that he never will. I vow to bring this chest to them when this is over, and a proper funeral will be held.

And then we lose another.

There was a second engineer woman, but it isn't until people started calling for her when I learned her name. Pilla. We never got along well after she found out I messed with the engine room. After Dalia died during Decker's attack, she wasn't quite the same person. She kept claiming to see the Wounded Woman. This sailor's myth speaks of a woman with a face like that of a stingray's underside—sunken eyes, a mouth stuck as a smile, and ribbed gills. She is known to float on her back in the water, calling to those who recently lost someone important to them. It's believed by the paranoid that she needs a person in grief to come with her, or consequences would follow. Others reported that Pilla saw the Wounded Woman, and because no sacrifice was given, she wholeheartedly believed the creature that attacked us was the consequence. To quell the Wounded Woman's desire, she wanted to give herself up to the ocean. Edia was the one who tried to talk some sense into her, but clearly failed. No one can find her. She must've tossed herself overboard.

This makes me the sole contributor to the engine room. Rubias orders me to start making any repairs to help get us sailing again. Spending hours alone in this heated chamber trying to fix it makes my mind wander. Deaths and doubts plague me. I see their faces, especially Wickit's, when I close my eyes, and they won't go away.

Without hesitation, Rubias orders us onward when the ship is repaired enough to sail.

〜〜〜〜〜〜〜〜〜〜〜〜

With a few more days of travel behind us, we come upon an island. Small, but it has lush trees and a beach. It's uninhabited, but there are signs of previous visitations, probably from nearby island tribes. How many of these pebbles are out here in the uncharted waters? I want to say it seems tranquil, but maybe that's a trick. A lure toward a great mouth ready to swallow us whole. Or maybe the lack of sleep is getting to me.

Tango tries to convince the captain to make a stop for the crew to rest and recover from the losses. Knowing how close we are to the ruins, Rubias declines. "This island has nothing we need." I go to speak with her one-on-one, but all she says to me is, "Get back to your post."

"I've misjudged you, captain," I say quiet enough for others not to hear. "I thought you cared about your crew."

"Don't act like you know what you're talking about just because you have some leagues traveled now," she spits. She looks to the horizon. "I can care again once this is over."

The drooping crew longingly stares at the island as we sail past.

There is an island worth stopping at. One with inhabitants. When they say this ocean is uncharted, what they mean is that they are unmapped by polar denizens. Islanders native to these waters know it like the koi knows its own spots. They've mastered living here, traversing islands for resources, and deterring beasts like the one we came up against a few nights ago. That's the reason why the captain has decided to speak to them. Any way to avoid being delayed is fuel for her fire.

But first, Tango is careful to identify through his oc-pipe whether or not we should avoid contact. Some tribalists gather on the beach and give a salute that we assume is a form of greeting. Tango sees a small pier—usually a sign of good faith among these tribes. The captain makes the decision to have a select few get on the dinghy and make landfall.

It is Rubias, Edia, the stormseer, Piston the quartermaster, and myself who are chosen to greet these folk. The selection was carefully made. The stormseer and Piston both come from tribal backgrounds, so there could be a shared language. However, she also wanted to avoid those in the crew who might approach too strongly and quickly, and especially those who might offend. Growing up, I had learned to be wary of tribalists in a similar manner to anarchists. In Tyro, even to my own father, barbarism and savagery was as frightening as chaos and piracy. Even now I'm trying to shake those thoughts from my head, because yet again the lies I was taught are proven wrong.

They are a welcoming but wary people. One treats us to some fruit rarely seen in the pole, and another gifts us leaf origami. Mine is some kind of beetle which I cradle in my palm. One woman with a face wrinkled like balled up parchment gives us a white paste for our skin to combat the boiling sun. And none demand anything in return. Then she hurries us along to the interior of the island where their habitats are located.

A cement-like mortar using primarily sand was used for the walls. The roofs are a stringy bundle of leaves. Campfires must be important to their nighttime culture. One is placed in front or to the side of each home. They have ash totems all over the island. It's similar to our cemetower, but their dead are burned first and added to the totems. There's a bustle to the island I never expected. It rivals that of the markets on a larger island. The only difference is how they treat one another. They have a much stronger bond. It's not like the spitefulness of Kameya or the quiet distrust in Tyro.

Even their politics is a treat to discover. The stormseer and Piston speak secondary languages that have distant ties to this area. They're able to understand a word here and there, but not necessarily the context.

However, together they pull enough information to discover this day is an important election day for the tribe. The crowd coalesces into a dense circle. Perhaps they're about to fight for some position of power. My immediate assumption is to the death, but as three people enter the circle with filled sacks, I feel foolish. They aren't fighting at all. Two men and one woman get closer to the center, but stop several feet from one another. They scatter different mixtures of grain in various patterns. When satisfied, the three back away into the crowd of congratulatory arms clapping their backs. Then it's quiet, and movement among the crowd slows.

"Don't move," whispers the stormseer into my ear.

Several birds flock to the circle. Their pronged talons skip across the ground as they choose their preferred grain. Beaks stab at the food—most gathered around a single pile of grain. There's murmuring in the crowd. Perhaps this means a winner is chosen. There's a large smile coming from the man who placed the feed. Still we do not move. One more bird flocks to the meal. This one is a gorgeous shade of white and blue. Larger than the others, as well. It chooses the other pile and squawks. The murmuring grows. Most hold looks of astonishment.

A single drum beat marks a certain passage of time, and the crowd no longer remains as statues. The woman who received the larger bird is awarded with a necklace of some kind, and many greet her with their version of congratulations. But the election is not over. There will be several rounds of this.

The stormseer says, "It seems we have had a much larger effect on this community than we meant."

"How so?" asks Edia.

"That bird was a cloud-tailed skrall. They are not native to these parts. It's been resting on our crow's nest for some time. It seems like this election is a point-based system. I assume these bird seed recipes are handed down from generation to generation with slight alterations over time. The one who received a larger number of birds probably would've won, but to have such a great crop year to attract a new species of bird to the island changed the outcome, giving the woman more points. Very interesting indeed."

Rubias says, "Aye, but we're not here to sight-see. We need to—"

There are several cracks like fireworks in the distance.

Edia asks, "Did you hear that?"

Everyone has stopped. Every person on the island and us four outsiders stare out at different segments of the ocean or sky. There is a long, silent gap of nothing before the terror hits all at once.

A native's home is blasted into pieces several paces away from us from a mortar shot. The tribe panics, and so too does Rubias. I can see in her face we're thinking the same thing. Was that from our ship? More mortar shots pound into the village, indiscriminately destroying things around the island.

As we run back to the shore, sand exploding behind us, Rubias confirms, "It's not ours. We don't have enough mortars to shoot so many."

The stormseer adds, "I agree. The shots seem to be coming from the south-east. We're docked to the north."

They're correct, of course, and we find the *Prey Empress* in its docile state, but the dots aboard are running around preparing for battle. We row back to it, and find our places within the war machine.

Finally on deck, we see who fires upon the island through our oc-pipes. Coming around is the largest warship I have ever seen, even considering the one on which we currently stand. The ram is like shark's teeth. Mortars set down the middle like a spine. Its offset sails are quite strange—although I can't deduce why at the moment. The gungills outnumber ours by twenty at the very least. In addition to those, there are devices I can't identify. It's a strange, hulking swimmer which could easily destroy us in our already harmed state.

"It's him," says Edia. "I'd know that ship anywhere. It's Pé Dutanté."

Rubias takes a moment to be shocked. Then regains herself and pipes orders through the ship. Our ship churns and churns, gaining speed and distance.

"Is he not coming after us?" say Shadir moving to the aft of the ship.

Some of us look upon the island as this titan of a ship sails around it. It takes its time and spends it by battering the island with mortars and cannons. The screaming grows ever more distant as we get away.

Edia breaks down. "We're outswimming him because he's... slaughtering them." She turns to Rubias. "They're dying, captain! We need to turn around and help them. Draw Pé's fire away from them."

Her plea is left ignored by a stern and steadfast Rubias. Instead, she commands, "Everyone get back to your posts! Our lives depend on it!"

Shadir says to me, "They were right about him. Monstrous. He'll be gaining on us soon, and then what? We can't outswim him forever."

"I think we'll be okay," I say to reassure him. "Rubias is the thorn in his boot."

Even if it has waned in recent days, my trust in her still holds.

THE STORM

The crewmate far above in the nest yips and yells. When Tango hears this, they exchange messages through hand signs. Tango rushes to the side of the ship and observes the horizon with his spyglass. Panicking, he rushes to Rubias's side and signs her a message. Her face warps into anger. Dutanté is still tailing us—a hunter with worthy prey.

We press on, giving the ship as much speed as we can, but the wind is against us. It will be against Pé too, but what matters is how long we can keep this up. We already started this chase burned out and exhausted. Crew morale is scraping the bottom of the barrel. My assumption is Pé's ship has enough storage and supplies to outlast us for the long haul. Rubias could order us to turn around for a fight, but no one here believes we could win that at this point.

The stormseer, with Ominix the cat on his shoulders, looks to the skies. "A storm is coming. It lays just over to the north-west. See those dark clouds over there?"

Because we need guidance through these uncharted waters, Shadir is close by Rubias at all times. He hears what the stormseer claims, and returns, "We aren't sailing there. We're going north-east."

The stormseer sniffs the air and studies the sky and wind. "It's moving. Its path will curve sharply and hit us."

Rubias eyes the distant storm. It seems so harmless that far away. "Are you sure?" she asks.

Shadir interrupts, "Nonsense. How can you tell that?"

"He's a stormseer who has trained his senses over a lifetime. Moreover, he is *my* stormseer. He's never been wrong before."

"Very well," says Shadir. "So we sail through it. Pé will have to do the same. The burden will be mirrored."

"Incorrect again," Edia says, prancing from out of the captain's cabin. "Pé Dutanté has a tempest-class warship. It's a rare kind. They can sail through storms without losing much speed at all."

That explains why the sails looked so strange. They can install rain shields on the sails and storm shelters for the crew to keep working without the force of the storm hindering them. If it wasn't full of pirates who wanted us dead, I'd marvel at the engineering feat.

Rubias shares a proud smile with her pupil. "It's called the *Carn o' War*. We've studied that ship more than most. It is an unfortunate coincidence. One that will see us lose this fight before we even begin."

I ask, "Is there nothing we can do?"

They're all looking to the captain for leadership. She got us into this mess, and now she needs to get us out.

Tango signs to the captain. Her eyes fall in somber contemplation. Disagreeing with whatever Tango suggested, Rubias orders, "Persevere. We don't know if we can outlast them until we try. Tie yourselves to a part of the ship if you must."

An exasperated Aldrezier climbs down from the mast, saying, "Have you been drinking seawater, captain? The storms at the pole are like being spat on compared to the ones out here."

"Don't test me," Rubias demands. "Do not forget I gave you a second chance."

"I'm only sayin' what everyone else is thinkin'. Isn't that allowed on your ship, or has this become a monarchy?"

Is he taking his shot to mutineer again? No, that wouldn't be wise at this time. The crew has been pushed non-stop since the Tontine Isle. Even the veterans have been slipping up.

The captain argues, "Our only chance is going through that storm and losing them. Pé has a satellite ship sailing behind as backup. We cannot defend ourselves against both."

Aldrezier is shouting now: "We're exhausted! You haven't let us rest. Pushing through that storm might kill us. I'm not suggesting we fight. We have to stop. Tie everything down. Get everyone into the hull. We wait it out."

I half expected someone like Aldrezier to sabotage us and join Pé's side. Not stand up for the rest of the crew. Perhaps I've misjudged him. Rubias had won back the loyalty of a man who mutinied against her. Now her obsession is about to lose it again.

Shadir says, "Pé is right behind us. He'll be boarding us as soon as the storm is over, maybe even before."

Rubias, trying to shake off the truth, says, "I can't lose this! Not while we're so close! Pé cannot do this to me again!"

"It's a futile escape!" says Aldrezier. "Your crew trusts you to make the decision that won't get them killed. We've already lost seven since leaving the pole. How many of us are you willing to sacrifice?"

Tango signs agreement, and a few other crewmates stop what they're doing to unify.

Even Edia nods her head, adding, "We can figure out a way, captain. We always do."

The captain rolls her head. She's been outnumbered. Without her usual gusto, she calls out, "Batten down the hatches."

The command echoes through the ship by the crew. They shuffle about to tie everything down and secure loose machinery. We are soon turtle-shelled and the crew files into the hull to wait out the storm. The captain stays in her quarters to wait for Dutanté. She wants to be the first to interact with him.

We know when the storm hits us by the flashes of lightning and whistling wind. Droplets of water come through the ceiling. A chill brushes through our huddled mass. Our collective stink is immediately noticeable. Edia is cross-legged in the corner. Tango peeps out the portholes, anxiously tapping a foot. The only person who doesn't look defeated is the chef who is still peeling potatoes. I wonder what's percolating through their minds, especially knowing the enemy is about to pounce. Maybe it's the same as me.

This is like waiting for death in our own coffin.

"Is anyone by a porthole?" asks Piston near the center of the huddle.

"Too much rain," says another peeking outside. "Can't see anythin'."

The stormseer attempts to settle down his hissing cat. He says, "The storms out here are the worst I've ever seen, but all storms pass eventually."

Low enough for only me to hear, Shadir says, "And then we face the next storm. People are going to die."

The crewmate by the porthole yells, "I see somethin'. It's a ship creepin' alon'side us."

We are invaded by Pé's crew wearing storm gear—an otherworldly bundle of waterproof coats, scarves, goggles, and boots. The weapons are various—from harpoons to pistols. A bloody-faced and rain-soaked Rubias opens the hatch. She is led down with a forceful hand on her shoulder.

I know who Pé is by his walk—a smug saunter. He peels back a rubber mask to reveal a pristine, mustachioed face. I can't tell if he has never been in a fight or if he is much too good in one to be injured. He fishes around the inside of his coat for a small towel and tosses it to Rubias to wipe up her wounds.

She hasn't given up yet. Hit a couple times, but not beaten. There is still an air of control about her, as if the situation is not at all lost—a nonchalance few could achieve.

Pé's voice is smooth with a Tontinian accent. "What a crew, Rubias.

They seem capable of giving mine a good fight. I expected nothing less from my most *formidable adversary*." Nothing but sarcasm in those hollow words. He doesn't consider Rubias to be an equal.

"Why are you here? How did you know where we were?" the captain asks.

"It started as a usual day. I woke up, made coffee, and docked to have a nice breakfast. However, this island on which I made port was my home island. The Tontine Isle, but of course you already know that. Suddenly, I was invited down to the courthouse. The council asked all kinds of strange questions about my past and some journal. They produced an interesting piece of evidence—a letter I wrote to you, of all people.

"I didn't much care for their accusations. Considering my home's navy is made up of a dozen carapace-class ironclads, and some of those ships are under my employment, I decided to sack them. It only took a couple of hours. Now the Tontine Isle has a new government. I'm surprised I hadn't decided to become a king before now. It suits me."

From her knees, Edia bounces up and sprints to the man, knife in hand. She yells as the attack is caught by Pé.

"Feisty, this one," the pirate laughs as he takes the knife away.

Her small fists uselessly hit against the man's torso as she weeps, "You killed her! You killed my ma!"

"I kill a lot of people, darling. She probably got in my way. Now hush up and don't make the same mistake."

One of his crew walks over and peels her off of him. She falls into a weeping ball on the floor.

Pé continues, "My next step, of course, was to find the man who started this ordeal to see if I could get some answers. The old man barely put up a fight at all. We... investigated him for a long while. He wouldn't give up any information—except what we already knew. You had been there two days before, and provided them with that letter. And then something curious caught my eye on his bookshelf. A journal out of place, and with a quick flip through the pages I realized it was not part of his family's library. It was ramblings by someone named Desja. Desja *Rubias*."

He drops the journal in front of Rubias. She looks to us, confused with eyes widened, and eventually settles on me. But I can't match her gaze for more than a second. My head lulls like it's a heavy bag on my shoulders. I hope to shrink away from her disappointment.

Pé's voice is giddy as he continues. "It was hardly discernible, but from what I gathered there is an island full of treasure like something from a child's tale. And it's somewhere past the boundary. I became very invested in this possibility. With some further torture—I apologize—with further investigation, the old man gave up a map. Shoddily made, but my navigator figured out the details. It took a couple days to catch up, but here we are. Up to speed."

"Is this true?" asks Aldrezier. "You led them straight to us, captain?"

Rubias admits nothing even as her crew becomes rowdy and angry. Shadir remains disappointed. He knew something like this could happen. However, the mistake is completely on me, not them.

Pé laughs, and says, "Perhaps I should take over this ship as my own and allow your own crew to throw you overboard."

"We won't betray our captain," says Piston.

Gridda elbows him, and adds, "This is the second time Rubias has gotten us captured. Perhaps she's losin' her expertise."

More infighting grows within the huddle, with no side taking the lead.

Under the growing tensions, Rubias slips in, "That island doesn't have what you think it does."

Pé waves his hand as if to swat away a lie he knows not to believe. There's nothing more she can do. Someone else has to step in.

I say, "I left the journal." But the squabbling continues. I stand defiantly, shouting, "I left the journal! Not the captain. I led them to us." This quells most of the unrest. "I stole the journal because I wanted more information. I forgot it at the Tontine Isle. It's my fault. I'm sorry—"

One of Pé's crew kicks me in the back, forcing me down to my knees again. The sting of his pointed boot lingers. Shadir shuffles over to check on me.

"How disappointing," says Pé. "I really was hoping to see that turn bloody. Either way, everyone in your crew is expendable to me. Don't forget that while you're helping us get to this treasure island of yours. We'll set sail as soon as this storm lets up." The man puts his hand on Rubias's cheek, looks into her golden eyes, and says, "It's too bad you don't go by Gildeye anymore. It suits you."

Gildeye?

Captain Gildeye?

The cellar...

The raid...

It's clear to me now. I had already met Isadora Rubias once before. Ten years ago.

THE HIDDEN ISLAND

The final two days of the journey are arduous. Under the watchful eyes of Pé's armed crew, we are worked to our limits. My good hand bleeds from rope burns. Their whips come down on us every time we slow down. As someone with one arm and one leg, I am slow often.

He has his satellite quarvette nearby at all times to outnumber us. Nothing else attacks us during our trip. Part of me wonders if there would be an opportunity to rebel if something did attack, but these are irrational thoughts from an exhausted, starving body. I fight myself to stay rational.

Pé thinks it is Rubias who knows exactly where the island is, not Shadir. We keep that our secret in fear of him executing her. Shadir consults Rubias whenever he can, but she isn't left alone very often. He has to give the stormseer ambiguous messages that are then given to the captain in passing. Bit by bit they are able to confer the direction of this dreaded island.

Because of this, I also haven't been able to confront her about what I've learned. She knows I know. After Pé said the name Gildeye, her first look was to see if I caught the exchange. Rubias kept it from me this entire time. My own betrayal seems paltry now.

"Land!" someone in the crow's nest yells.

Everyone on deck moves to one side of the ship and identifies it with their oc-pipes. Looking through mine, I can't really describe it as land—at least, not in the usual sense of land. There are huge stacks of mossy limestone and soil, each several planks wide and much taller than the length of any ship. They're like pillars, and between the gaps are ropes of vines, roots, and flora with leaves as big as a person. The trees are beautifully lush and vibrant, and strong enough to root into the walls of the stacks as easily as on top. This wall of limestone, wood, and vines creates an impenetrable fortress which surrounds and protects the island within. There is no way such a thing could be created by human hands, but I'm also hard-pressed in thinking it's a natural formation.

Our mouths fall agape. Even Pé's crew halts their whipping to look in awe upon this impending wall. Stopping short of it, Pé boards our ship again from the quarvette. He's armed with a suave, infuriating demeanor. He looks at others like they're nothing. It's that smug egotism of his I want to so badly retaliate against with every order he barks. But without a plan, such defiance would be a waste. Patience is our goal now.

"Well, *Captain Rubias*," the man says with a belittling tone. "It looks like this is it. Do we cut through this entanglement, or is there another opening."

Rubias needs no consultation with Shadir this time. He has fulfilled his end of the deal. Desja's journal would finally be of more use. She flips it open and scans the inky scratches, swimming through page after page until finally coming up for air with an answer. "They had to cut through last time. It has probably grown back by now. We go through."

Pé sighs. He wants the quicker payout. "Very well. Our two largest ships will stay outside the walls. Getting the quarvette through that might be easier and less of a risk. I want half of your crew on board there and half on here. I'll leave you all to figure out how best to go about getting through. And if the pace is not to my liking, this ship's population is going to dwindle."

I waste no time in piecing together an efficient method of hacking away at the brush. "Gather every machete and hatchet we can find on this ship!" I order.

The crew look to Rubias. She responds, "Do what the man says! With haste!" Then she gives me a quick nod before lending help in distributing the tools. Pé and his crew watch us carefully now that we have blades. I'm worried one of our people are going to try something too early, and that fear comes true a moment later.

"Do I have to do everything around here?" yells a familiar voice from near the edge of the ship. "You fat-bellied blaggard." It's Shadir, climbing the banister. He raises his machete. "We have our chance. Attack now. We can—"

A single shot cuts him off. His head flicks back and his body tumbles to the water below. Shadir is gone.

The smoking pistol is in Pé's hand. "If any of you have got similar thoughts as him, quell them now."

Rubias sneaks a curious look to me. I shrug. If he's got a plan, it wasn't shared with me. But I hope he'll be all right. There's no time to wait and see. We have to trust him.

After everyone changes ships the way Pé wanted, the satellite quarvette we now occupy is positioned to go straight in. Several crewmates are perched at the front to hack away at the roots and vines as we slug forward. When those crewmates get too exhausted to continue, they are relieved of duty and replaced immediately with fresh arms. Had it been a single layer of limestone and roots, we would've been through it quickly. Instead, there are many limestone stacks imperfectly aligned. We have to weave through them.

Halfway through, the ship catches on a particularly strong root down by the water. Tugging on it sends a crack up the stack to the left. High above, limestone gives way and crumbles down on us. Rubias scrambles to pull me out of the way. A few others move swiftly to avoid the raining stone. Our crewmate Hap, who is hanging forward off the banister, isn't able to get away in time. In an instant, he is gone, sucked under the ship from the falling soil and stone.

With a scrunched face, one of Pé's crew says, "No use mourning the loss of a savage. They'd never mourn you. Get back to work."

Hap was one of the few in our crew from a tribalist background. He was a good mate who loved being on this ship. And he mourned the loss of others just like the rest of us. But there is nothing we can do for now except carry on. He wouldn't want us to sacrifice the rest of the crew for vengeance.

In the evening, we finally cut through to the other side. Here we find a swampy lagoon surrounded by an island roughly the same size as my home island. But this rises to a single peak like a mountain, and every noticeable part is covered in a dark jungle.

Edia and I meet at the front of the ship and look down at the murky, frothy water below. It is uneasily calm. There are species no human has laid eyes on since my grandfather's crew came here decades ago. Species once thought lost to the flooding, now evolved to this one single habitat. And a deadly habitat it is—filled to the brim with predators. We will have to prepare ourselves for anything on this island.

It reminds me of the Obitzu Bayou, except more dangerous, which I didn't think was possible. Somehow, while trying to avoid the same fate as my father, I ended up in a place that is even worse. I laugh to myself.

"What?" Edia asks.

Without caring to explain, I say, "Just irony is all."

"Engaging conversation," the snappy girl says. She returns to her duties—which at this point is simply looking out for anything that might cause trouble.

We chug along. There's no strong wind to push us forward, so we rely on the rudders and propellers. Hopefully, the seaweed and muck below doesn't clog them up. Becalmed in this place would be shoddy luck. But we manage to get through, and arrive near the muddy beach of the island, anchoring before hitting shallow water.

"You the chestmaker?" asks Pé.

There is something about him that doesn't live up to Rubias. He's suave and imposing, sure, but it's not the same. It's like he doesn't seem real. He's pretending.

"I am."

"Come with me," he demands, and walks away without making sure I'm following.

He brings me over to the captain's cabin on this ship. The door is open, and inside I see Rubias studying her father's journal. Pé stands to the side and waves me in.

"Remember," he says, "I'll have guards stationed out here, and if anything goes awry, that girl who tried to stab me will be the first one fed to the beasts in the swamp." He winks, and leaves us somewhat alone.

"What do you want?" I ask. Harsh words, and the first I've spoken to her in days. I'm trying my best to keep it all in. I cannot make this about what I want to make it about. Not in the position we're in.

"A few days ago, Shadir reminded me of the kinds of animals we might encounter on the island, and how best to defend against them." She clears her throat. Why does she look so defeated? She's never looked this way. "There are these things called lurchpurr. Very territorial. Very aggressive. But we may be able to blind them and scare them away with a type of flare machine. Is it possible for you to craft that?"

"I would need time we don't have."

"You good with reading diagrams?"

"Salvatorres always make diagrams of their best works."

She hands over the journal. "Look at the marked page."

There's a diagram of something her father invented. I didn't know what it was the first time I saw it after stealing the journal, but now I can piece it together. Simpler than one would think. Desja might've been a genius. It requires some gunpowder and parts I can take off of the spotlights.

"With some help and minor changes, I can have them done in a couple hours."

The two musicians, Pelica and Arginon, help us pry the three spotlights off the ship. We set them down on the floor outside of the captain's cabin where we get the best lantern light. The three of them assist me, each taking one of the spotlights to work on, while I instruct and guide them. While looking over the diagram, I tell them how to safely dismantle the bulbs, take out the electrical wiring, and cinch the holes shut. We make gunpowder chambers out of pipes and do our best to rivet those in place. After making the final touches to them, the two musicians go off to get some deserved rest.

While I look over the flare machines, Rubias's prolonged silence boils an anger within me. When I'm ready to burst, she finally musters, "I'm sorry, Archie."

"You know how much your rusted apology means to me?"

"I know it's worth less than salt water, but that doesn't mean I'm not wrenching with guilt."

I check to see who might be in earshot. Some of Pé's crew lazily wander around, barely focused. "I'm not your kin, not even your crew. Yet I've been foolish in thinking I should give whatever it takes to help you. I sacrificed for you. Physically. Mentally. So I don't give a damn about your guilt."

Her golden eyes are glossier than normal. This time, it is she who avoids my gaze. "Please, let me tell you the tale. Let me explain it to you. I don't know if I'll ever get the chance after this."

"Might as well," I say, and sit cross-legged, pretending to inspect the flare machines in case anyone comes checking up on us.

Rubias also sits, and begins: "I never knew what to do with the stories my grandfather told me. I knew about Shadir being immortal. I knew there was something on this island that is a threat to this world. But what was I supposed to do? My brother Taegot and I just wanted to be fishers, but he drowned one day and that dream was dead."

I say, "If you're fixin' up a sob story, I don't want to hear it. Skip to the main bits."

"Aye. Main bits. It wasn't until I became a pirate captain when I started to take all of this seriously. I became obsessed with the idea of finding Shadir, or one of his maps, or something to get to this island. But my visits to Tyro yielded no results. Based on my knowledge of him and Gilligan, I figured he was somewhere in the archipelago, either in hiding or locked away. The best way to find him was to raid Tyro, but I was a novice captain. Barely any pull. No weight to throw around. Tyro had protections at the time. Good ones, too. So I had to wait. Built my fleet, and after a few years, I had around six or seven ships. Still not worth the risk based on a hunch. But fortune netted me a meeting with this woman. One of your charter barons speaking on behalf of the baron council."

I whip my head up. "Stellagard?"

"Perhaps. Don't remember a name, but we had aligned interests. I needed to search the island, and the barons needed something in return. She had called it 'balancing the island.' I remember that clearly because when she explained it further, I knew it was corruption. People of Tyro were starting to question them and the laws being implemented. There were dissenting voices, and the barons were not going to let that continue. So we struck a deal."

"Dissenting voices," I repeat. "People on the island were opposing the charter barons?" She nods. I have no memories of this, although I was probably too young to notice. "There was no spread of anarchist ideologies?"

"Your council wasn't afraid of anarchy. They were afraid of being deposed."

Piecing together the rest of what she said, something isn't sitting right with me. "So you searched for Shadir…"

"That's when I met you and your father. I knew fairly quickly you didn't know where he was. I assumed you didn't even know *who* he was."

"…but what did they get in return? What was gained from your deal? Was it to destabilize the archipelago?"

Rubias clenches her fists and closes her eyes. She doesn't want to tell me this part, but she knows she has to. "They gave us a list. About fifteen names and twenty buildings. The names were considered to be their biggest political threats. The loudest opposition. We had to burn down specific storefronts to destabilize the economy, and… the people on the list had to be killed. All of it would be covered up as collateral to a pirate raid, which they would then use to shore up their hold over you."

I observe the scarce pieces of the starry sky between the foliage above. "My father… was he on that list?"

With a croak in her voice, she says, "He was."

"Did you come to the cellar that day with the intent to kill him?"

"I did."

I knew what she was going to say, but it is still gut-wrenching to hear aloud. My father knew he was supposed to die that day. For years after that, he kept his head down and his tongue clamped. He never questioned anything again, until he did. And then Stellagard tied up her loose end and made it look like an accident by feeding him to the gators.

Rubias chose to walk away that night and leave her side of the deal unfulfilled, and for that I am grateful, but that does not clean the blood from her hands. Slowly at first, I respond, "You know what happens in that story after you leave? After you destroyed us and killed us? We destroyed and killed each other. I saw one person strangle his neighbor for taking fuel from his generator. I saw an old woman wrench bread out of the hands of a child because she was starving. People who usually came to our island to trade avoided us like we were plagued."

"I wish I could say I did not have my conviction at the time, but I did. I wish I could tell you I grew my morals from that. But the truth is, I sacrificed what I believed in to find this island. It remains to this day my greatest mistake."

Why is she crying more than me?

I get up to exit this conversation. But before I go find Pé, I want to say one final thing to her. "How many more of your own crew have you lost in your pursuit of this island?" I pause to linger on it. I want these words to bleed. "If it was your greatest mistake, then why didn't you learn from it?"

After Pé is informed the flare machines have been made, a small group of eight snugly fit into a dinghy and paddle to shore. Edia and I are included in this group because he underestimates a child and a half wooden chestmaker as hostages. Tango and Rubias are also chosen, and the final three are from his crew. This tactical move forced our primary and secondary leaders away from the already outnumbered crew.

The shore is muddy sand. It sticks to our boots when we cross it. The jungle is thick, dark. I can't see anywhere beyond our torchlight. What kind of animals are eyeing us at this very moment? Edia pulls the dinghy out of the water while I present the three flare machines to the group.

I say, "They're quite heavy. Put the strap over your shoulder like a bandersheef to distribute the weight. Pulling this lever on top opens the front, ignites a spark, and triggers the gunpowder which makes a blast of light. You just have to remember to refill it with gunpowder after every use. Also, don't tip it too far forward when you pull the lever. Lean it back or the gunpowder will fall out before being ignited."

"Most impressive," says Pé. "I think I'll have a place for you on my crew when we're done here."

The compliment slides off me like water off an otter. I casually respond, "I'd never follow someone like you."

"I wasn't asking." He points at Edia and I. "You two stay here. Watch the dinghy. Another group will be here soon with barrels to haul the gold away. Give them the third flare machine and show them which way we went. If either of you cause trouble, this lagoon will be your grave."

Brandishing torches, two flare machines, pistols, and machetes, the group marches into the jungle.

I can't tell how much time passes, but eventually Edia and I are anxious to know how far they've gone, or if they're still breathing. Pé should've at least waited for the morning light before disembarking the quarvette and plunging into a dangerous island. But questioning the greedy decisions of a man like that is an endless torrent.

"I don't like it out here," says Edia, breaking a long silence. She had found a clean spot to sit and hug her knees into her chest.

"If anything comes out, we'll hop in the dinghy and push off," I say. It's a failed attempt to comfort her, but I know she's less scared than myself. She always is.

She stretches out her legs and kicks at the sand. Her foot catches on something there. She plucks it from the grit and raises it toward the torchlight.

"What is that?"

"Just a rusty piece of metal."

I recognize it. "That's a cutlass. I saw it in one of those books at Sal's place. A kind of sword." I delicately take hold of it and clean the mud off. The brittle weapon falls apart. "It must be ancient."

Boredom and intrigue makes a fervent mix inside me. I walk around the beach waving the torch around to spot more metallic glints. Seeing one, I rush over to unbury the relic. My hand sieves the sand to reveal something newer, shinier. A coin. Digging around, I find a couple more.

"Are you glittergrabbing?" scoffs Edia.

I straighten myself up and brush off sand. Embarrassed, I stutter, "No, I'm just… curious. What do you make of these?" I hand over the coins.

She turns one over in her hand. Perplexed, she asks, "I thought no one has ever been here except for Shadir and his crew fifty-somethin' years ago."

"That's what I've been told."

"This is a gold coin from the Iveln Isle—a nation that used to be an anarchy and became a monarchy just thirty years ago. This coin has the face of a king on it. Other people have been here since."

"Strange," I say, pondering. "What do you know about this place? What has Rubias told you?"

She thinks for a second. "I know she lied to the crew about why we were searching for it. She told me I couldn't tell them. Said something on the island had to be destroyed, but wouldn't tell me what it was. A lot of gold and monsters. Honestly, I never cared all that much. Seemed like a dead-end fantasy until we received that message about you."

"That's about as much as I got too before I stole the journal. So she entrusted us with that information, but she wouldn't tell us what this thing is?"

"She assumed it would be dangerous for anyone to know the specific details. Clearly she was right, because now look at us. Under Pé's boot."

Feels like pieces gathered in a pile but not together. Evidence. Events. Legends. Like a historical puzzle box. Visualize it. Every moment. Every player in the game. Like all other problems, think around, not through. It's here, rolling around in my brain. It's…

"…a trap," I say, with a vague awareness of what I actually mean. It feels right. It's a trap for us to be here. But why? How?

A rustle of leaves and a splash of water steals our attention. To our right, something prowls. The flare machine is out of reach. All I wield is the torch.

A crackle of gunfire fills the air. My ears are fooled on the direction, but it's distant.

I refocus on the beast in the dark, now silently waiting for its chance to pounce. I won't let it. I run forward, screaming, waving my torch back and forth in an attempt to scare it off. But instead, it challenges my bluff and emerges.

"Keep your voice down!" says the beast.

I step back with my torch still outstretched. "Shadir?"

His face is gently illuminated. "Yes. Be quiet. The creatures on this island respond to noise. And you're making yourself sound like an easy snack."

A few others from our crew exit the brush as well—Noctis, Gridda, and Piston. Each have barrels strapped to their backs.

Edia says, "What happened to you?"

I add, "Why did you make yourself a target?"

Shadir smiles. "I needed to get shot. We were in snag. I had to stay behind to free our crew from Pé. After healing, I latched on to Pé's quarvette and snuck aboard. After you lot disembarked, I stealthily distributed weapons and we took control of the ship. I got these three to join me on the second dinghy. We landed just over there. The others?"

Edia answers, "They went off into the jungle some time ago."

"Then we have to catch up. They're not ready for what's in there."

"What is it?" I ask.

"I can't say. It's too dangerous."

"No. Enough with that! We're here now. We're already in danger."

Shadir pulls on my clothes, put his hand over my mouth, and whispers, "I just can't. We don't have time. Let's go."

I show Shadir the flare machine and he straps it on before we all dive into the jungle.

Our hasty ascent is pitch black with the occasional flash from the flare machine to light up the area like lightning strikes. In those fractions of time, we see the black fur of felines in the trees. It works wonders. The growling lurchpurr soon disperse as they leave to find prey more accepting of their place in the food chain.

I can hear one of Pé's crew say, "Who's coming up behind us?"

We caught up. They see our torches, but they can't fully discern who we are.

Pé emits a dissatisfied grunt. "I told them to wait for a couple hours before following us up."

Behind him comes a crunching sound followed by a splash. They all turn to find nothing but blood and pieces of a flare machine.

"That wasn't from a lurchpurr," says Rubias.

Tango signs, *Bigger.*

Pé orders, "Run back to those torches! We'll group together and fend off this beast."

They all sprint toward us, flare machine blazing—producing still images of an empty jungle. The strangest thing about the island is the silence. No insects buzzing, no birds chirping, and no rodents skittering about. But we know it's teeming with life. This place created the ultimate silent predators. And the apex just snatched a second one of Pé's crew.

Pé fires blindly at the creature. Noctis and Gridda take a couple shots too, but it's like shooting into a void.

"Help!" screams Pé's third and final ally, but they are scooped up, engulfed beyond our light, and returned as half a torso with the flare machine still attached and intact.

Rubias retrieves the machine and flashes it, showing a brief glimpse of trees and insects but nothing else. It's too quick.

When our two groups finally meet, Pé is horrified in a different way when he discovers we're not his crew.

"What have you done?" Pé raises his weapon to Shadir's face.

"You already tried that once," whispers the immortal man. Pé doesn't understand, but knows he's outnumbered. He doesn't struggle when Shadir takes the pistol.

"What's going on?" Rubias asks a little too loudly.

Shadir covers her mouth, and whispers, "They hear everything."

We wait in the cold dark for a plan to blossom.

Pé sees the barrels on the backs of our crew and loudly asks, "Are those for gold?"

Near him, Noctis is snatched up in the jaws of the beast. His flailing legs knock Pé to the ground. With one selfless final thought, Noctis shoots the keg on his own back. The explosion, although blinding, momentarily reveals saurian skin and reptilian features. The megafauna slumps to the ground. The force of the explosion was enough to kill it. Torches reveal a beast that had two heads before the explosion reduced it to one.

Rubias covers her mouth with a shaking hand as she sees the remains of both the beast and Noctis.

"Gunpowder keg?" Edia asks. She's trying to avoid looking at the gore spread across the jungle undergrowth.

Shadir says, "Yes."

"Is this what you had to kill?" I ask, hoping to get off this island as soon as possible.

He simply answers, "No," and continues on up the slope.

THE GOLDSIRE

The sun is rising when we finally reach the ruins of a temple near the summit. So much walking burns my legs and lungs. We didn't bring fresh water, so we look around for any kind of puddle that might be clear enough to drink from.

Shadir pauses at the crumbled entrance—a stone arch with moss and vines filling every crack. "This is it," he claims.

"Then let's go," urges Pé.

Rubias points a pistol at him. "You're no longer in charge here."

Pé responds, "Well we all want to go in there. Why is he waiting?"

"This quest isn't what you think it is. You had to go and nearly ruin it." Rubias looks over each one of us as she makes a decision. "I want everyone except for Shadir and I to stay here. We'll go in alone."

Our crew and Pé are confused by this suggestion. They still think we're here for treasure.

Edia snips, "What are you talking about, captain? I didn't do all that hiking for nothin'."

Gridda and Piston express their concerns with this idea as well.

Tango signs, *What is this about?*

She says, "I can't lose any more of you. I've sacrificed too much. Going any farther is too dangerous."

Gridda asks, "We've passed the dangerous part. What else could there be besides treasure?"

Rubias hesitates. I signal for her to tell us. We need to know the truth about what lies ahead. She forms a word with her mouth but can't force it out. Instead, she begs, "I need you to stay here, at least until we know the coast is clear."

Tango signs, *Coming with you,* and the others all agree.

Pé mocks, "Oh this is getting ridiculous. Sniveling over the lives of expendables? We're all going in and there's nothing you can do about it."

Rubias rescinds her argument.

"Let's get this over with," says Shadir. "And when we're inside, don't drink the water."

We enter the ruins single file, leaving the two flare machines by the arch. There isn't much to be amazed at. I expected artifacts of some kind from what I saw in the book I accidentally took from Sal's place. There are no broken-down generators or vehicles. No homes. No remains at all. Just stone. Stone plinths, walkways, pillars, and the arch—all overrun by wildlife.

The focal point where Shadir takes us is the entrance to a cave blocked by a large, metallic door. Part of it had been blown open. He enters the hole in the door, followed by Rubias, Pé, and the others. I enter last. The door is half a brick thick, and within the broken portion are frayed wires. It was once a mechanized door.

There's more evidence of the Arwellians deeper into the dark corridors. Littering the floor are more swords, tools, and other items I can't make out. Some look like they might be weapons, and others like mechanical armor. Or perhaps tools for farming and building.

Catching the eyes of the pirates is all the gold. They keep pausing to pick something up to inspect it. Coins, jewelry, crowns, wires, or chunks of it—scattered along the corridor and leading us to more. They rub the grime off the pieces with giddy anticipation.

Edia slips over to my side. "Look at these." She hands me some coins of all different shapes and sizes. "These are all modern, minted within this Star Koi calendar."

Even closer to our time than the coins on the beach.

I whisper, "Many people have been here, and some recently. Yet there is no knowledge of this place. No stories. No historical accounts. Nothing."

"Because no one has ever returned from here?"

"No, I don't think that's it. We would've seen abandoned ships or wreckage. It's because no one is physically capable of talking about it. Like Shadir and Rubias, they talk around it or avoid it completely."

"What can force people to stop talking about something?"

I don't know, but anything that can is as dangerous as Rubias fears.

Everyone has gone so far ahead I can no longer see them. I'm too slow with my peg leg. Edia helps me run to catch up. I hobble forward with her keeping me from tripping. There is a slight decline of the corridor, and it is more clear as we continue down that this place was once a natural cave which the Arwellians took over. There are trickles of water nearby, dripping off the ceilings or running down the walls.

We catch up to the others because they've stopped in a widened portion of the cavern. Something has netted their attention, widening their eyes and dropping their jaws. Shining back our torchlight are waves of gold. Coins. Crowns. Medallions. Nuggets. Anything one could imagine. The strangest thing about it all is the lack of anything else besides gold. No gemstones or silver or copper. It is gold and only gold.

Gridda puts her keg down and lies in it. Piston scoops up a handful and bites a piece to make sure it's real. Both of them are grinning from ear to ear. Even Pé seems to delight in this discovery, but also recognizes this moment of distraction as a way to escape. He takes small steps away from the group. Tango doesn't touch anything, but looks around in shock that this kind of place exists. Shadir and Rubias look for signs of something else.

I walk near them and ask, "Where is it?"

They don't answer because they don't know.

As Pé tries to slip away unseen, a growling wind stops him. Coins fall from an unknown height and tumble down the glittering slopes to Pé's feet. He backs away. A clawed, hairy hand smashes down directly in front of him. He yips and stumbles backward. Those fingers retreat into the darkness, scraping through ground and gold as it slithers away. Grunts and growls echo through the chamber.

We're not alone in this cavern.

A deep, rumbling voice vibrates the air. "I'd like to thank this bountiful feast for bringing itself to me."

Orbs of light flutter from a single source and float around the cavern, giving every corner visibility. In the dark, the cave felt infinite; in the light, it is much more confining. The lights illuminate the back wall of the cavern. With each orb comes a new limb of the beast uncovered. Two large feet, one sunk deep in the mud and another in gold—and four wriggling toes on each. Hairy arms and hands with fingernails like claws. Upon a throne of gold and stone it sits, hairy and colossal like the giant Ape Queen of legend. Atop its head is a crown of crooked horns. Yellow eyes dart, peering at each of our faces. Its back is connected to the walls with fleshy tendrils as if the creature is a part of the cave itself.

"What is that thing?" screams Pé.

The beast chuckles like an amused human. It says, "I am the father of your greed, the voice of your misdeeds, and the one who rules over you. I am the Goldsire."

That name. I read it in Desja's journal. I couldn't comprehend it at the time, but it is the name of the creature we have been looking for all along. This is what Rubias and Shadir hid from us. This is the danger they're so afraid of. But what is it?

Shadir notices the score in the gold and mud where the creature attacked Pé. He warns us, "Don't go past that mark. It can't reach us."

It can't move any farther than that without ripping itself off the wall.

"Welcome back, Shadir," grumbles the Goldsire. "I've been expecting you."

Shadir yells, "We've come to destroy you."

"You think that's what you've come to do. Part of my plan, it was." Humans smile when we're happy, but I think this thing smiles when it's hungry. Those two rows of teeth remind me of a shark's mouth.

"You're lying," says Shadir.

It laughs. "I play a part in every decision you make. You, them, everyone. Every poor decision, every mistake. I am inside your head."

A claw reaches into the piles of gold, pulls out a fistful, and chucks it at us. We're pelted by coins and nuggets, and after it settles we notice some of it squirms. Around our feet are small, golden things moving like worms. Along their backs are something akin to feathers dipped in a liquid gold. Shadir steps on one, splattering the ground with a rusty brown smear.

"Come to me," says the rumbling voice of the Goldsire. Each of the worms crawl and burrow back into the pile toward the beast. "You see, they obey my every command through telepathy. My endless days here have been fruitful in evolving these beings to my liking. The queen worm is in here." It points at its head, insinuating something inside its brain. "It feeds off me while I use its telepathic abilities to persuade the minds infected by its offspring." The clawed finger moves to point at us.

"A load of chum!" spits Rubias. "Even if you're telling the truth, how could you have infected everyone? We're spread out across the ocean."

"Ah... The offspring of Desja Rubias. Welcome." The Goldsire cherishes this moment. It enjoys praising itself, and finally has an audience to do that. It continues, "Before you humans existed, there were my kind ruling this land. Roaming, not fixed in place like I am now. I used to be an alchemist, one who tampers with the elements of the planet to create new ones. While I wasted away in here after the extinction of my species, I learned of a rising kind. Humans. They built their temple around me, and used me as their oracle. I found much joy in manipulating them. But after some time, many eras for you, they stopped coming. Abandoned me. Whether or not it was the flood that caused this change I am unsure."

Tango signs something to Rubias. She responds, but says nothing aloud. To distract the Goldsire from this fact, she interrupts its story. "You sure like to talk about yourself, don't you? But I'm not buyin' what you're sellin'. Prove it."

It reveals silvery grey stones on its palms. When it closes and reopens its grip, the stones are replaced with gold. But this is no sleight-of-hand.

He transformed those stones into it through real magic.

It continues, "Gold did not exist on this planet a few thousand years ago. Even before the floods. You humans traded with other metals, gemstones, jade. I transmuted the lead that lines these walls. I knew your greedy little paws could not help but take something like gold and make it a commodity. This shiny, intriguing thing.

"I placed these worm eggs within the gold pores. Within days of finding me on this island, human sailors were infected. You humans are so predisposed to pitiful desires. The greedy. The corrupt. The selfish. The obsessed. These are the easiest to manipulate... amplify... control. Mere suggestion in the minds of your leaders created the treasury. The perfect breeding ground for my influence."

"I've had enough of this nonsense," yells Pé. He steps over to be in the creature's line of sight. "You talk of manipulation and mind control. I don't believe it. Why are you still here, trapped, if you could've manipulated people to come free you? If we're under your control, why couldn't you stop the treasury from being robbed by pirates?" He takes another step forward.

Those people in the treasury, the bankers, acted like they were under control like a hive mind. They warned us about someone waiting for us. The Goldsire controls them from this distance. Could he have stopped us if he wanted?

It responds, "I am not trapped here. The planet sustains me. I do not live off of oxygen and water as you do. Therefore, this planet is not yet ripe for me."

I move between Shadir and Rubias to tell them, "He let us leave the treasury alive. He wanted us here."

Pé steps closer, and replies, "If you can control humans, why haven't you become the sole king of us? Because you can't. This is a braggadocio ploy!"

The Goldsire raises its voice—an earsplitting sound in this small cave. "I do not wish to be ruler of you pathetic creatures! You are an experiment. Someday, the planet will get rid of you, and my people will come out from the shadows. When that time comes, I will use what I've learned to control my own kind. I will be *their* king. Why would I be the king of bugs if I can be the king of gods?"

"Pé," says Rubias, but he ignores it and steps forward once again.

"Do you still not believe me?" asks the Goldsire.

"I am not scared of you," Pé responds with a snort. "I am outside of your reach. Outside of your control."

"My manipulations are subtle. A handshake. A prejudice. A gamble. Or even a few steps forward."

Pé's eyes widen as he looks down. He's across the line which marks the

Goldsire's reach. He turns to scramble away, but a clawed hand swoops down and brings the pirate to the mouth of the beast. I turn away but can hear the crunching of bone and gnashing of teeth. After swallowing a few bites, it releases a satisfied, steamy breath throughout the cavern. The fishy, metallic stench makes the air unbreathable for a few seconds. Our scrunched faces give the Goldsire a hearty chuckle.

"Who's next?" asks the beast to the feast.

There is a slight twitch in my muscles, and a sudden desire to get closer. It isn't much at all, not even a thought. More like muscle memory, or a subconscious reaction. If I wasn't looking out for it I wouldn't have noticed. But considering what we just saw, I know to ignore all of my emotions right now. Every action I make is questionable. Should I run, or does it want that? Should I try to come up with a plan, or stand still? No doubt the others are wondering the same. They're similarly paralyzed. This whole journey was forced by the Goldsire. We thought we were coming here to destroy it, but it wanted us to come.

Shadir adapts to this new reality. In a manner like acceptance of defeat, he asks, "What do you want from us? Why'd you bring us here?"

"The magic I put on you. I wanted to see its progression. You, Shadir, are still alive. That was successful. And the boy." It means me. Why? "What did I give your grandfather? I believe I called it *transference*. He could infuse objects with traits taken from other objects. Seems unlikely my magic was hereditary. Perhaps a few alterations are to be made. I'll need your bodies to study. The rest of you will be made into new experiments. How exciting. I've had time to think of new ones. I hope you're thirsty."

From my position, I can see Edia, Gridda, and Piston moving toward puddles of water with cupped hands. They can't stop themselves. He's forcing them to drink the water. Triggering their bodies to feel like they're dying of thirst. We're animals at the mercy of natural instincts.

"I will not let that happen!" yells Rubias. She points her pistol at the creature. Her trigger finger doesn't move. She's frozen until the tip of the pistol moves backward to her own chin.

"Stop," I yell. I hobble forward past the line where it could reach. "Let them go. I'll be your experiment."

Shadir yells, "Archie, no!"

"Do whatever you need to me, but let them go."

"Brave human," chuckles the beast. Its giant hand wraps around me. Its skin feels like sandpaper. I hold on to its knuckle hair as I am lifted much too close to its mouth. The stench of blood still lingers on its steamy breath. Fanged teeth are cleaned by a slithering, forked tongue. "I don't think I'll accept your proposition."

A giant thumb presses into my chest. Its grip tightens, lightens enough for me to breathe, and then tightens again. Every one of my joints are in pain while bones rub together and bend in wrong ways. The other hand plucks off both of my wooden arm.

"What ingenuity," the Goldsire mocks, and picks its teeth with it. After it gets a sliver of Pé out from between those fangs, it bends and snaps it between two fingers. Then it takes off the peg leg too, and flicks it away. "I can give you your real limbs back. Would you like to try that?"

The desire to be whole again is tempting, but I know the manner in which it would be done is nothing short of terrible. My defiance manifests as, "No. You will not control me. I am not your prey. And some day, someone will come to kill you. They'll succeed where we have failed."

"But what about your worth? Don't you want to feel valuable to them? Don't you want to be of use? I can make that happen. Be my emissary and spread my gospel, and you will regain your limbs."

I do. I want it. This could be what I've—

"Get out of my head, you rusty bastard!"

It lays me down right in front of its feet in the piles of gold. The tug in my brain is stronger. It wants me to do something. Beg, grovel, dance, kneel, cry, praise, run. With difficulty, I fight through each impulse successfully. I squirm and crawl away, but the uneven terrain is difficult with two limbs.

"Look at this one," says the Goldsire. "Strong-willed. More so than I've ever seen. Very well. You will not leave here alive. I wouldn't want you to pass on this evolutionary trait to offspring."

I keep up my resistance. Once again, those hairy fingers reach for me, but they stop short.

Chik, chik, chik.

The slapping of rock against rock reverberates around the room. The Goldsire looks at each of those in front of him. No one moves. Gridda, Edia, and Piston have all paused at their chosen source of water.

Chik, chik, chik.

"What is that?" it asks, searching the cavern for the echoing sound. Rubias still has her pistol at her chin. Shadir fights the impulses running through him.

Chik, chik, chik.

It soon finds the source at its side. Behind the throne there is a gap where more skin is attached to the cave wall. In that gap is a mute man slapping two stones together. The Goldsire looks at the barrel Tango hovers over.

It's one of the gunpowder kegs.

When the creature realizes what Tango is doing, it reaches around to grab the man who is somehow immune to the telepathy. His aversion to greed created the perfect blind spot in the Goldsire's plan. Tango gives the stones one last powerful strike.

"Tango!" yells Rubias. The distraction loosens the mental hold on her and she stumbles forward.

Chik.

There's a somber smile on Tango's face as the sparks ignite the gunpowder.

The eruption takes out a chunk of the throne, tears into the Goldsire's hip, and blows away its incoming left hand that nearly stopped it all. What follows is a multi-tonal moan from the Goldsire. Its feet moves for the first time in ages, heaving forward a mound of soil and gold, and pushing me away. It rips away from the cavern wall and falls to hand and knees. Ichor sputters from its spine. The mixture of putrid colors spilling from the organs in the wall spread like spilled paint. When the Goldsire's eyes open, it sees me underneath and in biting range.

A scream of agony exits its putrid mouth—this time something more akin to human. But that is short-lived. The yellow darting eyes turn frantic as it decides to eat me and rampage against the others.

Rubias yells, "Get out of the way, Archie!" She's points her pistol at the Goldsire.

There's another gunpowder barrel a plank away from me. The others must've thrown it into position. But I can't move. Shadir grabs hold and pulls me back, offering a defensive arm against the beast's incoming maw. A quick bite tears his arm away. Shadir, in a pain I understand all too well, wrenches me backward until we tumble down the dunes of fortune. As we slide down, the gold cascades over us as we curl into fetal positions. Rubias fires. I feel the explosive jolt before the heat. The gold offers some protection, but Shadir's back takes a lot of the impact. We're propelled out of the warped coins and trinkets onto the muddy cavern ground in front of Edia. She and Rubias help us up. I look back to see a slack-jawed giant clawing the ceiling and tearing at the walls in dying agony. All around us, the cavern walls crack and crumble.

"We're going to be caved in," says Edia, running ahead with the others.

Rubias and Shadir support me to hobble into the corridor.

"Go without me," I demand.

"Never," says Shadir.

I don't plead. I just try my best to go faster. Shadir's back and arm slowly heals, giving him more strength. Behind us, the walls crumble over the body of the Goldsire. The cave-in follows us through the tunnel. I can feel it in my bones, like the planet itself cracks.

"We're not going to make it!" yells Shadir.

We're nearing the door, but the corridor is crumbling above us.

"Throw him!" yells Rubias. It's a sacrificial move.

Together, before I have time to protest, they heave my light body forward. I land on the mossy stone outside, and I turn as quickly as possible to look back into the tunnel. A plume of dust billows out of the mountain. It's thick, but eventually clears.

Edia sticks her torch through the wired door.

In that soft light, bodies… gently moving, and coughing. They're alive. The cave-in settled just before cascading over Shadir and Rubias.

It takes us quite a bit of time to reach the ship. During which, we're too overcome with disbelief and shock to speak about what happened. And we grieved the loss of Tango. His sacrifice saved the rest of us. Gridda and Piston have urgent questions about it all, but Rubias promises to share everything at once with the rest of the crew.

Pé's quarvette was successfully taken earlier, so that at least is taken care of. There are too many of Pé's followers to be put in the brig, so they were tied up and are under guard.

Rubias turns to Shadir, who is helping me aboard from the dinghy, and asks, "Your doing?"

Shadir shrugs nonchalantly. "Pé had the numbers, but his crew didn't amount to anything when caught unawares."

Rubias is stunned with relief. For the first time in our journey, she gives a sincere look of admiration to Shadir.

He adds, "But we're not off the hook yet. We still have to get the rest of the crew on the *Empress*."

We make a plan to take control the other two ships waiting outside of the island wall. But no one is confident it can be done, especially not without losing more people. The plan is to make a hostage deal. All of Pé's crew for ours. Then everyone goes their separate way. To sweeten the deal, we can lie and say we still have a captured Pé in the brig, and threaten to only let him out once the rest of the transaction has been made. There are so many ways it can go wrong, but the only other option ends up with our bodies dyeing the ocean red.

We sail the quarvette back through the murky lagoon and steadily through the limestone stacks. Both the *Prey Empress* and the *Carn o' War* are positioned on either side of the exit with gungills ready to unleash on both flanks.

Rifles and pistols are immediately drawn against us, prompting our crew to draw their weapons in spite of Rubias telling everyone to stand down. Between the three ships, dozens of armed pirates yell at one another to put weapons down. Not one person fires a shot, but they're about to. Fingers are quivering on triggers.

"Captain?" I hear someone say on the *Carn o' War*. "Wait! Everyone stop! Lay down weapons!"

The three ships slowly do so.

The man who ordered it steps up on the banister—Aldrezier. At this point I realize the people holding the rifles and pistols against us are our own on both ships.

"What is happening?" shouts Rubias.

Aldrezier says, "I led the effort to reclaim the ships. Thought you might've been killed. We were ready send Pé to the ocean floor. You?"

"Pé's gone. We took over this ship."

"You're daft coming out slingin' pistols like that. We were about to kill ya!"

"Not if we had killed you first!"

Aldrezier laughs. We take a breath and then join in. And the three ships cheer for this triumph. Barring another sea creature attack, there will be no more loss of crew for the foreseeable future.

When Rubias helps me cross over to the *Prey Empress* on a thin plank, she says, "I think you owe me five gold coins."

I had completely forgotten about the bet. With everything on the line, Aldrezier came through. With certainty I made that bet, and so greatly did I lose it that I couldn't help but burst into laughter. Teetering on this thin plank over a dangerous sea, I can't stop myself to the point of tears. The wobbling nearly sends me below, but Rubias manages to hold me still and guide me across.

The captain is met with a barrage of questions from the crew—mostly about the fortune they were promised.

"There was gold," says Rubias. "Mounds of it." This got a cheer, until she continues. "But it was in a cave that collapsed."

"Then we go in and unbury it," says the stormseer. Ominix the cat is perched on his shoulder and gives an uncaring yawn.

"No. This island is dangerous. Too dangerous to be worth the risk."

"We're rusted pirates!" yells another. "We can handle it. We've come all this way."

She struggles to reveal the truth. Her mouth opens, but nothings comes out. For a moment, I worry the Goldsire's power still holds. She still can't force herself to make the revelation.

"Listen! All of Pé's crew, and himself, and... Tango and Noctis were all slain by the beasts of the island." The excitable air becomes stale after that. It's chilling news. Rubias waits for them to settle. "I've failed you all. I've failed those we lost. Because of what I've done, I don't deserve any of your trust."

Her head lulls with the weight of the grief that is finally hitting her all at once. It spreads through the crew.

After taking a moment to compose herself, she continues, "But I will fail you no longer. Listen closely. For now is the time I must tell you about Desja Rubias and the Goldsire."

And so she weaves her tale. Desja was a farmer who had dreams of being an archaeologist. With luck, he was employed by Shadir and Gilligan to discover the undiscovered out in the uncharted ocean. After facing similar threats to ours, they found the island and the Goldsire, drank the tainted water, and returned home.

Rubias sighs, relieved to have shared it all after so many years. "Today was the culmination of my entire life. I succeeded in my quest, and yet, it was so hollow because of what I sacrificed to do it. All Tango ever wanted was to be a captain of his own ship in my fleet. I thought he couldn't handle it because he was mute. He proved me wrong countless times, but I put my needs first and that anchored him. He sacrificed himself to complete my life, knowing it to be the end of his. So many others too. They put my need ahead of their own, and I abused that. It got them killed. I'm..." I don't think the crew has ever seen her cry before. They get teary eyed with her. "I'm so deeply sorry."

Some came to pat her on the shoulder or back. Others stayed back, wiping their wet cheeks.

Rubias changes her composure altogether. In a second, she warps back to a semblance of the woman I met many months ago. Steadfast and true, she says, "Your deck chief would not have wanted any of you to proceed onto the island. So we won't. But I promised you wealth. I will not break that promise. Pé Dutanté, the *great treasure hoarder*, is no longer alive. Any lesser pirate would assume his mass of wealth is lost forever. But I am Isadora Rubias, captain of the greatest crew on this planet. And I'll lead you all straight to his hoard, where you'll have your chests filled to the brim. No risk. All reward."

THE RAID

At the bow of the *Prey Mantas*, I look upon the harbor. Rubias and Shadir are next to me, armed.

"I don't know how I feel about this, Archie," says Shadir. "This isn't really what I had in mind when I said to make it a home."

I say, "It's what needs to be done," and wonder if I've picked up the wrong lessons from Rubias. I understand his hesitancy, but it's happening. "It is unguarded and vulnerable. If you disagree with this raid, hide in the captain's quarters until it's over."

Shadir stays, even as the flag is raised on the mast. The one indicating we are pirates. The flag of the Blackscabbard Fleet. And underneath it, a triangular flag with the depiction of a single boot. Around the archipelago, the same fleet flag is being raised on two dozen ships sailing into every major port of Tyro Archipelago. All imports and exports will be halted immediately. The *Prey Empress* circles the islands, watching for major opposing forces, such as Kingsguild or bounty hunters. But seeing the size of the force that we brought, even they won't see the benefit in assisting. This raid will commence.

The docks are fairly empty. We're able to anchor down in the Port of Krakau and lay the loading ramp without other vessels being an issue. I had sent word to Grifton ahead of time to make sure there was no panic among the people. We don't want the warning bells being raised or the charter barons will scurry like rats.

"What is that smell?" Rubias asks, scrunching her nose as we're coming down the ramp.

"The smell of home," I say fondly. Then the actual smell hits me. "Oh, actually that'd be the Obitzu Bayou."

Grifton bobs into view, with his single rope of hair bouncing around his shoulders.

"Archie!" he yells, bounding up to me and lifting me off the ground in such a large embrace. He puts me down carefully after noticing my arm and leg. "Your letters didn't mention this. What in the name of Bloody Baldeva happened to ya?"

"What didn't happen to him?" says Rubias. She embraces the man next—old friends meeting again after so long.

Grifton moves on to greet Edia who came down the ramp with a crate filled with some delicate materials.

"So the Artisan Pirate, eh? That's what they're calling you?" he asks me.

"Just a silly moniker I picked up," I casually deflect. Still not sure how I feel about that getting around. "And Krakau?" I ask, looking past him to the stores and houses. Some people are hesitantly watching from their doors.

Grifton says, "They know you're coming. I've spread word to every port across the archipelago."

I turn to the six crewmates still waiting on the ship. After giving them the signal, they come down the ramp. "Keep your weapons hidden," I remind them.

Through the Scarlet Muck and up the lane we march. The Krakau folk recognize me, but they're still surprised. They whisper and gossip, but no one runs or hides. I see the beggar girl who I protected from the charter barons before being taken by pirates. She's with a group of villeins who are getting their stilts and basket-scythes prepared for the day. She's a year older since the last time I saw her, but still way too young to be going into the bayou to work. I dig around in a pouch on my bandersheef and pull out a gold coin, which I fling to her. To the rest of the villeins, I suggest they stop and follow, and my crew drops coppercuts as we march farther up the lane to entice others. The citizens begin to crowd the lane, picking up the coppercuts like chickens following a feed trail.

Word spreads, and nearly everyone in Krakau follows us past the farms to the charter baron manor. The two-floor home has a balcony and a garden, and is surrounded by a wrought iron fence. At the gated entrance are two people with shotguns. I am unsure whether or not these are the same mercenaries who were here before.

We stop before them with the whole town lagging behind us. Confused, they raise their weapons slightly. Their eyes dart across each face.

I ask, "How much do they pay you?"

With an accent I can now recognize as Tontinian, one of them says, "One gold a day."

I unclip a pouch from the inside of my bucklecoat and toss it to him. "That's twenty gold for each of you to get lost."

The two look at each other, shrug, and then nod in agreement. They move around the crowd and head back to town. With the place now unguarded, the pirates and I push past the gate and encroach the manor while Shadir stays behind with Grifton to ensure people don't wander off. He doesn't tell them what our plan is, but makes sure to let them know they're not in danger.

Edia places down the crate she carried all this way. I nod to Rubias, who takes off the lid and passes out jars of oil. Everyone takes a fire bomb and lights their wicks on a lantern flame. When we're all in place, I give the signal.

The smell of oil and smoke spread through the air. The whoosh of thrown fire is followed by simultaneous breakage of glass as each fire bomb gets flung through a window of the manor. The flames crackle and spread up curtains and furniture before grabbing hold of the building's structural elements.

Two people rush out of the front door, one of them clutching a chest—Ozma—and the other coughing into a rag and cursing up a storm—Stellagard.

The latter yells, "You rusty bastards!" But the fury subsides into confusion when they see the rest of the town standing by.

Shadir and Grifton are still calming them down, telling them not to worry. But some are covering their mouths in shock, and others, I can't help but notice, are trying to hide their smiles.

Ozma yells, "What is this?" He puts down the chest and recognizes me. "*Archie?* What have you done? This is imbalance beyond belief."

"Clamp your tongue," I snap. Then I turn to the Krakau crowd. "The charter barons have been trying to make us cogs in a machine that produces a commodity off of which only they make money." I nudge the chest Ozma put on the ground, and ask, "What's in the chest?"

It's an ornate design, with brass straps and hinges and quartz inlays. He smirks, takes a key from his pocket and unlocks it. There is barely anything inside. Some coins, but not much. He says, "You see! Nothing but a dozen coppercuts after all your taxes are put to use. The charter laws and the bylaws of each island are carefully curated for balance and efficiency."

"Have you forgotten who I am?" I close the lid of the chest with my foot and flip the whole thing over so that the unassuming bottom is face up. There we find another key hole. The key Ozma has does not fit into it.

Stellagard steps forward, saying, "That is nothing but a mistake by the chestmaker!"

"This is a Salvatorre chest made by my father. It is no mistake."

I take out my lockpicking tools and get to work.

"This is an outrageous violation," she protests, and moves to do something about it but is met with Rubias's pistol.

Meanwhile, the blaze from the fire bombs has spread to consume the entirety of the manor. We are far enough to be safe, but the heat is unrelenting. A bead of sweat drips off my brow.

The lock clicks and I swing the chest open to reveal the real hoard of money they were hiding—an overflowing pile of gold and silver coins and a roll of papers. I pull out a roll and unravel them. Every current villein contract is here along with their hidden wealth. Krakau folk stumble over one another just to get a look, and when they do, their rage spreads.

Holding up the contracts, I say to the crowd, "We are not tools to be used and abused. We are not product. We cannot be made efficient like a machine. Our inefficiencies… our imbalances, so to speak, are what makes us who we are."

Stellagard says, "This is a farce! The chestmaker has planted this—"

Ozma yells, "Mother, stop speaking for me! I can handle this." He takes a few steps closer to the enraged crowd so they can hear him over the roar of the fire. "Whatever the case may be, Archie has invited chaos to overrule you. Look at who he has aligned himself with. Pirates! He wants anarchy. Are you willing to let this place become a pirate haven? Are you willing to let them destroy everything you've worked hard to maintain?"

This piece does subdue them a little. They will still fear the idea of anarchy to their dying days. That had been deeply ingrained in them.

I cut in, "I do not plan to leave the island in the hands of pirates."

"The chestmaker plans to rule us himself!" yells Ozma.

I motion for Stellagard's attention. I point to Rubias and ask, "Do you recognize this woman? At the time, you would've known her by Captain Gildeye."

She yells, "This is the pirate who raided us eleven years ago." She thinks this information will be used against me. It does stir something in the crowd, but I can turn it around.

"And how did you two meet?"

"Well, I… We never—"

Rubias interjects, "This woman met with me on behalf of all the charter barons to make a deal. We sacked the island eleven years ago on her order. A deal I deeply regret, but clearly she doesn't."

Over the growing fervor in the crowd, Ozma asks, "How many more lies are you going to weave?"

"Anarchy!" Stellagard yells. "What do you want if not total imbalance of the island?"

I raise my hand to settle everyone. Surprisingly, they listen. I command their attention.

"All I want is to be a chestmaker. I've traveled far in this past year, and have seen many different ways of the world. Different paths. I know not which is right or fair or good, and I'm still just as confused as any of you. But I have learned some things." I take the villein contracts over to the flames and throw them in, making sure not a single one is recoverable. That's the sign for Rubias to march her crew away. Before following her, I say to the crowd, "I leave the rest to all of you. You have been given the information to make a fair decision as citizens of Tyro Archipelago. If what you desire is the same as before, you are welcome to make that choice. But it is my hope to see something new come out of this."

The manor crumbles into charred rubble as we leave.

Over the next couple of days, we visit every island in Tyro with the same offer. All but one island elects new charter barons. Right away, they begin crafting a new charter and bylaws. Their biggest concern is that their trade partners, mostly the Aronians, might come and invade the archipelago in this transition state. Rubias offers a couple of her ships as protection until something else can be conceived.

And so, my journey comes to an end.

Salvatorre's Cases, Coffers, and Chests (No Coffins). The sign is askew.

I stand outside of the place I once called home. The place I grew up in. The place my father grew up in—and my grandfather. Generations of us have lived here and yet now it feels too small.

Next to me, Grifton says, "Acting as Krakau's new charter baron, I can say it's yours if you want it."

After adjusting the strap which hangs my chest off my back, I enter and look around. The place had been trashed. The door is bent off the hinges. There are broken windows and shelves. And the Scarlet Muck was tracked all throughout the house. Grifton, Shadir, Rubias, and Edia enter behind me. The captain wanted to come see the shop for herself, but there isn't much now to look at.

"It's been picked clean," I say. "All the chests are gone." I take a look into my workroom. "Most of my tools are gone too."

Grifton, rubbing the back of his head, says, "Shortly after you disappeared, some people came and broke in. Took everything."

"The scammers," says Shadir. "Bastards couldn't find the money they lost, so they took everything else."

Grifton adds, "Charter barons did nothing to stop them. As far as they were concerned, it was less for them to clear out before they found someone else to live here. They never did. Who would want to move here just to be under a villein contract?" After a moment of silence, he asks, "You do still want it, right?"

Now all their eyes are on me. I look down to avoid the attention, and spot a button on the floor. I lean over to pick it up. It had come off the cuff that day. I rub its smooth surface.

Rubias still wants me to join her crew for good. I have chosen to forgive her for lying to me, and she made amends by lending me her fleet to liberate Tyro. I am grateful to have discovered the world, but my passion is being a chestmaker. I left to find a new home, but now I'm stuck deciding between two. She awaits my decision, but I suspect she already knows what I'm going to say before I do. She's cunning like that.

"I think…"

Edia snaps, "Speak up, driftwood. Can't hear you."

Louder, I say, "I think it's going to cost a lot to make this place a shop again." I take the chest strapped on my back and put it down on the counter. I unlock it and flip it open.

Grifton's eyes shine. He says, "How did you—"

"As I said, I've been through a lot." I dig through the pile of gold and silver and stack together an amount I think is more than satisfying.

It was a long way back, and much work to be done. After leaving the Arwellian ruin behind, we first stopped at the tribalist island decimated by Pé to help them rebuild. We gave them the *Carn o' War* to use as they pleased. Then we met up with the fully repaired *Prey Mantas* and took Pé's treasure, which was hidden on a small island not too far from the Tontine Isle. Half was distributed to the crew and the rest was given back to the Tontinians to lessen the impact of Pé's coup. We spread the news of the pirate hoarder's demise so that all bounty hunters knew there was nothing to gain for coming after us. I created more chests for the crew, and remade my limbs better than before. There were a couple snags on the journey back, but nothing quite as perilous on the flesh as before. And finally, I convinced Rubias to go far out of the way to Wickit's home island so that I could deliver the news and his chest with a part of my share inside.

So much of this treasure was spent or divided up or given away as we sailed back, but even after all of that, I still have plenty left over.

"Such a foolish thing to keep in chest," I say, holding a small amount of the leftover coins. "I can think of many things far more deserving of being treasured than this." I hand the small fortune over to Grifton. "Here. I hope this will cover the next couple of months of taxes, and maybe you could help me find some quality materials. I think I'll be sticking around."

Edia mocks, "Kind of a fixer-upper, isn't it? I say ditch it."

"As much as I would like to sail with you all, this is my home." Now knowing more about the world, I want to bring some of that here. The good parts, that is. Not the monstrous ones.

Embarrassed that her hidden meaning had been unraveled, she stutters, "That's not what I'm trying to say at all, driftwood!" She explores the kitchen area in the next room to hide her reddened face.

Grifton's shocked expression transforms into one of warm happiness. "Very well, young Salvatorre. You'll have to come by for a conch of coffee and tell me all about your travels."

"I will, but if I'm staying, I'll also need my favorite employee," I say. Shadir smirks. "This is his home too."

"Of course he can stay! Now, I'll be off to find those materials you need." The new charter baron, elected by the people of Krakau, bounds out of the shop.

Shadir says to Rubias, "Since you're here, mind giving us a hand?"

She nods, and the four of us begin the long process of cleaning the shop. A few neighbors passing by see this and offer to help. This inspires a few others to also join in, and after a few minutes, my home is filled with the neighbors I once feared helping replace my windows and fix my door and shelves. I try to pay everyone, but they decline. They are happy to do it free of charge.

After reclaiming my home, it's time for the pirates to leave. On the docks, we say goodbye to Edia and Rubias. We stand next to the *Prey Mantas* with its loading ramp down and its crew hard at work readying to set sail. Far off in the distance is the *Prey Empress* awaiting their captain's return.

Rubias says, "Archie, if you ever get bored of the land life, tell Grifton. He knows how to contact me."

"I will. Perhaps I'll hop aboard from time to time. See how a pirate's life is really like."

"Shadir… same offer doesn't apply to you."

He chuckles, and says, "Trust me, I'm fine with that."

She adds, "It's been a pleasure to have you on the *Prey Empress*. I don't think the ease-seats have ever looked as good." She laughs at her own jest, punctuated with a snort.

He says, "Well, I am an expert now," and laughs with her. Then he winks. What strange alternate realm have I crossed over into where these two get along? I'd be lying if I said I didn't picture them as a romantic couple for a fraction of a second, but that would've been a strange combination considering she's a pirate and twice his age. No, wait. He is twice her age. What a strange voyage this has been.

I turn to Edia. "Good luck with your apprenticeship. I'm sure you'll be a grand captain within the year."

Edia, clearly not adept at goodbyes, says with a straight face, "You need more varnish on your leg." With that, she walks up the loading ramp, but turns back for a split second to see if I looked down at my leg, which I did. She hides a smile.

Isadora Rubias puts something in my hand and closes my fingers around it before boarding the *Prey Mantas*. After they depart on their new voyage, I look at what she pressed into my palm. Shiny metal loops like rings. Her cherished nick-knucks. A wonderful gift from the most intriguing person I have ever known.

"How about an afternoon visit to the cemetower," Shadir suggests.

"I'd like that."

So we make that venture, and while Shadir visits my grandfather's plot, I visit my father for the first time in a long while. Even though I know he's not really there, and can't hear me, it is lethargic being able to share the tale about my trip with pirates to strange islands. It feels weird to do this knowing how much he'd object if he were alive. He would faint at the sight of me. But perhaps he'd also be proud of me for bringing back some semblance of the island he once knew and loved.

Shadir finds me cross-legged on the ground and finishing my story.

I ask, "Were you able to say what you needed to say this time?"

He nods.

"Then let's go home." I hop to my feet and dust myself off, but before we go down the stairs, I turn back and say to my father, "I'm going to become the greatest chestmaker in the world."

EPILOGUE

There is an update in the newspaper regarding the five-army standoff surrounding the Central Maritime Treasury. Apparently a pirate fleet has joined the fray to lay claim to it. This pirate captain claims to have the Goddess Doubloon and thinks that is some kind of indicator of having ownership on the CMT. What a mess we've made.

The door chimes.

"Where my chesh a'?" spouts the crooked mouth on a man much bigger than me—as usual.

"It's right here. Just finished polishing the wood for you," I say, putting the newspaper down. It's a smaller chest like a puzzle box. A lot of work and pride gets put into something like this. "That'll be forty coppercuts. Or thirty coppercuts and fifty nickelcuts. Or—"

"Too expenshive." His speech is slurred like a drunkard, although he doesn't seem to have had a drink. Maybe he's lost one too many fights.

"I charge what I'm worth."

"Don't you know me, boy?" He giggles while a waterfall of drool falls off his bottom lip.

I look him up and down. "I don't know who you are, but I do know you." The kind of person who doesn't pay up.

"They ca' me Chumface. Tuffesht fighter in the Aronian colisheum."

He takes the chest straight out of my hands and meets me eye to eye. I avert my gaze. He kicks my wooden leg, and I buckle.

"Too eashy," he says, turning his back to me.

I slip my hand into my pocket and retrieve a small tube. I place something in one end, aim, and blow. The dart whistles to its target, puncturing the man's neck and injecting him with a strong dose of sleep venom from the Obitzu Bayou toads. He falls face first, but I doubt he'll notice any difference when he wakes in a few hours.

"Shadir!" I yell.

He sprints up from the cellar and groans. "Another one?"

I shrug. "My chests are highly sought, even among the unsavory."

He turns the man over. "What did you do to him? Did you use the nick-knucks?"

"He came in like that. They call him Chumface," I say, mockingly.

"Ah. Heard of him. I'll barrow him down to the charter baron office. Maybe there's an extradition reward out for him somewhere." He leaves to get the wheelbarrow.

On the floor is a new track of mud. I find the broom and sweep it out the front door.

AFTERWORD

Thank you for reading my debut novel, *The Chestmaker*. I've worked on this for quite some time now. I have notes about an "artisan pirate" story dating back to 2017. I was inspired by many things. *Sea of Thieves, One Piece, Pirates of the Caribbean, Treasure Island…* I can't exactly pinpoint one major influence. However, I can say I began actually writing it as an experiment of sorts.

It started during my time getting a teaching degree; this was sometime in or around 2020. At some point, an assignment gave me an idea. This idea was to write the same story told in two different genres: pirate fantasy and space opera. The former became *The Chestmaker*, and the latter became something I have tentatively titled *Celestial Bonfire*. Both would be traveling adventures where the characters can experience different cultures or dangerous places and use their expertise to help along the way. I wrote a scene of each to test it out, and got a positive reaction from others.

At first it was going to be two novellas in one book, but as this story was revised, I realized how much more I needed to flesh out the world and characters. Thus, *The Chestmaker* grew past the point of novella. Then I hit a wall with my writing, and shelved both projects for some time. It wasn't until after I got my Master's in Publishing that I thought this book could be my first published novel. But I had to finish editing it, and so went on that arduous journey again. I even wrote a short story prequel for Archie, which got an honorable mention in the Writers of the Future contest.

The other story, *Celestial Bonfire*, which I hope to release someday, is about a young woman around Archie's age who finds a hidden cryogenic freezer on the rundown space station that she reluctantly calls home. I challenged myself to figure out how the plot in *The Chestmaker* could be transferred into my favorite genre—space opera. Islands equal planets. Pirates equal space pirates. The great flooding of the world equals the heat death of the universe. And so on…

I had so much fun with this kind of thinking, and I believe many writers out there can benefit from this experimental writing exercise. I've also considered translating it into a weird west style novel, but I'm not 100% sure that will actually get done. I've already got so many other ideas to try out.

So if you enjoyed *The Chestmaker*, keep an eye out not just for potential sequels and short stories, but also for its spiritual twin. And thank you for braving the seas with me and Archie.

J. L. Smyser

(Stay tuned for a 'post-film' interview with the cast of *The Chestmaker*.)

CAST INTERVIEW TRANSCRIPTION

Interviewer: Welcome, I am here with some members of the cast of *The Chestmaker*. We have here: Archie, Isadora, Shadir, Edia, and Ozma (who also played the Goldsire). Very excited to see you all. Thanks for sitting down with me today.

Isadora: Pleasure to be here.

Archie: Thanks for having us.

Interviewer: We did ask Tango to join as well, but unfortunately he is filming another role at this moment. Well, fortunate for him and unfortunate for us, I suppose. Good for him though, right?

Isadora: Absolutely earned, and I'm glad he's getting his moment in the spotlight. His performance was phenomenal. I loved our scenes together. Very funny, too.

Interviewer: Oh was he?

Isadora: Yeah, anytime we were between scenes he'd be doing physical gags and all that. Cracked up the whole crew.

Edia: He also taught me some sign language, which was great.

Interviewer: Edia, I know you had some school to do during all this. What was that like juggling both?

Edia: It was weird. Going from a pirate ship to math homework feels like such a downgrade.

Interviewer: Do you feel like you see a lot of yourself in the character?

Edia: Well, kind of. Maybe not that much. I think she is a much braver version of myself. I don't think I'd be the kind of person to try and stab a pirate lord, or whatever Pé was called. I don't think that would be me. But I did improvise some lines that they kept in, so some of it is me in a way.

Interviewer: What about you, Archie? This was you first lead role. What about yourself did you bring to this character?

Archie: What drew me to the character in the first place was his views on art. I'm a very artistic person myself. So the struggle that he goes through with understanding what his art means and how to pursue his passion in a place that doesn't value it resonated with me. And especially after he loses an arm and needs to reconcile with that, I really felt that. It hit me deeply, and I was excited to explore that.

Interviewer: Speaking of the arm, and the leg too, what was it like filming with the prosthetics?

Archie: Oh, very strange. I had to put my arm behind my back and my knee up on the peg leg with my leg up behind me. You don't realize how much you rely on everything for balance and mobility until you have it restricted like that. I got it down eventually, and it'll be easier for any potential sequels, but it was a challenge at first. But it was nothing like Ozma's costume and prosthetics while playing the Goldsire.

Shadir: He spent eight hours in a chair getting all that makeup on, and then spent several more hours doing the scene. For multiple days in a row.

Ozma: Well, we wanted it to be more realistic than mo-cap, so we went practical. It wasn't so bad, really. That character was hardly in the story. It only took three days to finish that scene.

Interviewer: That's still a lot of time in the chair. Would you have liked to do more scenes with this character?

Ozma: I believe there was some discussion—it was such an interesting character to play, by the way—but there was some discussion of that during the writing process. How much do you put in a character like that? So grandiose. So influential. It makes sense for a character like that to be in it more. But ultimately it would've just dragged on if they stayed in that cave any longer. I think Smyser knew he needed to have another thing to do at the end of the book to finish everything off, and that's when he came up with the raid and the charter baron characters were created.

Interviewer: Oh really? Ozma and Stellagard were late additions?

Isadora: The charter barons weren't much of a villainous force in the first couple of drafts, so I've heard. They were just mentioned. I believe it was from a short story prequel where this character shows up for the first time. So after that, those characters were added to the main story. There needed to be an obstacle for Archie on his home island before he left and something to come back to and overcome in the end.

Ozma: I was already cast as Goldsire, so they decided I should fill that role too. I'm not sure if this was something symbolic or just convenience.

Shadir: I like to think that Ozma was Archie's personal Goldsire, and so to have a similar face, even if it was under a pound of makeup, helped make that connection.

Interviewer: What draws you into playing villains?

Ozma: Well they're all so terribly interesting, aren't they? Ozma was this sniveling kind of character way in over his head. But the real villain there was my character's mother, still puppeteering him from the shadows. And, in a way, the Goldsire did the same thing but on a much grander scale.

Isadora: But then you get so many other villainous characters packed into this story, as well. Decker was an interesting addition. A newby in the pirate world, and yet making big waves, pun intended. And Pé Dutanté came in with that sophisticated ruthlessness that I think is iconic.

Interviewer: But the real villains of the story are, in a way, the systems that are in place that force these beings into existence.

Archie: Yeah, I think that is spot on. It was a major stressor on Archie seeing how all these places he visits are so hostile in different ways. It's why he had to make his home rather than find a new one.

Interviewer: The set design was wonderful. Were there any that were your favorite?

Edia: The *Prey Empress* was huge! Walking onto it for the first time blew my mind. And everything was so detailed.

Isadora: I agree. It doesn't necessarily show in the story, but the craftsmanship of the *Prey Empress* was really well done.

Archie: Maybe there is a bias here, but I loved the Port Ov Krakau. It was very cozy. I could see myself living there… post ending.

Shadir: I enjoyed the ruins. We didn't spend much time on the outside, but it was cool. And the cave with all the gold in it was amazing with a bunch of different easter eggs hidden around.

Ozma: Ruins for me as well. But also the hidden island as a whole was magnificent.

Shadir: But also the CMT castle was really strange and compelling. I want to see what happens with that after what our characters did.

Interviewer: Shadir, besides the Goldsire, you had the only character who had some form of magic in this fantasy world. What was it like playing that?

Shadir: Well it wasn't really magic as one might expect, you know? It's quite different than, say, shooting lightning out of your hands. But, yeah, I think it would be interesting to see more characters like that. More varied abilities. Maybe even different species like in other fantasy series. Not sure how those might be incorporated, but there is a whole world out there beyond the southern pole. So maybe that will be explored in potential sequels.

Interviewer: Last question on that note. Are there any other stories you'd like to have told in this world?

Isadora: Oh definitely some kind of prequel for Rubias. I think her dynamic with Pé could be explored further. Maybe set during their time under Dane Lurious's command.

Edia: A time skip for Edia someday. See what she's up to when she's older and becomes a captain.

Ozma: I think focusing on new characters from other islands could be interesting.

Shadir: I always thought a cozy, slice-of-life book would be nice for something like Archie and Shadir. I don't think my character is likely to go on any more adventures.

Archie: That would be nice, but I would also like to see what awaits in the rest of the world. There are so many other islands to explore. Maybe even something going on up in the north pole! I'd also like to see Archie become some kind of mentor figure, perhaps. So anything like that.

Interviewer: Excellent. Thank you all again for sitting down with me.

J. L. Smyser is a teacher and co-owner of Blue Feathered Quill Publishing. He squeezes in his writing time by scribbling on any scraps of paper or sticky notes, and the cats that use him as furniture are his muses. The curious reader will be able to find his short stories in various anthologies, or other works he helped bring into the world at bfqpub.com. On any given day, you can find him somewhere in Colorado trying his best.